## Also By Jass Richards

*This Will Not Look Good on My Resume*

*The Blasphemy Tour* (forthcoming)

# The Road Trip Dialogues

# The Road Trip Dialogues

Jass Richards

Magenta

The Road Trip Dialogues


ISBN 978-1-926891-42-2

Published by Magenta

Magenta



www.jassrichards.com

Cover design by Stephen James Price based on a concept by Jass Richards

Formatting and layout design by Book Looks Design

Bits on page 100 from www.despair.com

Library and Archives Canada Cataloguing in Publication

Richards, Jass
The road trip dialogues / Jass Richards.

ISBN 978-1-926891-42-2

I. Title.

PS8635.I268R63 2011 C813'.6 C2011-902511-6

Thanks to Bill — for his younger self.

She pulled on the door to the auto shop from the outside, and he pulled from the inside. Thus demonstrating the law of reality that says when two or more people do exactly the same thing, it has no effect whatsoever on the world at large.

"Dylan?" she then said through the glass. Amazed.

"Rev?" he said back. Equally amazed.

They tried again. As people who want to change the world at large do. Only this time they both pushed. Demonstrating exactly the kind of teamwork they'd perfected back in teacher's college. They eventually coordinated their actions and were face to face.

She was so not a hugger and he just kind of was, so you know how that part went.

"Well," she said. And then didn't say anything else.

So that hadn't changed, he thought. Happily, he realized. Her capacity for small talk had always approached nonexistent.

"What are you doing here?" she said next. Okay, that sounded wrong, she thought, fully aware of her arrested social development, but not really giving a damn.

She took in the well-worn jeans, the lime green t-shirt, and the second-hand suit coat he managed to make so very his own. Still loose and lean. The pink rat's tail was gone though.

"I thought you were teaching up in, what was it—Nelson?"

"Yeah..."

"You were all excited about it. Small community, informal school. I was a bit surprised, actually. Thought you'd go for the action of some inner city school."

"Yeah, well, that must've been Monday."

She waited.

"Tuesday I joined a bunch of drunken Indians," he smiled cheerfully, the Irish lilt still in his voice, "and we formed a band."

She broke into a grin. Typical Dylan, really.

"What'd you call yourselves?"

"A Bunch of Drunken Indians."

She burst out laughing.

"I didn't know you played an instrument," she said in the ensuing silence.

He hesitated. She waited again, sure it would be good.

"Tambourine."

This time she snort-laughed.

"Still haven't lost the laugh, I see." He started giggling then.

"Nor you."

They stood there grinning at each other. And then just sort of picked up where they'd left off some twenty years ago.

"Hang on—" Rev went to the counter, paid for her new brakes, then joined Dylan standing outside.

He'd gotten a couple cans from the nearby vending machine and handed her one.

"Thanks," she said. She noticed then the knapsack slung over his shoulder, a larger bag at his feet. "So. You need a ride?"

He looked around, as if he were considering what to do next with his life. "Okay," he said.

She led the way to her car. It was a black Saturn, polka-dotted with—

He studied it. "What in god's name did you do—" he walked around it, "to piss off an armada of pigeons?"

"It's globs of pine tar."

"Oh." He leaned forward to take a better look. "So it is. Doesn't this place clean your car before they give it back?"

"I asked them not to."

"Right. And you did that because..."

"It's my anti-theft device."

"Ah." He considered that. "Good idea."

She unlocked the back door for him to throw his bags in. "Besides, in the summer, it's all sticky and a real bitch to get off. Better to do it in the winter when it gets all hard and you can just flick it off."

He looked at her expectantly.

"I'm not standing in twenty-below to clean my car," she said. But what she meant was, I'm not an idiot.

"Cars are not meant to be clean," she continued. "They stay outside all the time. Where it's dirty. Where there's gravel roads. And mud puddles. Which they go right through without a moment's hesitation. Most of the time."

She got in and reached over to unlock the passenger door. "You're going to want me to cut my grass and sweep my driveway next."

"You have grass and a driveway?" He got in.

"Well, not exactly. But if I did." She pulled out of the lot and onto the highway.

"So what, exactly, do you have?"

She looked over and just—beamed. "A cabin on a lake in a forest."

"No," he said. "What you always wanted!" He smiled broadly, happy for her.

She nodded. "My dream come true. Been there for over ten years now. And you?"

"I'm sort of between dreams."

"But what about—"

"It's in storage."

"What—your dreams?" She grinned.

"No, my stuff." He grinned back.

"You got stuff?"

"Everybody's got stuff."

"MY GOD, LAST TIME I SAW YOU," she glanced over and thought back, "you were—blurry."

"That's because we were drinking tequila under the table." He took a slug of his pop.

"Riiiight," she drew the word out, remembering. The cafeteria had been pathetically made over for a graduation party of all the bright-eyed and bushy-tailed new teachers. He was a History and Psych major, she a Philosophy and Lit major. He was going to make history a hands-on course, an experience! His students would not fail to learn from the past! They would not be compelled to repeat it! And she was going to make philosophy not just a new course, for high school, but a mandatory one. What could be more important than learning how to think? Logically, critically. And what could be more relevant than learning how to figure out right and wrong? They were both taking 'Society, Challenge, and Change' as one of their teaching subjects. And they couldn't wait to get into the classroom.

"Did you ever finish your History thesis?" she asked. "Didn't you get into the B.Ed. program on the condition that you finish your Honour's thesis and get your B.A.?"

"And I got the Nelson job on the condition that I get the B.Ed.," he said proudly.

"Don't tell me," she said. "You never finished it." She glanced over. Then waited.

"I forgot what it was about."

She snort-laughed again. He giggled.

They'd left the town and were on an empty stretch of highway, nothing but forest and rock.

"And what about the getting married and having kids thing? I remember you were so in love with this girl...." Rev thought back. "Wasn't she Japanese? That's right, you were learning to speak Japanese! And you insisted on being faithful..." she trailed off, eyes on the road ahead.

He looked over and smiled, then looked back out the window.

"Yeah, well. She wanted to move to Japan."

"And you wanted to move to Manitoba."

"Actually, I went to Japan. About a year or so later."

"And?"

"Turns out I hadn't learned to speak Japanese."

She glanced over again.

"Hm. And there's been no one else?"

"Oh there was, from time to time. But women have these—" he gestured vaguely, "expectations—"

"What, that you have a steady job and support them?"

"Yes!"

"And—"

"And I much prefer *un*steady jobs."

She grinned.

"And you?" he asked. "You *weren't* going to get married and have kids." He had a horrible thought. "You didn't, did you?" He looked over in alarm.

"No," she said. With 'absolutely not' in her tone. "Men have these—" she gestured vaguely, "expectations—"

"What, that they'd have a steady job and support you?"

"Yes!"

"And—"

"And I could never be a kept woman."

"No. You have trouble enough being a woman," he grinned out the window.

"What's that supposed—well, yeah," she conceded cheerfully. "Remember—"

"Remember—" he said at the same time. They grinned at each other. "Professor Bixby's report, right?" Dylan pursed his lips. "'Miss Reveille needs to work on her professional appearance. A bit of make-up and some jewelry would help.'"

"I still can't believe he said that," she said.

"Hey, I offered to lend you my earring—"

She looked over. "You've stopped wearing it."

"Yeah, well, for a while there it sort of got appropriated as a symbol—and now—"

"Things don't mean what they used to," she said.

He nodded.

"THOUGH I HAVE TO SAY," she continued after a comfortable bit of silence, "I look around and all the women my age have these nice homes, and they drive those expensive stupid mini-van things, which they keep in a garage, and they have furniture—"

"You don't have furniture?"

"I have stuff that functions as furniture."

"Well then," he said conclusively.

"Okay, yeah, but, what gets me is they all act so—entitled. And I just want to shake them and say hey, if it weren't for your husband, you wouldn't have any of this!" She stopped talking for a moment as she changed lanes to pass an expensive stupid mini-van thing. "I hate these things," she muttered. "Can't see around them to the road ahead. It's like driving behind a truck." She zipped back out of the oncoming lane, then continued. "And yet I don't know where I went wrong. Because if I haven't been home raising kids for twenty years, I should be the man. I mean *I* should be able to afford that nice house, that garage—"

"Not that you'd want a garage."

"No, but."

"Or real furniture."

"Well—" she wasn't so sure about that. "But how do they do it? How is it that all these men have all that stuff *and* money left over to totally support someone else? I've been barely able to support myself."

"What do you mean? All these years I've been taking comfort in the knowledge that at least one of us—you haven't been teaching? All these years? You never answered my letter."

"You sent a letter?"

"Yeah, telling you about the band."

"I never got it. 'Course I moved a lot the first few years—well, until the cabin, actually. I thought maybe you'd written—so I sent another letter."

"I only got the first one. 'Course we went on tour—"

She looked at him.

"What?"

"You're telling me there are people who *wanted* to hear A Bunch of Drunken Indians?"

"Well, when you put it that way—" he paused. "But it must have happened. Otherwise—never mind."

She glanced over, grinned again, then resumed her update. "I did get a teaching job. It was just part-time though. But that was exactly what I wanted. Because, as you recall, I was working on my first novel. I was going to be a writer," she said with mock enthusiasm. Mocking enthusiasm. "Yes I was."

"What happened?"

"Well you know what it was like back then. We were lucky if we got any kind of teaching job. Unless we wanted to teach English overseas. End of my first year, I was declared redundant."

"There were two of you?" He giggled. Then said, "I meant what happened to the 'going to be a writer' part."

"Oh, I am a writer."

He waited.

"I write the questions that go on the LSAT."

"You became a lawyer?"

"No, I don't know anything about the law. Well, I do, but—"

"Ah-hah! I thought so!" He seemed so—pleased. "Misdemeanour?"

"Yeah—how did—" She glanced in the rear-view mirror before making a lane change to pass another stupid mini-van thing.

"The principal—" she sighed as she started the explanation. "I'd become a sub and after a few months of a day here and there, I got a long-term placement at one school—the principal caught me teaching my grade ten boys how to put on a condom."

"All of them at once?"

"Yes—no!" She reached over and cuffed him one. "It was a late and lazy Friday afternoon, and some of them were hubba-hubba-ing about their hot dates for the weekend, and I said something like 'You guys *do* know how to use a condom, right? 'Cuz if you put it on wrong, it'll bust, and you'll end up a daddy.'"

"Bet that got their attention."

"It did indeed."

"So the principal laid charges?"

"I was 'corrupting minors.'"

"Socrates would be proud. Still, it seems a bit over-reacting."

"Well—"

"It wasn't the first time." He waited.

"I refused to stand for the anthem," she said. "Every goddamned morning they wanted us to proclaim our allegiance. You'd think we were in the Soviet Union. Or the States. 'Nationalism is—"

"—an infantile disease,'" he finished the quote. "And the next time?"

"Well, the long-term placement got turned into a short-term placement—"

"Isn't it usually the other way around?"

"Smart ass. At the next school," she continued then, "I started a discussion club. I chose abortion as the opening topic."

"Well, you can't do that at St. Mary's of the Eternally Blessed Virgin Who Never Goes To First Base Not Even If She Really Really Wants To. *Especially* If She Really Really Wants To—" he stopped then.

She looked over at him with inquiring eyebrows, but he didn't elaborate. Didn't really need to.

"It was a public school," she said. "A regular public high school. Next time, it was something else. I can't remember."

"Yes you can."

"Yes I can. The next time—oh it doesn't matter. The next time, when I—" she paused to find the right word, "left, I offered to sponsor an annual Award for Independent Thought. To be given each year to a graduating student chosen by the teaching staff. Each May, I'd send a book prize for the award. They'd give it out at the graduation ceremony in June."

"And?"

"The Awards Committee refused my offer. They said it would be too complicated to administer."

"Ah, well, they're administrators. The May-June thing probably stumped them."

"So if you aren't a lawyer," he said after a while, "how can you write the questions that go on the LSAT?"

"I write the questions for the critical reasoning part. You know, 'If

X, Y, and Z are true, what must also be true?' or 'Which of the following conclusions can be drawn from the information provided above?'"

"Multiple-choice questions? I love multiple-choice questions! No, wait a minute. I hate multiple-choice questions!"

"And they certainly don't all go on the LSAT. I send in my quota per month, they go through first review, second review, sensitivity review, edit, penultimate review, re-edit, and ultimate review. If the question makes it that far, if the on-site team is convinced the question would stand up in a court of law—"

"You have to defend your work in a court of law?"

"Well, it turns out the LSAT test-takers are a litigious bunch. Go figure."

He grinned.

She passed a transport truck on an uphill. "But no, not me. The onsite-staff. That's why they're so picky about accepting questions. They have to be able to say, for example, that in item 34, the question itself is perfectly clear and totally unambiguous, there's no way it could be justifiably interpreted to mean anything other than what it means, and that option (B), for example, is absolutely and demonstrably correct, no ifs, ands, or buts about it, and each of the other options is just as demonstrably *in*correct.'"

"That sounds—exhausting."

"Yeah."

"But you like it."

"I do," she looked over and smiled. "It makes my neurons sing."

"Ah, well, neurons singing, that's always a good thing."

"And when they buy a question, I get paid well. 'Course when they don't—"

"So you have a flexible income."

"Exactly. But it's a job I can do whenever I want and wherever I want. And I don't have to deal with people."

"Because you have no people skills."

"I do not," she agreed.

"Which is why you went into teaching," he grinned.

"Okay," she looked over at him, "that was a wrong turn. I so wanted to make a difference, you know? But I didn't. I couldn't. And I figured that out," she said, proudly. "After ten years."

"So whatever happened to—*ten years*?" He put his hand on the dashboard as if to absorb an impact.

"That's how long it took, remember? For real jobs to come around again. The ones with benefits and a pension plan. But, since I wasn't exactly bright-eyed and bushy-tailed anymore—"

"No, I imagine by that point you were walking into the schools with a loaded rifle, taking aim at the principal, and screaming 'Leave the kids alone!'" He tilted his can and finished it.

"How did you know?" she dead-panned.

Pop sprayed out his nose.

"So when I got out of prison *that* time—"

He started choking, so she gave him a moment to recover.

"—I was de-certified."

"I can see how walking into the classroom with a loaded rifle might have that consequence."

"Well I just got so tired of the—resistance. Schools are such hostile environments," she added.

He raised his eyebrows at the irony.

"That explains it," he said then.

"What."

"Well, you're still angry."

She flared at him.

"Just a little," he pulled back as his eyebrows got singed.

"'Course I'm angry. Aren't you?" She looked over at him. "And if not, why not? What happened to you? I mean—after Japan...” she tried to cue him.

He shrugged. “I wasn’t as persistent as you. I didn’t try as hard.” He looked out the window. “I’m not entitled to be angry.”

“Hm,” she nodded thoughtfully. “We’ll come back to that.”

He grinned.

“So whatever happened to the novel,” he said after a bit. “Did you finish it?”

“I did. *Portrait of an Artist as a Young Woman*. It’s in my desk drawer. Unpublished, unknown, unread.”

“How—appropriate.”

“Isn’t it just.”

“Couldn’t get a publisher?”

She snorted. “Twenty years and I still can’t get an agent.”

“Um, you ever think it just might not be very good?” he said a little delicately.

“Of course. But apparently that’s not an obstacle to getting something published.”

“Good point.” He looked out the window again.

“So what about you,” she asked again. “Are you still playing,” she couldn't keep a straight face, “the tambourine?”

“No, alas, my tambourine days are over.”

She waited.

“Carpal tunnel syndrome.”

She burst out laughing, and a snort escaped.

“Well,” he resumed, “I too have a flexible income.”

“Doing?”

“Oh, this and that. And a good deal more of this than that. For a while I was a dj at a radio station.”

“Oh yeah? That must’ve been cool.”

“It was. I did social commentary. I’d play ‘I Can’t Get No

Satisfaction' followed by 'You Can't Always Get What You Want.' Or the Carpenters' 'We've Only Just Begun' followed by Deana Carter's 'Did I Shave My Legs For This' followed by Neville's 'Everybody Plays the Fool.' Then one day, I played 'I'll Be There,' 'I Am Here,' and 'Here I Am,' followed by 'What Am I Doing Here?'—and—it was all just so confusing." He paused.

"And so then you were not there?" Rev said helpfully.

"And so then I was not there. At the moment, I'm a freelance reporter."

"Yeah? How did that come about?"

"Well I started in Obits. 'John Smith led an unbelievably boring life. And now it's over.' They saw right away I had a gift."

"So they fired you."

He nodded. "Thus I became a freelance reporter."

"Ah. Though I was after an explanation more for the reporter part than the freelance part."

"Ah. Well, I wrote an article about something, and it got published. And I got paid. So I wrote another article. About something else," he clarified, "and it got published as well. And I got paid again. So I wrote—"

"Got it. It was that easy to get published, eh?" There was, of course, a tinge of sour envy in her voice.

He looked over, regretting immediately his insensitivity. "Well, remember that we established the irrelevance of quality."

"Yeah, yeah." She was not convinced. Either that or she was convinced.

"So what do you report on?"

"Oh, this and that."

"And a good deal more of this than that, I'll wager."

He grinned over at her.

"SO WHATEVER HAPPENED TO LEECH?" she asked after a while.

"I don't know. I didn't stay in touch with anyone. Everyone was so…so. Present company excluded."

They were both quiet for a bit.

"We would've made the best teachers," Rev said. Sadly. Bitterly.

"Which is why we quit or were fired," he replied.

"Or declared redundant," she qualified, defensively.

"Same thing. They could've declared the football equipment redundant instead."

"Seeing as there were already a number of ways in which young men could display their stupidity," she agreed.

"Or the football *team*," he said.

"Seeing as."

"I bet he became a principal," he said then.

"Who?"

"Leech."

"But he borrowed your notes even for classes he attended!" she said. Then she sighed. "You're probably right."

They drove on. After a while, when the sad and bitter had dissipated somewhat, she thought to ask, "So where are we going?"

"I don't know, you're driving," he said. Grinning.

"So your car—"

"Died. I left it at that shop to be a multiple-organ transplant donor."

"Oh. But you—"

"Where were you going before you met me?" He grinned at how that came out. So did she.

"Actually, I was on my way to Montreal. To see the fireworks."

"You're driving to Montreal," he repeated with some disbelief, "to see fireworks. But that's so—oh, yeah," he said then, "they have that international competition. I've heard about that. Lots of sparkles and—okay," he said after a moment.

"Okay what."

"Let's go see the fireworks."

She smiled. It was so—Dylan.

"So you speak French then?" he asked.

"Probably as good as you speak Japanese."

"Then we'll do fine. How hard can it be to ask for directions to see the—" he exploded his hand and made some noises.

She glanced over. "The re-enactment of the War of 1812?"

"No, silly. The War of 1812 wasn't in Montreal. Or in 1812."

She shot him a look.

"Okay, yeah, it was in 1812. But it's not something most students know, I can tell you that."

They drove for a bit.

"Hey, before we go to the fireworks," he pointed just up the highway to their left, "let's go to the ice cream place."

"Okay," she slowed and pulled into the small parking lot. When they walked in, they saw it was the local hang-out. An assortment of teenagers occupied the corner with a table. Gangsta rap was pumping from a jukebox at the far end.

"That's—confusing," Rev commented.

"What?"

"Rap coming from a jukebox."

"Hm. But the Fonz would approve."

"Think so? I don't know." She took in the sullen-looking teenagers sulking in the corner. "The Fonz was basically a happy person, don't you think?"

The teenagers looked back at her belligerently.

"It wasn't just the principals, was it," Dylan said.

"No," she confessed. "At first, yes. But eventually—no."

She brushed the pain away and went up to the display freezer. She cruised by slowly, reading the names and looking at each of the open round cartons.

"Do you have soft ice cream?" Dylan asked the young woman behind the counter.

"Yeah, but only in vanilla."

"That's fine. I'll have a soft cone in vanilla." His eye was caught then by the containers of ice cream condiments. "With pink sprinkles," he added delightfully.

He heard the snicker and turned to see the smirk. "Fag," one of them said.

"Why, because I'm getting vanilla? Or because I'm getting a soft cone. Or is it the pink sprinkles? Just curious."

They laughed and jostled each other.

"Whichever," he continued, "you realize you're being totally irrational, yes? Because what could the flavor or consistency of the ice cream I prefer—or the color of my sprinkles—possibly have to do with my sexual orientation?"

Rev turned to look at the boys. They were not amused. She tried to catch Dylan's eye, but surely he knew. He couldn't help himself. She understood. Or did once. If it moves, teach it.

"I'll have the Chocolate Almond Deluscious," she turned back to the woman, unable to watch.

The woman gave Dylan his vanilla cone, then scooped out Rev's cone. While they were paying, the boys shuffled out. Good. No, not good. They were clustered around the door.

"We can eat our cones here," Rev suggested.

"Don't be silly. The décor is awful."

"But I don't have my rifle," she muttered.

Dylan went to the door, and opened it, but the boys didn't move to make room for their exit.

"Excuse me," he said, reasonably enough.

"No. We don't excuse fags."

Dylan paused a moment. "I thought we went over that." Then he smooshed his ice cream cone into the biggest guy's face and yelled to Rev, "Run away! Run away!"

They sprinted to her car and got in.

"Lock the doors!" she shouted at him.

"Drive!" he shouted at her, tumbling into the back seat to get the locks.

She zoomed out of the small lot and back onto the highway. He clambered back into the front seat, then looked behind them to assure himself that they had not had a car.

"What the hell were you thinking?" she demanded.

"That it was too bad we didn't have a cow we could throw over the castle wall at them?"

She looked at him then burst out laughing. "Wasn't it a killer rabbit?"

"No, the killer rabbit was before, wasn't it?"

"No, don't they go up to the castle wall—oh, hell, I can't remember."

"Okay then."

"Okay then what."

"Okay then we have to find a video store, rent *The Holy Grail*, and find a motel for the night."

"Yeah," she looked around vaguely. "My eyes don't like driving in the dark these days. I hate this growing old shit," she added.

"Me too. But before we grow old, we have to find another ice cream place. I want my pink sprinkles."

Rev rather smugly picked up her Chocolate Almond Deluscious cone from the drink resting place. Dylan looked at her in amazement.

"It's chocolate," she said. What more need she say?

THEY DROVE ANOTHER HOUR BEFORE they found another ice cream place. It was in the next town, and it wasn't so much an ice cream place as a corner store that had an ice cream counter. As for the pink sprinkles, Dylan had to improvise. He bought a little box of cake decorations, no doubt made in the 1950s, and sprinkled its contents on his vanilla cone.

Conveniently enough, the store also had an aisle of videos for rent. Which was surprising, Rev thought, since most people in the area must be getting more movies than they could ever watch through satellite TV. There wouldn't be any cable service, and she suspected that until they got closer to—somewhere else—anyone with an aerial would be getting only two or three stations. Even DVD rentals were becoming passé. They looked through the comedy section, which was understandably old, but apparently Monty Python was older still.

"Excuse me," Dylan absently waved his cone to get the attention of the young man behind the counter. And almost lost it, again. "You don't by any chance have *Monty Python and the Holy Grail*, do you?"

"Yeah, it's in the half-price bin. Sarah brought in Don's old collection for sale. Buck a piece."

"Don doesn't want them anymore?" Dylan couldn't believe anyone would give up their Monty Python collection.

"Don died."

"Ah." He was momentarily disconcerted, then started searching for the *Holy Grail* in the half-price bin.

"Is there a motel in this town?" Rev asked in the meantime.

"Another half mile. End of town."

"Thanks," she said, as Dylan cried out, "Aha!"

They paid for the video, left the store, walked back to the car, then drove the half mile to the motel.

"Do you find it personally disturbing that Monty Python fans are dying already?" Dylan asked.

"Yes."

"Hm."

She pulled into the small parking lot of the motel at the end of town. He grabbed his bag out of the back seat, and she got hers from out of the trunk. They walked into the office, a quasi-apartment attached to a row of five motel rooms, and rang the little bell on the cluttered desk. It didn't sound loud enough, given the hockey game coming from behind the curtain. So they rang it again. When the play stopped and a commercial came on, the motel guy came out from the back.

"Hi there, we'd like a room for the night, please," Rev said.

The motel guy shuffled over to the cluttered desk and looked at a handwritten list of sorts.

"Only a double left."

"That's fine," she said. She filled out the paperwork and gave the guy her credit card. It took a few tries for the swipe to take, but eventually her payment was processed.

He gave her a key. "Unit #5, at the end. Check out's by two."

"Thank you, kind sir," Dylan said, as they walked to the door.

"Here," he reached out his hand to Rev, "give me that. You move the car." She gave him her bag and went back to her car. He walked down to unit five, stopping on the way to get a couple cans of Pepsi from the vending machine. She met him at the door, then had to convince the key that it was indeed made for Unit #5. Dylan tossed her bag on one bed and his on the other.

"Well, that explains the video rentals," he said, nodding at the old TV and VHS player chained to a cabinet. He put the video into the player and flopped back onto one of the beds, as she headed to the washroom.

"You still smoke?" he called out to her, sitting up then and tugging his knapsack toward him.

"Oh man, you've got a joint? How big is it?" she hurried back into the room. "Is it a Cheech and Chong joint?"

He laughed as he handed her a can. "They only had Pepsi."

"Don't you love the free market? It lets companies buy the freedom of distributors." She took the can and popped its lid. "Thanks."

Dylan got up to press the 'play' button—there didn't seem to be a remote—then settled back onto the bed. He pulled a baggie out of his knapsack and a book of matches. As he lit up, Rev arranged the pillows of the other bed against the bedboard.

"Oh don't be silly, I can't reach that far." He lamely held out the joint to her in the space between the beds.

She picked up the pillows from her bed and tossed them beside his against the bedboard. Settling herself companionably beside him, she took the joint.

She drew in. "Last time I smoked," she said as she exhaled, "I was doing my laundry. Took forever to get my shirts onto their hangers. Have you ever noticed how complex a spatial task that is? Matching the two shoulders of a shirt with the three corners of the hangers. It was kind of like playing musical chairs. One corner was going to be left out, and I couldn't figure out which of the five it should be. Around and around I went."

"So why'd you stop?"

"I got dizzy."

"I meant—"

"The guy I was with, we split, and then it was forever until I came across someone else who had a connection. And then, well, the next day is a total write-off in terms of lucidity."

"You still notice a difference?" he giggled. "What with the growing old shit?"

"Oh shut up."

They watched the movie, drank their Pepsi, and smoked the joint.

"Bring out your dead. Bring out your dead."

"To Don!" Dylan said soberly.

"To Don!" Rev echoed.

Then the Requiem scene followed and they both lost it when the first monk slammed himself in the head. By the third one, Rev had tears in her eyes from laughing so hard.

"To Don!" she gasped.

"To Don!" Dylan echoed.

About an hour later, Dylan called out, "Here it comes!" The cow came flying over the castle wall and they both collapsed again in giggles.

"You know what we forgot?" Dylan said.

"The airspeed velocity of an African swallow?" Rev suggested.

"Doritos."

"Ah."

"And pizza."

"Do you think the local place is still open?" she asked.

"Did you see a local place?"

"Well, of course. By definition any place we see here is a local place."

"Good point." He considered that. "Okay, did you see a local *pizza* place, *that's* what we need to determine," inordinately pleased with himself for identifying the obvious.

"No I didn't see a local pizza place." She ruminated on that for a moment. "But that doesn't mean one doesn't exist."

"You got an A in Epistemology, didn't you."

"I got an A in everything."

"Okay, put on your shoes. We'll go look."

"I'm not driving."

"Of course not. The whole town is just half a mile."

"Okay, I can do that. I can walk half a mile."

"I should think so."

"But I have to piddle before we leave."

"I should think so. Piddle *after* we leave and you'll be charged with another misdemeanour."

"Do you think piddling in public is a misdemeanour?" she called out through the bathroom door.

"Well it should be. Don't you think it's a lapse in decorum, a mis-demeanor?" he giggled. "A *mis*-demeanour. A misdemeanour is a mis-demeanour. Perspicuity," he added. And giggled again.

She came out of the washroom.

"Perspicuity," he said again. "It sounds funny," he explained.

"Especially coming from you," she agreed. "Okay, I found the door out of the washroom. Now we have to find the door out of the room. And it won't be the same one," she added.

"That's a helpful clue. It adds," he sputtered with delight, "perspicuity."

"Maybe we should just order out for the pizza," she suggested, suddenly daunted by the quest they were embarking upon.

He looked at the phone, doubtful. "Can *you* negotiate all those numbers? They're very little."

"Good point. Okay, here's the door."

They stumbled out of Unit #5.

"Okay, which way?" she asked.

"To the holy grail! To the pizza!"

"Yeah, but which way?"

Dylan pondered as he looked one way, then another, then another. "Forward! It's always easier to walk forward than it is to walk backward!"

She agreed and they walked forward onto the walkway that joined their unit to the walkway running along all five units. When they got to the corner, Rev stopped.

"Having hanger flashbacks?" Dylan asked her with concern.

"Yes. I am the shirt."

"And I am the walrus. Let's go this way," he suggested. They turned left and walked into bush.

"Okay, now let's go this way," he suggested. They turned around. "Isn't that the highway I see in yonder distance?"

"I believe so," she said. "Isn't that where we need to go?"

"I believe so," he replied. "Engage! Warp speed five!"

They stumbled along the motel walkway to the highway.

"Okay, so far so good," he proclaimed. "We have come a long way."

"And no one's thrown a cow at us yet."

"The night is young," he cautioned. "And there are cows about."

"Which way now?"

They looked at the highway stretching in both directions. They looked behind them, and they looked in front of them.

"Up!" Dylan shouted. They looked up. "Ah, stars."

"Oh, look," Rev said, "there's a bunch in the shape of a—cluster."

"Is it moving? Are the aliens coming to get us yet? I want to go home," he cried.

"Okay, but before we do, let's get some pizza."

"Right. Good idea. I'm hungry."

They turned right and started walking along the shoulder of the highway.

"Okay, we have to be careful to keep the gravel under our feet. You remember what happened to the rabbit in *Watership Down*."

"But it wasn't a killer rabbit."

"No. But it was road kill just the same."

"Look! Pizza Pizza Pizza!" he cried out.

"I think there's only two of them."

"How fortuitous. Because we need only one of them."

They kept walking, toward the Pizza Pizza sign.

"Keep our eyes on the pizza and our feet on the gravel," she said, "and we'll be fine."

"Feet on the pizza, eyes in the gravel, we'll be fine," he agreed.

Eventually, they reached their goal.

"We're here!" he shouted triumphantly as he burst through the door.

"Yeah," the young man behind the counter said, clearly not as enthused about it as Dylan. "And what can I get for you this evening?" The script had definitely lost its sparkle.

"Pizza pizza pizza!" Dylan cried out.

"Just one," Rev clarified. With perspicuity.

"But a really, really big one!" Dylan insisted. "I'm so hungry," he confessed to Rev.

"Duh," Rev giggled. "We just walked all the way here from the motel," she explained to the guy.

"A whole quarter-mile," he said dryly. "Bet you could eat a horse."

"Or a cow!" Dylan burst into giggles. "Throw one over the castle wall!"

The young man started to smile then. "Riiight," he said. "So that'll be one family size pizza, with the works, two cans of Pepsi, and two bags of Doritos."

"Yes!" Dylan cried out. "No! Four bags of Doritos! We need *four* bags of Doritos."

The young man smiled more broadly then. "Can you carry all of that all the way back to the motel?" he asked as he started making their pizza, plopping one of the ready lumps of pizza dough onto a floured table. "I mean, I'm off in ten minutes. We close at midnight. I could deliver on my way home."

"Could you? Yes! Deliver! That's a very good idea!" Dylan turned to

Rev. "He's going to bring the pizza to us. Instead of the other way around."

"Wow."

"All right, then." Dylan was pleased. "That's settled. Now what?"

The guy chuckled. "Why don't you take a seat and I'll deliver you two as well."

"Brilliant!" Dylan said. "But you can't put us in a flat box. We're not road kill yet."

"Okay," he smiled. He finished making their pizza and put it into the oven as Dylan and Rev found the little table in the corner and sat down. Rev started examining the cross bars under the chair's seat. The way they intersected in the corners then went off in different directions.

"Wow," she said.

"I'm so hungry," Dylan moaned.

A bag of Doritos came flying at them from behind the counter.

"Look!" Dylan said to Rev, "We are blessed! Doritos fell from the sky and landed on my head."

The young man burst into giggles.

Ten minutes later, he was bundling Dylan, Rev, a family size pizza, two cans of Pepsi, and three bags of Doritos into his beat-up Neon.

He drove back to the motel.

"Which—do you remember which unit you're in?"

"The one near the bush," Dylan said.

"We walked into the bush. Before."

"Before we walked out of the bush."

"Okay, here we are. Do you have your key?"

"Oh no! I forgot to take the key!" Rev cried.

"That's okay! I forgot to lock the door!" Dylan said.

Sure enough, the door was unlocked. They walked in.

"Come in, come in, good kind sir! Here, have a Pepsi!" He opened one of the cans and gave it to the young man. He opened the pizza box.

"And have a slice! Have a seat!" He gestured vaguely to the room. "Have a name! I mean, what's your name?"

"Shaun." He moved the chair from against the wall closer to the bed upon which Dylan and Rev had settled.

"And you live around here?"

"Yeah, just down the highway a bit. I live with my grandpar—I live with my grandmother. My grandfather passed away."

"So did Don," Dylan said.

"You knew him?"

"Who?"

"Don."

"No. The guy at the video store said—"

"Wait a minute—you're Don's son?" Rev figured it out. She wrote for the LSAT, after all.

"Grandson."

"*Grand*son? Just how old was Don?" Dylan asked.

"I don't know. 'Bout your age, I guess."

"Cannot be! *We're* about your age!"

Shaun laughed. "You got that right."

Dylan pulled his knapsack onto the bed and began rummaging through it. "Ah, the last one." He pulled out a crumpled joint. "Alas. No matter," he reached for the matches, lying on the table between the beds. "Here, join us." He lit up, then passed it to Shaun. Shaun took it, drew in deeply, then passed it to Rev. She took a small drag, then got up to press 'play' on the VCR.

"To Don," she said, lifting her can of Pepsi. Dylan echoed her, waving the joint.

"To Don," Shaun said, raising his slice of pizza. "My grand-dad."

They watched the rest of video as they ate, drank, and smoked.

The killer rabbit scene came on.

"Run away!" Dylan cried out. "Run away!"

Shaun's eyes began to tear.

"It's okay," Dylan noticed. "It's just a flesh wound," he said, then collapsed in giggles. Shaun couldn't help joining him.

"He'd've loved this," he said when he recovered. "This is perfect." He looked at Rev and Dylan. "Thank you so much, you guys."

Dylan and Rev nodded a 'you're welcome.'

The video played to the end, then started its automatic rewind.

Dylan got up, pressed the eject button, then put the video back in its box.

"Here," he said, handing it to Shaun who'd also gotten up. "Your grandmother shouldn't've given them all away. Though I can understand why she might've. But you should have this one."

"Yeah. Thanks." Shaun turned to leave. "Hey. On your way out of town tomorrow?" he half-said, half-asked. Rev nodded confirmation. "Stop at the grey bungalow. I can replenish your supply if you'd like."

"Good man. We'd like. Till tomorrow, then." Dylan put his hand on Shaun's shoulder at the door.

SO THE NEXT MORNING WHEN they headed out, they looked for the grey bungalow. Rev stopped at the corner store.

"This building is neither grey, nor a bungalow," Dylan looked over at Rev. She didn't respond. "Which of the following conclusions can be drawn from the information provided?" he added helpfully.

"That you're neither color-blind nor architecturally challenged. Be out in a second," she said.

She returned with a bag full of videos. "The rest of Don's collection. Shaun should have them."

"He should indeed. Nice idea. No, wait, you're not a nice person. What was it you said to Professor Tally when he criticized your deskside manner? 'Being nice is highly—stupid.'" He giggled, remembering the scene.

"So this is a *good* idea," he amended. Then paused. "No wait, are you a *good* person?" She didn't reply as she pulled out of the parking lot.

"Okay, we'll come back to that," Dylan said.

They drove up the highway a short bit.

"Thar she blows!" He called out gaily as a grey bungalow came in sight. "Anchors ahoy, away, aloft!" She pulled into the driveway behind Shaun's Neon.

When they knocked at the door, a woman perhaps a little older than Rev answered the door. She looked a lot like Emmy Lou Harris.

"Hi. You must be Dylan and Rev," she said warmly. "Shaun told me you'd be coming by."

"He did?" Dylan was surprised.

"Hi," Rev reached out to shake her hand, "you must be—"

"Sarah," she shook Rev's hand. "Come on in." She led the way to the back of the house into a kitchen. "Have a seat. You want some breakfast?"

"But it's only—" Dylan looked at his watch, "three o'clock."

"Point?"

"Taken." Dylan grinned.

"We don't want to put you to any trouble," Rev said.

"No trouble at all," she said, as she opened the fridge and took out two pizza boxes. "Pepperoni and mushroom or olives and pineapple," she said as she set them on the table.

"Oh wow. Thanks." Rev took a slice with olives and pineapple. Dylan opted for pepperoni and mushroom. Sarah got three bottles of beer from the fridge, then joined them at the table, taking a slice of the olives and pineapple.

"The breakfast of champions!" Rev raised her slice in a toast.

"You've got your grain, your dairy, your veggies, and your fruit," Sarah agreed. "And it comes readi-made," she added.

"Yeah, courtesy of the pizza elves." Shaun appeared in the doorway, looking like he'd just gotten up. "Hi."

"Hi yourself." Rev said.

"Good morrow, kind sir," Dylan said.

"Hey, I brought you these," Rev gave him the bag. He looked inside.

"Thanks. I—" Then he looked at Sarah.

Sarah glanced at the bag and knew immediately what was inside. "I should never have given them away. I'm sorry," she said to Shaun. "It just—it just hurt too much to watch them," she said to Rev and Dylan. "I thought it would be nice, you know, like having him here. But it was exactly like *not* having him. You keep them, Shaun." He nodded, then left to put the bag in his room.

"So what do you two do?" Sarah took a bite of her pizza. "I mean besides get stoned and watch Monty Python movies," she grinned, a little painfully.

"I write for the LSAT," Rev volunteered. Which sounded so very implausible at the moment.

"And I'm a freelance reporter," Dylan said.

"And what do you report on—where do you go for your stories?"

"Oh, here, there—" he said, then couldn't resist adding lamely, "and everywhere."

"Who let the dogs out?" Sarah said casually to Rev. Then grinned at a delighted Dylan.

"She speaks song titles!" Dylan said to Rev.

"Used to play in a band," Sarah replied.

"What inst—" Rev was suddenly afraid to ask.

"Tambourine!" Dylan guessed.

"Bass guitar," Sarah said.

"Ah."

"A real instrument," Rev said to Dylan.

"Well, barely," Sarah admitted.

"And now? What do you do now?" Rev asked.

"Well I used to do a lot of grassroots feminist stuff. Worked at a women's shelter for a while, then did some research and report writing for the women's directorate. Even did a stint with Studio D. At the NFB."

"Yes, I know it," Rev said. "It is no more."

"Well it's no longer needed, don't you know? We live in a postfeminist world," she said sarcastically.

"Oh yeah, I must've missed that. Tell me again how many of us are CEOs and Supreme Court justices."

Sarah laughed. "One day we're all moving forward, even the men are finally starting to get it, then the next, we're all a bunch of whiners 'cuz it's all good now." Sarah took a swig of her beer. Then burped.

Rev hesitated for the shortest of moments, then rose to the challenge, prepared, and let out a better one.

"Oh is that all you've got?" Sarah took another swallow of her beer and let out a whallop.

Shaun had reappeared in the doorway and rolled his eyes.

"Don't you hate it when the women get all prissy?" Dylan said to him.

Shaun let out a giggle as he stepped up to the table, took a slice of the pepperoni and mushroom, then went back to lean in the doorway.

"It shouldn't be so surprising though," Dylan said at what was apparently intermission. They both looked at him wondering what exactly he was referring to. Could be a number of things. "I mean, the same thing happened with the blacks, didn't it. As soon as slavery became illegal and they got the vote, it was like, okay, you're all good now. Racism is dead. As if changing the law was all it would take. Not many black CEOs either," he added.

"But more, I'll bet," Rev responded.

"Well, yeah," he agreed. "Women are the niggers of the world."

"Imagine," Sarah inserted dryly.

"She's good," Dylan said to Rev, smiling broadly at Sarah.

"You ain't seen nothin' yet," she replied.

"Hot stuff," he said, and Sarah grinned.

"Look at the Hillary versus Obama thing," Dylan continued the conversation. "We'd rather a black than a woman. Of course, I'm oversimplifying, but—"

"But there's some truth in that, I think," Sarah said.

"Which is why Michael Moore's idea was so great," Rev said. "Oprah should've run."

"I hadn't heard that," Dylan said. "Wouldn't that've been interesting." They paused for thought.

"You know what I hate the most?" Sarah asked. "We tried so hard to get women treated like the adults we are," she let out another really impressive burp, "to get rid of the 'girl' in 'Girl Friday' and—everywhere," she grinned at Dylan, "and today's 'girls' actually *like* being called girls. They think they've fixed the pejorative subtext by spelling it 'grrls.'"

"Like that'll do it," Rev agreed. "Look at the way Dylan phrased the contest: as between Hillary and Obama. Everyone referred to her by her first name, but they referred to him by his last name."

"So?" Shaun spoke up.

"Well, first names subordinate," Sarah explained. "They don't confer the formality, the respect, that last names do. They're used by superordinates to subordinates. You don't call your boss 'Jim,' you say 'Mr. Paruso.'" Then she added. "Don't you?"

"Yeah," he said.

"But he calls you Shaun, doesn't he."

"Yeah!" he said.

"No," Dylan said to him quickly, anticipating. "Don't. At least not until you're ready to get fired."

"And notice how 'Miss Paruso' just wouldn't sound so—authoritative," Sarah continued. "Though 'Ms. Paruso' isn't that much better."

"Yeah, that was a wrong move, going for Ms.," Rev said. "We should've pushed for nothing at all. Or a gender neutral prefix. I used to teach and I can't tell you how tired I got of being called 'Ms.' in the classroom. 'Female person' this and 'Female person' that. And 'Male person' whatever. What's so goddamned important about our sex that it has to be part of our names?"

"It's like an identity card, isn't it. It declares our status," Sarah said. "Appropriate in apartheid."

"Once gender becomes so unimportant it's *not* routinely part of your very name, *that'll* mean we're in a post-feminist world. Imagine going around and calling people 'Blue-eyed Paruso' and 'Brown-eyed Smith' or whatever."

"Why would you—oh," Shaun understood.

"You know, I said to the woman at the bank the other day, when she was filling out my new account application, and she paused to confirm that I preferred Ms., I said actually I prefer nothing at all, I didn't really like 'Female Person' being part of my name."

"What'd she say?"

"She said, 'Oh is that what it means?'" Rev paused. "And she was *our age*!"

Sarah looked disgusted. "What the hell did she think it meant?"

"Well, she didn't think," Rev replied. "That's the problem."

"And the real kicker is that it's considered polite," Sarah said a moment later. "Just try *not* using it and see what happens. Polite to identify someone by their sexual organs," she hmphed.

"On *Star Trek*, they call Captain Janeway 'sir'—don't they?" Shaun had been thinking. "When she gives an order, don't they say 'Yes, sir'?"

Dylan seemed to run a replay in his mind. "No, I think it's 'Yes Ma'am'—but it sounds like 'Yes sir'—they make it carry the same respect and authority."

"But see, why can't they just call her 'Captain'?" Rev asked. "Whether it's Janeway who gives the command or Jean Luc Picard, why can't they just say 'Yes, Cap'n'?"

"Funny how you know Picard's first name but not Janeway's," Dylan pointed out. "Just the opposite of the Hillary and Obama thing."

"That is weird," Rev said, thinking. "What *is* Janeway's first name?"

None of them knew Captain Janeway's first name.

"Maybe they've never used it," Dylan suggested. "Maybe they're aware of the Hillary/Obama thing."

"No, that can't be right," Rev said, "because they've made her name *Jane*way. As if they have to soften her role as commander. Make sure everyone knows she's still a woman."

"Have you guys seen *The Mentalist*?" Shaun asked. "His name is Patrick Jayne. So they're often calling him Jayne. It's a bit weird, but okay actually."

"That's right!" Dylan said. "And once when someone hesitated, when they were told his name was Jayne, he actually *said* 'Jayne, like the girl.'"

"But then he added, '*Patrick* Jayne,'" Shaun remembered the scene. "Still."

"So what do you do now?" Dylan asked Sarah.

"Well, most of the organizations that used to contract my services no longer exist. The women's shelter went under too. Lack of funding. But," she sighed, "men still beat up women, so there's still a need. If we can't provide shelter, I figure we should at least provide self-defense."

"You teach women's self defense?"

"No," she replied, "I sell Taser guns."

"Woh," Rev said.

"Well expecting women to physically fight back—we don't even *play* fight with each other, it's not in our—well it's probably not in our nature *or* our nurture. We do have superior hand-eye coordination though. So why not use what we've got?"

"Good point."

"But aren't there—don't Taser guns sometimes kill?"

They both looked at Dylan pointedly.

"Do you want to or shall I?" Sarah asked Rev.

"Three women a day," Shaun spoke up. "Are killed by their partners," he added.

They both looked at him.

"Hey, I know stuff!" he said defensively.

"Why not just shoot the guy with a tranquilizer dart though," Dylan suggested, "then run away." He grinned at Rev.

"Turns out when the guy wakes up," Sarah said, "he tracks her down, she who had the nerve to leave him, and he shoots her. With a bullet gun. Go figure," she added dryly

They finished their slices and drank their beer.

"So, um, do you wanna come out back?" Shaun asked Dylan.

"Yeah, let's go out back," Sarah said. They all got up and trudged out the back door. At which Rev stopped dead. And stared at the Harley-Davidson. The candy-apple red Harley-Davidson.

"You drive?" Sarah asked.

"Used to. Until I needed a new roof. Sold the bike. The roads where I live are all gravel anyway."

Sarah nodded. "Like driving on ball bearings. No fun."

Rev started circling the Harley.

"You're drooling," Dylan said.

"Am not," she said, wiping her mouth. When she got around to the other side, she burst out laughing.

"Yeah," Sarah said, "they asked me to design something for the Take Back the Night march. And I did that instead. I call it—"

"TAKING BACK THE FINGER!" Rev said with delight.

It was a man's hand, with the third finger extended, but curled just enough. Painted onto the gas tank at just the right place—

"It's perfect! Absolutely perfect!"

Dylan nudged Shaun. "Take note," he said quietly.

"Noted," Shaun said, and nodded slightly.

"Wanna take it for a spin?" Sarah asked. "Left out the driveway and left again, and you're on paved secondary roads for quite a while."

"Could I?"

"Sure," Sarah said. "I'll get the key." She went back into the house, while Shaun and Dylan carried on to the little greenhouse out back. She returned with key and helmet.

"Here, it'll probably fit," she handed Rev her helmet.

Rev got onto the Harley, couldn't help grinning as she straddled the gas tank, then turned the ignition. A broad smile burst across her face. She slowly wheeled it around and drove out of the driveway.

BY THE TIME REV HAD returned, it was close to six o'clock. Dylan, Shaun, and Sarah were sitting on the porch.

"Lunch!" Dylan called out as he raised a bottle of beer and another slice of pizza.

"Be there in a minute," Rev said as she carefully set the kickstand, then put her left foot on the ground, lifted her right leg, and—fell off the bike.

Sarah burst out laughing, choking on her beer.

"Rev?" Dylan heard her swearing somewhere on the other side of the Harley.

"I sit in one position for more than ten goddamned minutes and I turn to fucking cement," she said by way of explanation. From the pavement. "One of these days I'm going to break something just getting off the damned couch," she said as she walked stiffly toward the porch. "I hate this growing old shit," she added.

"Yeah, well, what're you gonna do," Sarah commiserated. "Here, have a beer. Good ride?"

"Yeah, apart from the falling off part." She sat down, slowly. "Thank you so much," she said. "It was wonderful." She took the bottle of beer Sarah held out to her, and helped herself to a slice of pizza.

"I was going to ask if you've got a print or some sort of copy of your—finger. It's just so—delightful. But," she waved to the Harley, "that's the only place it should be, really."

"Yeah, it's what they call site-specific art," Sarah grinned.

Once they'd finished lunch, they stood up to make their departure.

"Well, look, thanks," Rev said. "For the beer, the pizza, the ride—"

"The conversation, the replenishing," Dylan nodded to Shaun.

"It's been a pleasure meeting you both," Sarah said.

Dylan nodded his agreement. "Well," he said, then broke into silly song, "'Always look on the bright side, of life.'" Sarah recognized the bit and smiled, her eyes welling up just a bit. Shaun burst into a goofy grin.

"Thanks," Sarah said warmly, stepping forward to hug them both. "You're good people."

"HERE," REV TOSSED THE KEYS to Dylan, as they walked out to her car. "You drive. I want to bask in the Harley experience a bit longer."

"Can't," he said. Apologetically. "I sampled the merchandise."

She sighed, as she got in on the driver's side.

"Sorry. Just a little bit. It seemed the thing to do."

She turned the ignition and put the car in reverse.

"Usually I have my bike for times like this. It's not such a problem then. I just take a little longer to get to where I'm going. Should I indeed remember where I'm going—"

She started backing out.

"Vroom, vroom?" Dylan said helpfully.

"Oh shut up," she grinned. Once at the end of the driveway, she paused. "Which way?"

"Not the way we came from. If we want to keep going."

"Right."

"Really? That made sense?"

"Oddly enough," she said. Then, after a moment—"And which way did we come from?"

"I don't know. I sampled the merchandise, remember?"

"Right." She looked to the right and then to the left. Then to the right again.

"If school was spatial instead of verbal, you'd've been in the special class, wouldn't you've been."

"Shut up," she grinned. "Just let me think a minute. I turned—left! I turned left onto their driveway. So that means—"

"So that means you turn right now."

"No it doesn't. It means I turn left now."

"But then you'd be making a circle. Left and left again."

"And they say men are the ones with all the spatial ability. God help us." She turned left out of the driveway.

"Tell me if you recognize anything."

"Ah, brilliant idea." He looked out the window. "Nope. I've never seen anything like this before. Rock. Forest. Fields of green stuff. How wonderful. Oh, oh, a cow! We must getting near the castle."

They drove for a while, each lost in their thoughts. Dylan considerably more so than Rev.

"It'll be getting dark soon."

"Yes it will." He paused. "And then what happens? I mean apart from everything disappearing."

"Well," she said after a moment, "that's not really inconsequential, is it. I mean as an empiricist, I've always found night to require a great leap of faith."

"It does, doesn't it," he agreed, clearly thinking about some other aspect of night that required a leap of faith.

"I don't like driving at night, remember?"

"Oh yeah. Because you're so very old. Well then we'll just stop at the next motel."

"Since we've put in so very many miles today already—good idea. Remind me," she said then, "to call ahead to the dorm in Montreal to change my dates."

"You're staying in a dorm?"

"Yeah. During the summer, it's real cheap to stay at one of the university dorms. And I'd planned to stay a whole week—the fireworks are Wednesdays and Saturdays, so I thought I'd stay a week—well, a week plus a day—and see three of them."

"Ah."

She drove for a while. They passed more rock and forest, but no motels.

"So since all of your stuff is in storage," she asked, "does that mean your lease was up and you're between apartments or something?"

"Something. Not exactly."

"You didn't get evicted—did you?" She looked over.

"Hey!" he said with indignation. "Yeah," he confessed. "The landlord turned out to be specist. Specieist. Speciesist?" Dylan paused, considering. "He turned out to be stupid."

"You had a dog and it was a 'no pets allowed' apartment?"

"I didn't so much have the dog as the dog had me, but yeah. Bob wasn't allowed."

"But I bet kids were allowed," Rev said. "And yet dogs can be taught to sit on request."

"They come when you call."

"They get fixed well before they hit puberty."

"Interesting word that. 'Fixed.'"

"Isn't it. So what kind of dog is Bob?"

"The big and goofy kind."

"A lab."

"Yes! How did you—"

"And a *black* lab, I'll bet. They're goofier than the golden labs."

"Isn't that a bit—racist?"

"No. It's a bit—colorist."

"Hm."

"So where is Bob? Don't tell me you left him in storage with all of your stuff."

"No, of course not!"

Rev waited.

"He left me. For a dog named Fifi. Can you believe it?" Dylan was so insulted. "Fifi!! Can't blame him, really," he continued. "She lived on a farm, with lots of—" he gestured, "stuff to do. And a bunch of kids. Bob loves kids. It was never going to last anyway."

"So you're looking for a new apartment?"

"No, that was years ago, me and Bob."

"So you're—"

"I'm a house-sitter."

"What's a house-sitter?"

"Someone who sits houses. These LSAT people, do they buy *any* of your questions?"

"Shut up," she grinned back. "Okay, so what does a house-sitter do? What do you actually *do* when you sit a house?"

"Well, I look after it." He paused. "I live in it."

"So you sit in it."

"That's really all a house wants."

"To be sat in."

"To be lived in. Oh sure, it might need a plumber or an electrician from time to time."

"And you do the maintenance while you're living in these houses?"

"Oh god no, I don't know a hammer from a screwdriver. But I know how to *call* a plumber. And an electrician. That's the important thing."

"And how do you find these houses to sit?"

"I joined a house-sitting network. You sign up, post your qualifications, your availability, and some such, and people who need a house-sitter contact you. Usually it's people who really want a live-in dog sitter—which is fine with me. I miss Bob. But sometimes it's rich people who want their house to be occupied while they're away so someone's there to be killed when the thieves come."

"And it pays well, this house-sitting business?"

"Oh, it doesn't pay at all. But nor do I have to pay."

"Ah. Don't you miss your stuff?" she asked after a moment.

"Well, I used to. But since I got a laptop—and one of those mp3 thingamajigs, well, there's my music. I join libraries wherever I am, so there's my books. The houses always have a TV and they're already furnished so I don't need that part of my stuff. Clothes I take with me. I was never into the thirty pairs of shoes thing, so that's cool."

"But don't you miss having—home?"

"Sometimes. But don't you miss traveling about? Don't you get bored staying at home all the time?"

"Sometimes. Hence the trip to Montreal to see the fireworks."

"Yeah about that, he said after a moment."

"What?"

"Well it kinda surprises me. I mean, it's so—frivolous. I expected to find you—I don't know, bringing democracy to the Third World."

"Yeah, well," she paused to pass a car. "I tried, remember? Ten years? So, now, well, I eventually realized that the capacity for pleasure is—not universal. I used to think that people who weren't pure hedonists were just denying themselves, out of some moral duty. Turns out they don't *have* a capacity for pleasure. So they're not denying themselves. In fact, they *are* hedonists. It's just not pleasure they seek." She paused a moment. "That sounds—"

"Very Catholic."

"Yeah well. So my point is I do. Have a capacity for pleasure. And of course it's always a shame, perhaps it's even remiss of one, not to actualize one's potential. It's like someone with higher intelligence limiting herself to factory work. Out of some moral duty. Because others have to work in a factory, and it's wrong to be elitist, to set oneself apart, to not do one's share of the shit work. But that would be like cutting off an arm because everyone else has only one arm. How stupid is that."

Dylan was trying to follow her logic.

"So once I was in a position to—once I started having a bit of money left over, and now what with the mobility of the LSAT job—well here I am, on my way to Montreal to see the fireworks."

She looked over at him. He was unconvinced. 'Course so was she.

"So by not bringing democracy to the Third World," she summarized, "I'm actualizing my unique potential."

"Ah." Dylan thought it through a bit, then said, "*I* have the capacity for pleasure."

"Okay, my *rare* potential," she amended. Then paused. "You have the capacity for silly shit."

He grinned.

"Which is also rare," she continued. "Especially in men."

Dylan started to protest, but then changed his mind.

"Men don't—I don't know, maybe they *have* a capacity for pleasure," she said, "but they get pleasure mostly from conquest. From power. They can't just sit in a boat in the middle of the lake, they have to be fishing. Catching and killing things. They can't just go for a walk in the forest, they have to go hunting. Catching and—"

"Got it."

"Or they have to take pictures, with some complicated camera-tool-surrogate. They can't just—enjoy. They have to make everything *work*.

"And retired men—they're the worst. I used to think that living where there are a lot of retired people, on the lake, it'd be quiet. But my god, they have to be cutting their grass or trimming their weeds or repairing this or building that—and all with power tools. Every day, all day, I hear lawn mowers and those irritating weed things and power saws and chain saws and those nail gun things and—"

She eased up on the gas pedal, took a breath, then got back on track. "Even when they're—even when they're playing Bach for god's sake. Every chamber group, every symphony orchestra I've ever seen, the men all look so damned serious. Can't they just—smile? Enjoy? Must everything be work?"

"Well it is work. They look so serious because they're concentrating. It's hard to play Bach," Dylan said. "Especially on a tambourine."

She grinned. But was not deterred. "Maybe," she said. "Or maybe they just have to make everything they do so damned important. Because that means *they're* so damned important. They even put on a serious face when they tie their shoelaces."

"That's because they're concentrating so hard! I'm telling you!"

"Maybe they have no capacity for pleasure because they have no concept of beauty. A couple weekends ago, someone put fluorescent-orange spray-painted bleach bottles all over the lake marking the deadheads. I suspect—"

"Wait a minute," Dylan said. "There are Grateful fans—in your lake?"

"There are waterlogged trees that poke up to just below the surface."

"Ah."

"I suspect it didn't even occur to him," she continued, "that he had totally wrecked the—the beauty. This beautiful, *beautiful* lake—full of trees, reflecting in the water when it gets impossibly still, and full of sun sparkles when the breeze ripples across, sometimes the mist, and the moonlight—and then there were these goddamned spray-painted bleach bottles everywhere."

"Well why didn't you just go sink them all?"

She cast a glance in his direction.

"Right. Of course. Bad for the environment. Better to just untie them all and take them to the dump."

She cast another glance in his direction.

"And if I'd pointed that out to him," she continued, "that he'd wrecked the beauty—he would have laughed at me. Not in malice. He just genuinely would have thought I was kidding. He would have been completely incapable of taking the point, or me, come to think of it, seriously.

"Same as when I asked another guy not to cut down a bunch of trees on the slope that stretches out onto the little peninsula. He said they were dead anyway. He totally didn't get that I loved the view, that trees stretching out onto the lake were so much more beautiful than a clear cut scar of stumps would be."

"Not to mention that dead or not, they would have been holding the bank in place. What happened when he cut them down?"

"Oh he never got around to it. He was out one afternoon zooming around in his loud obnoxious motorboat from one fishing spot to another and he hit a deadhead. Flew overboard."

Dylan burst out laughing. Then tried to stop. Couldn't quite.

"And it's not at anyone else's expense," Rev continued.

"What isn't?" He didn't follow.

"My hedonism. I stay in my own little world, the pleasures I enjoy don't detrimentally affect anyone else. Okay, I'm putting myself first, but what's wrong with that?" she demanded. "I mean, why should I put others before myself, why should I spend my time trying to please others instead of myself? What kind of low self esteem does that imply? Are other people worth more than me? Are they better than me? No, they are not. And I have extensive evidence indicating that."

"You don't have to justify your hedonism," Dylan said somewhat defensively.

"But I do. I mean, what do I do with the guilt then?"

"Ah." He understood then. "How can you enjoy fireworks when so many don't have food."

"Well if I had a name and an address, I could mail a bag of food every day," she said, missing that it was a rhetorical question. "But even then, I couldn't be sure the kid would get the package. Some guy along the way might confiscate it and sell it for his own profit.

"Plus, I can't feed them all," she continued. "'Oh but you don't have to feed them all. If each one of us took care of just one of them—'"

"'Adopt a—'"

"Right. Well there's a reason I didn't have any kids of my own."

"You don't like kids. Which is why you went into teaching."

"Which is why—at the high school level," she protested. "They're teenagers then. Kids are so…immature."

"Well," he agreed, "kind of by definition." He looked over at her. "These LSAT people—"

"But high school students aren't kids. They're adolescents. Going through the throws of existential crises."

"That's throes, with an 'e.'"

"How do you know how I spelled it?" she looked over at him. "And they're not. Throes. They're throws. Really hard throws that make you smash head first into brick walls. But my point is that by high school, they're more mature. They can tell you to fuck off."

He glanced over. She did have a half-grin on her face.

"But my *real* point is," she continued after pausing to pass a car, "—what was my real point?"

"The reason you didn't have any kids."

"Right."

"And it is?"

"I don't want to be responsible for another human being. Is that so selfish?" She looked over at him. "I mean, where does it say we should become responsible for others? What's the logic of that morality?"

Dylan shrugged. He didn't have any kids either.

"So, all these starving kids I'm supposed to feed. Well I didn't make them. If their parents hadn't've made them, they wouldn't be starving. The guilt is on them for knowingly—*knowingly*—creating something that would most probably starve to death.

"I used to be persuaded by Singer's argument," she continued. "You know, the responsibility of affluence—"

"Yes, I know it."

"Well," she paused again to pass another car, "I used to be persuaded. At least persuaded enough to feel guilty. Because I didn't have much money to give anyway. And part of me wanted to stay poor so I wouldn't have to—anything extra I earned I'd feel compelled to give away, so—but then I heard some developing-world guy say to some first-world organization or government body, 'It's our right to have children, and it's your responsibility to feed them.' *Excuse me?*" She glared at Dylan.

He glanced at the speedometer and mutely pointed. She eased off the gas pedal.

"So I'd consider it," she said. "Feeding the hungry children," she clarified. "But only after their parents get sterilized. Because otherwise they'll just keep making more hungry children. And I'm supposed to keep feeding them? I don't think so.

"*And* only after their parents get penalized," she added. "As I say, they're the ones that did wrong in the first place."

"But the kids are innocent victims," Dylan ventured. "If their own parents don't take responsibility for them, wouldn't it be nice if someone else did?"

"Nice? Yeah. But morally required? I don't think so."

"And you're not a nice person."

"No, I am not."

"You're an angry person."

"Yes, I—" she looked over at him. "Yes," she conceded, "I am. Still." She sighed.

AFTER A WHILE OF JUST STARING ahead into the darkness, Dylan cried out, "Look! Lights! The spaceship has landed. Dad's come back for me!"

As they approached the town, Rev said, "Okay, keep your eyes open for the motel."

"How do you know there will be a motel?"

"It's the rule. Every small town has a gas station, a beer store, a corner store, and a motel."

"And there it is!" he said. "The Paradise Motel. Oh please," he added, "who are they kidding?"

The parking area was full of potholes, the building needed a coat of paint, and two of the five units were boarded up. A third had police tape around it.

She slowed down and pulled off the highway.

"Careful," he called out as she opened her door. "Don't fall out of the car."

"Oh shut up."

She exited the car successfully, and they walked to the office.

"One night please," Dylan said to the woman behind the—card table. "You got the last one," he said to Rev, as he pulled out his credit card.

The woman handed him a pen and nodded at the clipboard bearing blank registration forms. He filled in the information required while she processed his card.

"Check out's at two. Here's your key. Unit #5. Right at the end."

Rev and Dylan looked at each other. Then headed out the door.

A minute later, they entered the room and tossed their bags onto the beds.

Dylan collapsed back onto one of the beds. "I'm exhausted. All that driving. Oh my!"

Rev snickered from the washroom.

"Hey, a TV *and* a remote!" He sat up, got cross-legged, turned on the TV, and picked up the remote.

'Cover me!' A cop show.

'The man was last seen leaving the store—' News.

"How do you do that?" she asked him.

He looked at her. "You press the button here. See? This little mark, the one that points up? That means up a channel. Go figure. And this little mark—"

"Shut up, I meant how do you sit like that."

"You can't sit cross-legged?"

"Not if I want to—not fall over when I get up."

"Hm."

'I told her she has nothing to worry about—' A soap opera.

'The rain should hold off until later this evening—' A weather report.

"Not bad," Dylan said, bunching up the pillows and getting comfortable for some serious play. "But I can do better." He continued clicking the remote.

'And then I told her she should just do it, I said—'

'Engage!'

"That's a bit better—"

Rev watched for a moment, trying to figure out what the hell he was doing.

'Your Honour, I fail to see the relevance—'

'Oh—that was nice,' a woman moaned. 'And it can get even nicer,' a man's voice responded. 'Here, let me help you with that—'

'He shoots! He scores!'

Dylan burst out laughing. So did Rev, finally understanding.

'Yeah, somebody's gotta do it.'

"Oh, a triple!" Dylan cried out.

"Let me try!" she said, settling beside him. He handed her the remote. She clicked it.

'Turn left! There he is!'

'... would announce that the government bail-out has gotten the green light—'

A child's face filled the screen, serious. 'And that would be wrong.'

"Yeah! Good one!" Dylan laughed again. "My turn."

Rev handed him the remote.

'Oh, please.' It was Alan Shore, the lawyer from *Boston Legal*.

"Oh stay here. I love this show," Rev said.

'Am I to understand,' Alan Shore continued, 'that you would have my client, or indeed anyone who is unfortunate enough to have a gun pointed at him or her, to first ask "Gee, is that a real gun or a toy gun?" And then, I suppose, one must ask "And is it loaded or not?" And then, surely, "And does this person really intend to shoot me or is he just bluffing?" By which time, if it had been real, and loaded, and pointed with full intent, my client, or indeed anyone, would be dead!' He looked expectantly at the prosecuting attorney. With his Alan Shore look.

"I generally check out any new lawyer show," Rev said, "but when I found out Spader was in this one—I've liked him since *Sex, Lies, and Videotape*. He always makes his characters so—interesting."

"Did you see *The Secretary*?"

"Yes!"

'Your client should have known Bobby had no intent of really killing him,' the prosecuting attorney was speaking, 'because this is not Sri Lanka. This is the U. S. of A. And we don't arm our children.'

'Oh please,' Alan Shore said. 'As we speak, I suspect there are hundreds, thousands, of fathers teaching their young sons how to use a gun. No doubt believing it'll make a man of him. What *kind* of man—I don't really want to get into at the moment.'

"Shatner almost turned me off watching it—he's such an arrogant asshole."

"But he's making fun of exactly that in the show. Denny Crane," Dylan mimicked with full-chested ego.

"Yeah, I finally realized that. Still."

"Don't you love it how they keep casting actors with a past—"

"—that they—"

"Like Magnum PI singing showtunes."

"Yes! And Dan Fielding—"

"—being the normal one."

That gave them pause.

"And Betty White," Dylan said.

"Isn't she perfect? All those snide comments coming out of that white-haired red-lipsticked little old lady—"

"Who used to be such a naïve Norwegian..." he searched for the word, "bumpkiss."

"And of course Shirley Schmidt being Murphy Brown."

"Yeah, but she *is* Murphy Brown," Dylan said. "There's no play there."

"You're right," Rev realized. "So she should've been cast as—a Phyllis Shaffley?"

"Oh, the horror."

'Use of force is justified,' Alan Shore was saying, 'when a person *reasonably believes* that it's necessary. "Reasonably" according to whom? According to the community? But Mr. Mendis was new to our community. In the community in which he lived most of his life, children don't play with guns. They carry real ones. Ms. O'Neill has argued that it's the standards of *our* community that should prevail. Well then surely we have a responsibility to newcomers to tell them about our community. In citizenship classes, we should be sure to say "Welcome to our country. By the way, we have made killing into a game for our youngsters. You should know that about us."'

"This is a good one," Rev said. "And it must be a new one. I haven't seen it before." They watched a bit more.

'Furthermore, with all due respect, Your Honour, I question the wisdom, indeed the reasonableness, of using a sick standard over well, no, scratch that. A country that conscripts its children into its armies and gives them real guns compared to a country that says "Here's a gun, go have fun pretending to kill people"—it's a toss up as to which is the more sick, isn't it.'

Commercials came on.

"You know I've always regretted that she wasn't cast for *Commander in Chief*," Rev said.

"Who?"

"Murphy Brown. Candace Bergen."

"And what was *Commander in Chief* about?" Dylan asked.

"You didn't watch that? A woman President! Geena Davis played the part."

"Really? How could I have missed it?"

"Well, it lasted only one season. No surprise. She did such a good job."

"Ah. And we can't have that," he understood.

"But then I realized," Rev continued, "it's because she's tall. Candace Bergen wasn't tall enough."

"What? You're saying Geena Davis got the part because she's tall?"

"Happens all the time," Rev said. "Short men don't have power. Or rather, people don't grant short people power."

"Bill Gates isn't all that tall, is he? And what about Eisenhower? He was in a wheelchair. Can't get much shorter than that," Dylan giggled. Just a little shame-facedly.

"Exceptions," Rev glossed over his objections. "I've always thought if most women were taller than most men—instead of the other way around—what a difference that would have made. No more patriarchy."

"You think it's all just because we're—taller?"

"Well, it's not that far from saying it's just because you're bigger. An argument often made. You're not, by the way."

"What, bigger?"

"Yeah. Think about it. Look around. At real men and women. Think of all the married couples you know. Makes an easy comparison. The woman usually has the bigger chest measurement, yeah?"

"Okay, yeah—"

"And bigger hips."

He nodded.

"And thighs."

He had to nod once again.

"But," Rev said, "the man is taller. Think back to when you've had to look up at someone. Didn't you find yourself just sort of naturally being, well not subservient exactly, but—it's hard to take the dominant role when you have to look up at someone. Maybe because it's reminiscent of being a child."

"Hm..." Dylan was thinking.

"And since most men are taller than most women, women have to look up to men almost all the time."

He hadn't considered that.

"I saw a program once about short men. And parents who put their sons through hell to gain them an extra few inches. They actually break their bones and then stretch them during the healing process. There were all these heart-rending stories about how awful it is to go through life short. Well, fuck, women all over the world go through life being short. -er. It *is* important."

My god but there were a lot of commercials.

"So," she continued, "if male infants started being born smaller and ended up, on average, five feet—"

"You think men would start feeling subordinate to women because of having to look up at them all the time."

*Boston Legal* returned.

"You know who they should get?" Rev said after a while. "They should get Hazel, or the maid from *The Brady Bunch*, or, oh, oh—Edith. From *All in the Family*. You know, Archie Bunker. They should get Edith to play a topnotch hotshot lawyer."

"That would be so—so something," he said. "And Data! They

should get Data to play a stand-up comedian!"

"Perfect!" Rev laughed. "And Lassie! Lassie should play a police dog gone bad!"

"I know who they should get," Dylan said a moment later. "Johnny Fever."

"What, to play some 'Just say no' zealot?" Rev snort-laughed.

"Speaking of which," Dylan reached for his knapsack and rummaged inside it for his stash. "Just say yes?"

"Yes," Rev said, then got up—and down—"Shit!" she said from the floor.

Dylan burst out laughing. She glared at him as she peered over the bed.

"Hey, I'm not—" he protested then changed his mind. Because he was. "How can you fall off a bed?" He waved the baggie, papers, and matches. "We haven't even started yet."

"Because my muscles turn to cement, remember?"

"Are you sure that's the explanation? It doesn't sound very—plausible. Medically speaking," he added.

She got up, stiffly, and walked over to the TV table. She opened the drawer and pulled out a phone book and a variety of flyers from fast food delivery places.

"Good idea," Dylan said. "Let's arrange for food *before* we—before."

"Oh look, dinnerware too!" She pulled out some paper plates, some plastic cutlery, and a wad of napkins, and tossed them onto the bed.

"Pizza Fantastico or Doug's Pizza?" She'd quickly narrowed it down to the pizza places. Then selected Pizza Fantastico without waiting for Dylan's answer. He smiled to himself.

"Hi," she said after a minute. "Could I order a large, half pepperoni and mushroom, half green olives and pineapple. And two bottles of Pepsi."

Dylan had lit a joint and taken a draw, and was waving it wildly as he held in the smoke.

"Oh, right, and do you have any Doritos?" She paused. "That'll do. Two—three bags please."

"No Doritos?" he asked glumly as she hung up.

"Cheesy Fritos instead."

"That'll do," he said happily.

*Boston Legal* had ended and Rev picked up the remote. "Let's play with the remote some more."

'All the kids are doing it, mom—' A young voice protested from the TV.

Dylan laughed delightedly. "A halfer!"

"What's a heifer?"

"No, a halfer. The juxtaposition was half you, half TV. Counts more that way." He handed her the joint.

"What *is* a heifer?" he said after a moment.

They thought about it.

"A castrated male cow?" Rev offered, as she exhaled.

"But it wouldn't be a cow then."

"Right. It would be—" she suddenly took the next exit. "We don't have a word for castrating a female!" She snorted with disgust. "Figures. Not important enough. Females are never important enough. And certainly our sexual—or reproductive—capacity isn't important enough to name losing it."

"Now wait, wait just a minute," he groped for the thought as he waved the joint. "Your sexual and reproductive capacity *is* important. You were complaining just the other day—or today—about how it's the *only* thing that's important! *Captain* Reveille."

"Right. You're right. So why don't we have a word for it?"

"We do. Slut, hussy, whore, prostitute—"

"For *losing* it."

"We do have a word for losing it," he chuckled. "Losing it."

"That's two words."

"Not if you say them fast."

"Speed doesn't determine number!"

"Right. Okay, not if you say them together. Losingit. Loo-singit." He giggled. "Loo-*sing*-it."

They were both silent for a moment. Probably trying to remember what word they were looking for.

"Spacing determines number?" Rev finally said. "Physical proximity determines independence? That's so...physicalist."

"Gelding," Dylan announced in response.

"What?"

"Isn't a castrated male called a gelding?"

"If it's a horse."

"Right." Then after another moment, "Oh, oh—" he waved the joint in the air.

"They should get him," Rev said.

"Who?" He stopped waving the joint.

"What's-his-name from *Welcome Back, Kotter*. The oh, oh guy."

"Oh yeah."

"What *was* his name?"

"Oh, oh," Dylan said, remembering where he was a moment earlier, amazingly enough, "maybe a heifer is a breed thing. You know, like jersey and guernsey and chocolate and vanilla—and palomino," he said with relish. "Pa-lo-mi-no," he said slowly. Then he said it quickly. "Palomino. Perspicuity." He giggled. "Losingit."

"Bull, cow, calf," Rev announced. "They go together," she said proudly.

"Good. That's good. Let's do it that way. Stallion, mare, pony."

"Not pony, you ass, colt."

"Mr. Ass, Ms. Ass, and Baby Ass. Good, this is working. We're going to figure out heifer any minute now."

In the silence, he said, "I needed Mr. and Ms. there, because—"

"Yeah yeah, get your laptop out," she said. "Let's look it up."

Dylan snagged his knapsack and pulled it toward him.

"Don't you just love…" he said after a long while, then trailed off.

"We put satellites way up high," he resumed, "out in space, so we can find out *right now* what a heifer is."

She leaned over his shoulder to look.

"A heifer is a halfer!" she cried out in glee. "Half a bull. A castrated male male-cow."

"No, that's the line for steer." He grabbed a plastic knife to use as a pointer.

"A heifer is," he read aloud, "'a female cow—' Isn't that redundant? Didn't we have that worked out at least? '—before she's had her first calf.'"

Rev leaned back with disgust. "We have a different word for that?"

Then the rant poured out of her. "Oh sure, of course, yeah, whether or not a female actually becomes a mother, that's so fucking important because it defines her, right? I mean if she's not somebody's mom or somebody's wife, she doesn't exist. Is that what they're saying?"

There was a knock at the door. She grabbed the knife from him. "Pizza's here!"

Half way to the door, she stopped. "It's hysterectomized!"

"What's hysterectomized?" Dylan looked around in horror.

*"That's* the same as castrated. And that's where hysterical comes from?" she said then in disbelief. "It's *men* who get hysterical when they get castrated!"

"Screaming in high-pitched voices and all," Dylan agreed.

"Neutered," he suggested.

"No that refers to both." Rev remembered then that she was on her way to the door. “Spayed! Spayed and crastrated!” she said with triumph, as she opened the door, waving the plastic knife in the air.

The pizza guy took a couple steps backward. Then ever so slowly, eyes locked on hers, he set the pizza box on the ground, the Pepsi and Cheesy Fritos on top. Ever so slowly, he straightened up. Then ran for his car like a bat out of hell.

“Pizza’s free!” she cried out gaily to Dylan.

THEY WERE CHECKED OUT and on the road again the next day. Bright and early. By two. Dylan was surfing the internet.

“Find anything interesting?”

“Maybe—I’m seeing if there’s anything to do in Elliot Lake.”

“Hm. We could go watch the tailings glow.”

He looked over at her. “Are you nuts? They don’t glow. They twinkle.”

She smiled.

“Funny how that used to be such a big thing. A pile of radioactive nuclear waste six feet high stretching from coast to coast. Elliott Lake as Canada’s premier retirement community because no one would live there except old people who would die of something else before the radiation got them. And now,” she said, “no one even knows what the word tailings means.” She sighed.

“Maybe not true. There’s a demonstration.” He clicked away at the keys. “Oh. It’s not actually in Elliott Lake. It’s at the university in Sudbury.”

“The students at Laurentian are protesting nuclear waste?” She was impressed.

“Not sure...” he was clicking away. “But we should go.”

“Why? I mean what’s the point?”

“Well, you know. To send a message.”

“To who?”

"The people in power," he said grandly. "You used to—"

"Oh please. They won't pay any attention except to consider mounting a PR campaign to counter whatever damage to their precious reputation might have occurred. And said campaign will be far more effective because they've got far money to spend. On spin.

"And anyway," she continued, "what possible message can be sent by a bunch of people carrying signs and shouting. You can't say much on a sign. You certainly can't present a convincing argument, there's no room for reasons. Or evidence. And do we really expect people to change their minds, their policies and practices, *without* argument or evidence? Do we really *want* them to be so stupid?"

"No. But the point is not to make a point, but just to raise the question. Or maybe it is to make a point—to present the conclusion to arguments presented elsewhere. In a way that will get the media's attention."

"So, what, the conclusion to those arguments presented elsewhere will become a headline. And the point of that is—?"

"Okay maybe it's not so much a display of reason as a display of emotion. It's saying, hey, we're angry and we're—"

"—going to walk around in a circle carrying signs. That's how angry we are."

"You think they should walk around in a circle carrying something else? AK-47s maybe?"

"Yes! No. I don't know. Maybe I've become a hedonist because I'm too cowardly—no, too selfish—to become a terrorist."

"Too selfish?"

"Yeah. I like doing what I want when I want. Being in prison would mean I couldn't."

"It also means I'd have to live with other people," she added. "A lot of other people. If I were ever in prison, I'd do something to get solitary confinement. I've never understood how that's a punishment. Why do people find it so awful to be all by themselves for a few hours? My god—"

"Okay, here we go," Dylan interrupted, focused on his laptop. "They're protesting the debt."

"What, the national debt?" She was surprised.

Dylan clicked away. "Doesn't say exactly. Still, we should go."

"But why? After everything I've said?"

"Because *That Magazine* will pay me $1,000 if I write an article about it," he said just a little sheepishly.

They're both silent.

"Which magazine?"

So a couple hours later, they pulled into the main entrance of the university campus. There was no sign of the demonstration. There were no signs to the demonstration.

"Gee, this is a really good way to get the media's attention," Rev said. "Don't tell them where you are."

"Well, let's just drive around. The campus can't be that big. Or the demonstration that small."

So they drove around and eventually saw something going on at the end of the sports field. They drove toward it and parked in a spot not far away. Dylan grabbed his camera and a notebook from out of his knapsack.

As they approached, they heard music blaring out over a sound system. Several tables were set up with what Rev assumed was literature, petitions, and so forth, and there were a couple large striped circus tents. More tables inside? Rainy day back-up? About a hundred students seemed to be in attendance. Most were standing around in clusters, some were throwing a football back and forth, and a few were rather despondently walking in a circle, carrying signs that said simply 'NO MORE DEBT!!'

"Well, that'll make the world a better place," Rev said dryly.

Dylan took a few pictures, then they walked up to one of the tables.

"Hi there. I'm doing a piece for *That Magazine*. Can you tell me—" he had his pen poised, "what debt you're protesting?"

She just looked at him.

"The national debt?" He tried again. "Corporate debt?"

"Student debt."

Rev was stunned. "*Student* debt? You're protesting *your own* debt?"

"Yeah."

"But—why?"

"We have a right to be debt-free!" One of them said with gusto.

"On what basis?"

That stopped them.

"What?"

"On what grounds do you claim the right to be debt-free?"

"What do you mean?"

"Well, did you inherit the debt—is it a debt you bear through no fault of your own?"

"It's our student debt," she said, as if talking to a child.

"I understand that," Rev replied. As if talking to a child. "But debt is typically incurred when you buy something and choose to defer payment. That deferred payment is your debt. So when you say you have the right to be debt-free, are you suggesting you have a right to get things without paying for them?"

"What?"

"This is hopeless," Rev said to Dylan. "Let's go before I shoot her."

"University should be free!" the other student called out as they turned away. Rev turned back.

"Okay, well that's something else altogether. Some countries do have state-paid university. Much like we have state-paid elementary and high school. But in those countries," she couldn't help adding, "I think you have to have a certain grade point average to get in. Or stay in." She paused. And saw she needed to say it. "Do you have a—grade point average?"

"What?"

"Let's mingle," Dylan suggested. "Maybe—"

A burst of chanting suddenly came from one of the tents. They looked at each other in confusion. Shouldn't the chanting come from those carrying the signs? As they approached the tent, they heard it more clearly.

"Chugga hugga chugga hugga..."

"I *thought* that sounded like 'Hell no, we won't go,'" Rev said. "It's a beer tent. They've got a beer tent. At a demonstration. This is like a fucking picnic," she said as they walked toward the tent.

"Do you think they've got food?" Dylan asked hopefully. Rev glared at him.

"What? I'm hungry. We buy food and it goes to the cause. Of no more debt," he added lamely. "That's what the Americans do, isn't it?" he resumed cheerfully. "In the middle of every recession, or depression—you know I've never really understood the difference—whenever they don't have any money, they go shopping. The President urges them to do just that. You've lost your job? You can't pay your rent? Go buy stuff. It's the American way."

They'd arrived at the tent, and once inside, they saw that yes indeed, there was food. One table was full of extra large pizza boxes, most already opened, and another was full of beverages. They went up to buy a slice of pizza.

"How much is the pizza," Dylan asked. To no one in particular, since there wasn't anyone standing behind the table.

A student walked up to the table at that moment, helped himself to a couple slices, then walked away.

"It's free?" Rev asked. Of no one in particular. "How can they provide free pizza if they're all in so much debt they're protesting about it?"

"Maybe it's coming out of their student union fees or something?"

"I'd be pissed about that. I think."

"Ah." Dylan pointed then to the bright banner hanging across the table. "Courtesy of their sponsors." He took a few steps back to take a picture.

"What? Sponsors? Demonstrations have sponsors now?"

He shrugged. They each grabbed a slice, and a bottle of beer, what the hell, and sat down at one of the tables.

"Chugga hugga chugga hugga!" came from the boisterous table in the corner. Dylan put his slice down for a moment and took another picture.

"No one's here because they care about changing the world, making it a better place," Rev complained. "Half the guys are here to pick up some chick and the other half are here just for the party."

"What, you don't think that was true during the 60s too?"

Rev's pizza stopped half way to her mouth. Which was left hanging open. Oh my god, she thought. He was right. All those sit-ins were just parties. Music, drugs, sex. The issues were just an excuse, a cover.

"They didn't change," she murmured.

"What?"

"I've always wondered what made all those radical idealists change when they got into positions of power twenty years later," she said. "That they did is what—I mean, if *they* couldn't change the world—But they didn't. Change. They weren't idealists in the first place. They were just opportunists. All of them. Oh god," she moaned. It was worse than she'd thought.

"All those 'Make Love Not War' signs," she carried on, into hell. "It was *personal*. The political is always fucking personal! No one cares about anything beyond themselves!"

"I've got to sit down," she said.

"You are sitting down," Dylan pointed out.

"Did I just blow your mind?" Dylan asked then, as her pizza lay limp in her hand, forgotten. "You really hadn't considered that possibility before?"

"'Course not. I'm not a guy."

"Oh are we back to that then?" He could get really angry about this, he thought. "You think women are so much better? They weren't there to get laid too?"

"No, you're right," she conceded. "In the sixties, yeah, okay. They'd gotten the pill. But all the demonstrations before the sixties, before the pill, the men—oh my god, there weren't any!" she suddenly realized. "It was always women. See?" she said somewhat triumphantly. "Men didn't demonstrate until sex was to be had."

"What? What images are you calling up? There were pre-sixties demonstrations that men participated in!"

"Name one." She begged him. "The only pictures that come to *my* mind are women demonstrating for the vote and for temperance."

"Civil rights—sixties," he anticipated her.

"Viet Nam," she said. "Sixties."

They were both silent then, trying to think of something.

"You're right," Dylan finally said in defeat. "We *are* the scum of the earth. No, wait a minute, what was there to demonstrate about, before the 60s?"

"What I said! The vote! If women marched against sending men to Viet Nam, there's no reason men couldn't march to get women the vote. But they didn't. There wasn't a party to be had. And temperance—well, okay, maybe even I wouldn't've—though wait, it was more a child support issue than a drink is evil issue. And what about the bomb? World War II? Hell, World War I!"

"But even women didn't demonstrate against World War I. Did they?"

"Well they might've. But it wouldn't've made the news. So we'll never know. History's like that," she added sarcastically.

"About a lot of things," he pointed out.

They finished their pizza and beer in silence.

"So shall we venture into the other tent?" Dylan asked. "Or are we afraid to."

"Can't be worse," she got up. They tossed their paper plates and napkins into a huge garbage bin and put their empties into one of the cartons beside the table. They left the food and drink tent, and headed to the other one set up a short distance away.

"Oh but it can," he said as they paused in the doorway. There was a shiny new car on display, and a tallish man was standing nearby, dressed in attire emblazoned with the logo of what must've been the local car dealership, waving booklets of raffle tickets. Dylan took a picture.

"Only fifty bucks a book," the man called out. "Chances are good!"

"Fifty bucks?" Rev repeated. "He thinks students at a protest about their debt are going to pay *fifty bucks* for a raffle ticket?"

They watched then in disbelief as three students proceeded to do just that. Dylan took another picture. Then he looked up from his camera viewfinder.

"Wait a minute—isn't that—" he looked into his camera again, zooming in. "Isn't that Martin Bourge?"

"Who's Martin Bourge?"

"He was in our class. Remember? Tall guy, longish blond hair. He was specializing in—wasn't he in Art?" Dylan said with some surprise.

They walked up to the man and saw by his name tag that he was indeed Martin Bourge.

"Martin," Dylan said, extending his hand. "What are—We're—Dylan and Rev. From—"

"Dylan? Rev?" He looked from one to the other. "From teachers' college?" Martin was equally surprised. "Hey," he shook Dylan's hand enthusiastically, obviously in sales mode, then reached out to do the same with Rev. "What are you—you guys are—you guys are *profs* here?"

"Well, it wouldn't be completely in the twilight zone," Dylan responded with some indignation.

"No, no, I just meant—"

"Would it?" he turned to Rev.

Martin turned his attention to another couple of students who had wandered up to buy tickets.

"So you're—" he turned his attention back to the two of them.

"We were just passing through," Dylan explained, "found out about the demonstration, thought we'd check it out—"

Rev exploded. "What the hell are you doing having a raffle for a *new car* at a *student* demonstration about student *debt*??"

"I'm with the local car dealership here," he said, totally missing her point. "We're sponsoring the demo," he said cheerfully. "Though I have to say, what with only a couple hundred in attendance, we're likely to lose on this one—hey you wanna buy a ticket? You don't have to be a student." He tried to hustle them.

Then he suddenly caught up with the tone in Rev's voice. "Hey, students have to have cars too."

"Whatever happened to taking your bike?" Dylan asked.

"In winter?"

"Can do."

"There's the bus," Rev suggested.

"Oh please," he raised his voice so nearby students could hear, "who wants to take the bus when you can have this nice new car?"

Rev opened her mouth—

"Let's go before you shoot him," Dylan said.

"You were in *Art*!" Rev cried out at him as Dylan tugged her out of the tent.

"Hey, I got five kids to support," Martin cried out back at her. "A man's gotta do what he's gotta do."

"What?" she turned and headed back. "Don't use your kids as an excuse. You chose that expense. And there's lots else you could do—" Dylan turned her around again.

"What?" she said to Dylan. "It's not like a stork dumped the kids on him."

"You're right. And it's too bad he didn't have an English teacher who some Friday afternoon—"

She stomped across the field. "'I've got kids to support'" she whined. "I'm so fucking tired of hearing that. Men use it to justify—"

"Surely women too."

"Yeah, but not as often."

"Because she has some man to say it."

"Yeah, well. My point is who the hell is responsible for that state of affairs? It was his, or her, choice to make a bunch of kids to support. And yet because of it, they get paid more. The whole breadwinner salary thing."

"That doesn't still happen, does it? Pay equity, discrimination laws, and all that?"

"Not overtly, I guess, no. But don't you think people, bosses, treat married men differently than single men? And all women? Somehow it's the married man who's thought of first when there's a new position to fill or when there's overtime to be had."

"Hm." He lengthened his stride to keep up with her.

"And what I want to know is why should their choices trump mine. I've got a manuscript to support. Why are his expense-incurring choices more legitimate, more justifying, than mine? It would takes as much money to print and market my book as it does to feed and clothe his kid."

"Possibly more."

"Plus his kids'll probably do a lot more damage to the rest of us than my book would. Resource consumption alone—"

"That—"

"I've got to chip in for their vaccinations, I've got to chip in for their education, I'm even expected to give them right of way when they're playing in the streets."

She unlocked the car doors and they got in.

"You do—" he looked at her, "give them right of way—when they're playing in the streets. Don't you?"

REV WAS DEEP IN THOUGHT an hour later as they drove along, and Dylan was working on his laptop.

"Unemployment," he said.

"What?"

"There were demonstrations against unemployment. During the depression. Lots of labor issues. Lots of men." He turned his laptop toward her.

"Okay."

"Okay."

He continued to tap away.

"You were going to spend a week in Montreal, right?" he said a bit later.

"Yeah, why."

"How would you like to spend the whole month there instead?"

"Well," she looked over at him, "that'd be nice, but I can't really afford a whole month of—well I wouldn't want to spend a whole month in the dorm—"

"What if you—what if we can spend it in a house? On—" he checked his laptop, "Ellesmere. Someone wants a housesit for the month of July while they go on holiday. They've got a couple cats and lots of plants—are you okay with cats?"

"I'm more a dog person, but I wouldn't kill the cats," she said. "I'd probably kill the plants though."

He looked at her. "Why in—"

"Not intentionally. I just forget to water them. And then I drown them. To compensate. But July, that's like—soon, isn't it?"

"I don't know, is it?" He checked his laptop. "It is. Soon. It's tomorrow. So it's probably already been taken, but I can ask—" he ended hopefully.

Rev though a moment. "Yeah. I mean, if you'd like," she looked over at him. "July in Montreal might be nice." She smiled at the road ahead.

"Okay," Dylan started to compose a query, smiling at his laptop.

"Could we get there in time though? If they say yes?"

"Good point. Let me—" he tapped away. Then he looked out the window. "Where are we? Mapquest wants to know."

"I don't know. We haven't come to any towns yet. Since we left Sudbury. Have we? Come to any towns? I know we left Sudbury," she added.

"I don't think so". He tapped away again. "Okay, if we make North Bay by tonight—we can do that, right? Isn't North Bay just a couple hours from Sudbury? If we make North Bay tonight, it'll take us 7 hours tomorrow."

"That's—do-able."

"We'll make it an early and unsilly night. Pretend we're *really* old. And I can drive too. We can take turns."

His laptop beeped.

"That was quick," he checked his email. "Okay! They still need someone, and they've looked at my profile, and they're convinced I'm a mature, responsible person—"

Rev snorted.

"—well, that's what I said I was, in my profile," Dylan interjected, "—who won't kill their cats. So…" he skimmed through the message, "if we can be there by—oh—their flight leaves tomorrow morning. Early."

"We can't make it by then. Can we? I mean, even if we drive all night—"

"Sure we could. Two plus seven equals nine. And it's—" he looked at his watch, "7:00 now, so we'd get there at—four in the morning. Which means," he anticipated her objection, "we can even pull over at some point and sleep for a few hours."

He looked at her encouragingly.

"Okay," she said. "Let's do it!" She increased her speed. "'Head out on the highway,'" she tried to imitate Steppenwolf's gravelly voice, "'lookin' for adventure!'" Then settled for just saying "Vroom, vroom."

Dylan smiled happily and sent off an email accepting the housesit.

"So where did we go wrong?" she asked half an hour later.

"What do you mean?"

"Well here we are, two reasonably capable people who set out to make a difference. To change the world for the better. And here we are, some twenty years later, and I'm on my way to see pretty sparkles in the sky and you want to go to a demonstration only for the money."

"Well, not *only*—do you mean 'we' personally or 'we' as a species?" he asked.

She looked at him helplessly.

"Okay, let's do one then the other." He girded his loins. Figuratively speaking.

"Well *I* didn't make a difference," she started, "because I was stupid." She paused for just a second. "And we as a whole haven't changed the world because we're stupid." She paused for a longer second. "Oh man that was—too easy."

"Frighteningly so." He paused for a second. "Okay, but what do you mean when you say you were stupid. How were you stupid?"

"Let me count the ways," she groaned. "Well. Okay. Let's start with something simple. I was going to get Philosophy into the high schools, right? Get it on the curriculum, maybe even make it a mandatory course in grade eleven or twelve. So I wrote a letter to the Ministry of Education suggesting that, they said no, and that was that. I realized I have no idea how to change the world because I don't know how to work the system. I take 'no' for an answer. 'No' means 'no' to me. All my life, I've politely knocked on the front door, and if no one answered, I've walked away. Probably why I haven't gotten published."

She slowed on an uphill as she neared a laboring truck in front of her, then at the top of the hill, it zoomed away. She caught up with it on the next flat, but couldn't pass it because it was a curve. She waited until they'd driven through the curve, then once an oncoming car had gone by, she pulled out to pass the truck.

"But," she continued as she tucked back in front of the truck, "I couldn't even change the world one person at a time, one student at a time. I did not become Teacher of the Year. I do not have students that keep in touch and tell me how much I changed their lives."

"Well, that might just have been because you never got a full-time position. You were always just the sub—"

"Exactly. See? I couldn't even get to first base. As for other stuff. I joined the local green party and managed to infuriate the guy in charge during the first meeting." She anticipated Dylan's question. "I don't know how. I said something. Or asked something. Every time I open my mouth, people think I'm—*men* think I'm challenging them. And they invariably do not respond well to being challenged by a woman."

"What kinds of things did you say? Or ask?"

"Who knows," she said with frustration. "It doesn't take much. If a woman asks a simple question of clarification, of a man, it's taken as a challenge. If she goes so far as to suggest an alternative, an improvement, let alone come right out and say hey, you're a fuckin' idiot, well, look out! Anyway, I stopped going to meetings. It was clear I wasn't wanted."

"And you only go where you're wanted?"

"Hm. Well, no, it was also clear there'd be no point. It was clear that whatever I said wasn't going to be taken—constructively. That would be conceding. To a woman."

She stewed a bit on that point, and Dylan had nothing to say. She was probably right. Men competed all the time. Certainly most conversations he'd had with men seemed to be a contest. Maybe that's why they talked about sports so much, he mused. It lent itself well to the subtext.

"And I eventually came to believe," she continued, "that all the letters I might write on behalf of political prisoners being tortured or seals being slaughtered or forests being clearcut or women being denied abortions—they wouldn't make a damn bit of difference. The people in power will do what they want. Perhaps at some point, popular opinion against them will matter—it won't be in their best interest *not* to change—but it takes more than letters. Or even media coverage. I mean when there's a job—a *job*—called 'lobbyist' and 'media consultant'—when people have done studies on exactly what kind of pressure is effective, and how much, and when—what chance does a simple letter have?"

"So you're blaming the people in power."

"Okay, yeah. They're the ones, the only ones, that *can* change the world. By definition. They're people in *power*. So they have the *power*—"

"Got it," he put an end to her babbling. "So if the world doesn't change, it's because those in power don't want it to. And the Margaret Sangers and Ghandis of the world—they're what, myths?"

"Well, not myths, but—flukes? I don't know. No, maybe they are myths. Maybe they've been made out to have single-handedly changed things, because we like to believe a single person can make a difference, an single *ordinary* person, but maybe there's more to the story than that. Maybe they had power—connections, money—we don't know about. Or maybe other factors were in play that were just as decisive as whatever it is they did."

"Hm," he replied. Then said, "Okay, let's come back to them later. For now, let's stick with the 'only people in power can change the world' hypothesis. And you didn't want to become a person in power because..."

"I didn't know how. It's too complicated. I'd never succeed. It's like 'You can't get there from here.'"

They crossed over a bridge and Rev slowed down for the beautiful view of a lake. The sun was sparkling on the water.

"For one, I suspect I couldn't afford it."

"So it takes money to become powerful. It takes economic power to get political power." He paused then, thinking. "Is political power really just economic power? So it's not power per se, but money? Does it all come down to money?"

"Well, money has power, that's for sure," she took up his line of thinking. "Money buys things. When you're in power, you can award contracts to your friends. You can even buy your competition, isn't that what mergers and acquisitions are all about? Hostile takeovers? They're just economic invasions."

She paused then, as she passed another truck.

"They should be illegal," she added. "Economic invasions," she clarified. "Anyway, with the competition, the alternatives, bought, and thus controlled, they cease to be competition. So your way wins. You get what you want."

"Cities dependent on fossil-fuelled carbon dioxide-emitting cars instead of electric streetcars," Dylan suggested. "For example. And oil furnaces as the standard instead of heat pumps and solar panels."

"But money can do good too," Rev backtracked. "It could've been used to develop the electric transit system instead. And solar power. I mean why did we have Viagra before we had Plan B?"

"So it's not money per se," Dylan said, "but what the people with money use it for. So the people in power don't want to use it for good? They don't want the world to change? So we need to figure out why that's so."

"Because the world the way is enabled them to have that money. And get that power. The only people who want to rock the boat are those not in the boat."

They rounded the next curve then and Rev suddenly slowed down. The road ahead of them, the very long flat stretch of road ahead of them, was completely backed up with cars. There was no telling for how far, as the line went out of their sight around the next curve. Many drivers had turned off their ignition.

"Accident?" she wondered.

"Or road work," Dylan suggested.

"At this time of day?"

"Come summer, they often work overtime, right up 'til dark. Makes up for the time lost all winter."

"Oh right. Well, either way, looks like we'll be here quite a while." She turned off her ignition too.

"Switch?" Dylan asked?

"Yeah. Might as well." Rev opened her door. And fell onto the pavement.

"Careful," Dylan said, then exploded into laughter.

"Oh shut up."

She got up slowly and did some exaggerated stretching as she moved around to the other side.

"You look like a School of Silly Walks drop-out."

"But I got an A in everything!" To prove it, she started to—walk silly. Her left leg drew a circle in the air then shot off to the side at the last moment, and her right leg dragged behind with each step. Dylan started doing an elaborate version of what looked like 'I'm a Little Teapot' before each very little step.

Their concentration was suddenly broken by a car door ahead slamming shut.

"Uh-oh," Dylan said, mid-teapot.

They watched in disbelief then as a man started—walking—toward them. He looked like an octopus trying to do a split leap. Or leaps. Another door opened and closed. A woman started moving along the line of stopped cars, doing a barely controlled double deep knee bend with a 360 turn sort of in the middle. Rev and Dylan looked at each other, mouths open. Three more people got out of their cars and—they didn't join in so much, since no one actually acknowledged anyone else—but they—

Just then a pick-up truck, with half a dozen scruffy no-neck guys sitting in the back among stacks of orange pylons, drove up slowly on the shoulder. It slowed down for a moment as it passed them. A few seconds up the road it stopped and backed up.

"No," Dylan said with incredulity, as the driver got out, followed by every one of the guys in the back. They attempted a group silly walk. And failed brilliantly. Dylan and Rev started giggling, then they, and everyone else, started applauding, broad smiles all round. The guys did a silly group bow, got back into their truck, then carried on up the road. The others returned to their cars.

"Well, that was a—moment," she said as he got into the driver's seat.

"It was indeed," Dylan said, still rather stunned.

They sat for a while then, basking in it.

"This is going to put us at least an hour behind," she finally said. "Could they maybe just leave the key somewhere?"

"That would be a good idea but people usually like to actually meet the person first. It's risky enough with just the profile to go on. Though in my case," he said proudly, "I've got references attached."

"What, from a Bunch of Drunken Indians?"

He giggled. "From happy houses I've previously sat in," he said then with mock indignation. "But I'll fire off an email telling them we've been unavoidably delayed," he reached into the backseat for his laptop. "Maybe the neighbours can check us out on their behalf when we arrive—shit."

"What?" She looked into the back seat.

But he was looking over at her. "We're gonna look like shit when we arrive."

"So we stop at a Tim Hortons first, freshen up in their washroom, and drink a gallon of their coffee. We can do perky for the meet."

He looked at her dubiously.

"Or at least presentable. We can do presentable. Can't we?"

ABOUT AN HOUR LATER, the road crews had stopped for the day—seeing as it was night—and traffic had resumed its normal flow. And an hour after that, they'd switched again.

“So it’s the world the way it is, the system,” Dylan resumed their conversation settling into the passenger seat, “and not the people. But what exactly about the system?”

“Its capitalist nature?” Rev suggested. “That’s what enables people to become unfairly rich, right? And I’m not just talking about inheritance, though that pisses me off too. It’s taken me twenty years to get what some kids had given to them at eighteen. A car and a house, say.”

“Talk about a head start.”

“Exactly. Though I’m not sure I want to say parents can’t give the fruits of their labour to their kids—or that they can give only so much—but if I’d had $100,000 just given to me, maybe I could’ve—well, maybe I could’ve created some self-sustaining foundation that does good.”

“You could’ve started with half that—”

“Except that I don’t know how to make money make money. Do you? I mean, I just know how to earn money. Rich people seem to know how to make it without earning it. Because it’s impossible that they’ve earned their millions.”

“Right. So how is it that some parents have so much to give. That’s the question. How is it some people make so much money.”

“I don’t know, and that’s the problem, isn’t it. Or at least another problem. I don’t know how to work the economic system. But, okay, there’s no ceiling on salaries. For starters. CEOs make a hundred times what people in their companies make. It’s impossible to work a hundred times more hours, it’s impossible to work a hundred times harder in any given hour, it’s unlikely their contribution is a hundred times more important—by no standard of value is it justified that they make a hundred times as much.”

“Try five hundred times,” Dylan said. “And it’s got nothing to do with education or experience,” he added. “I used to think salaries were commensurate with—well, they're not commensurate with anything. Like you said."

"And bonuses," Rev said. "There's another one. A project manager gets a $50,000 bonus if the bridge gets done ahead of schedule. So he comes down hard on his subordinates to work harder, faster, they cut corners, on quality, safety, and on and on. It complicates things. It makes it really hard to do the right thing.

"Even the commission salespeople get," she continued. "People push you to buy shit you don't need because they get a commission every time you do. I mean even among the best of us, who would be able to resist? Who wouldn't talk themselves into it, just this one time, for the greater good, my kid needs braces, it's not for me—I mean, really, if McDonald's or Shell offered to pay you half a million or even just ten thousand dollars to say just one sentence for one of their ads, wouldn't you do it?"

"No. Maybe. Yeah. Then I could use the money for something—"

"Would you? Really? 'Cuz I don't know that I would. I mean, twenty years ago, yeah, I know I would've. But now?"

A pair of headlights appeared in the distance. "Good thing it's not snowing," she said.

Dylan looked over at the apparent non sequitur.

"Looks like you're traveling at warp speed through the universe, but makes it harder to—"

Once the car had gone by, she resumed. "And there's no ceiling on profit. The very notion of profit is wrong. It's a surplus. It means you got more out of something than you put in. But if that's the case, someone else is getting less, right? Pathetic wages, for example."

"And it's not just at the corporate level," Dylan suggested. "It's also at the personal level. Rich people buy stocks like poor people buy lottery tickets."

"The stock market is just a casino for rich people."

"So that's how they make money make money."

"Have you ever read Marilyn Waring's stuff?" she asked.

Dylan shook his head.

"It's a real eye-opener. Those excess profits are possible, in large part, because of the messed up accounting system. The whole externalities thing that lets them 'write off' the consequences. I. e., not pay for them. Someone can build a plant and reap the profits of whatever it produces, but not have to pay for cleaning up the river it pollutes. The whole nuclear energy industry is built on an agreement with insurance companies that it won't be held responsible for any accidents resulting from flaws in the construction or what have you. So the people in power reap the profits, but taxpayers have to bear the losses."

"Government bail-outs," Dylan said.

"Exactly. They make that practice, that reality, so very obvious. *That's* what those students should have been protesting," Rev added.

"Plus," she continued after the briefest of moments, "the system's set up so it's so much harder to do good. There's no profit in giving medicines away."

"Or feeding the hungry. But," Dylan said, "I'm not sure it's the capitalist system that's to blame. Communism didn't work out too well either. People in power found a way to abuse it. For their own personal gain. There's nothing in the capitalist system that *forces* people to take such salaries or not clean up the mess they make."

"True," Rev agreed. They drove in silence for a bit.

"Plus I just don't know anymore," she said with a sigh. "I mean I actually bought shares in Ballard Fuel Systems. First stock market stuff I ever did. I wanted to put my money where my mouth is, you know? The hydrogen fuel cell. So green. No fossil fuels, just hydrogen emissions. Turns out the hydrogen puts holes in the ozone.

"And maybe plastic bags are better than paper bags. I mean, on the one hand, yeah, plastic bags are bad: they're made from oil, which is a limited resource, and the manufacturing process is so very polluting, and they don't decompose in the dump. But paper bags require cutting down trees. Which we need because they suck up carbon dioxide and produce oxygen. And clear-cutting wrecks the animal habitats, and it increases erosion, which means we lose topsoil, and though theoretically it's a renewable resource, replanting doesn't seem to work well."

A few moments later, they saw in the distance what was, hopefully, North Bay. Lights on each side of the highway, in any case.

"Let's make a pit stop," Dylan said, as Rev slowed down. He pointed to the grocery store ahead on their left. "I'm thirsty. And we need—sustenance."

"Is it open?"

"Looks like."

"We need gas too. Okay, you get food and drink while I get gas." She dropped him off in front of the grocery store and drove to the gas station conveniently located right across the road. She pulled in front of a pump, popped open the gas tank cap, and got out of the car. Without falling.

She took the pump gun off its hook—then stared at the pump. Regular or Ethanol. Fossil fuel: limited resources and bad emissions. She flipped up the Ethanol thing. But *food* as fuel? When the world is starving? She flipped it back down again and flipped up the Regular thing. But they probably wouldn't get the food anyway. Maybe it would just rot in the field. So it might as well be turned into fuel. She flipped down the Regular thing and flipped up the Ethanol thing. But doesn't it take a lot of energy and what have you to process the corn or whatever into fuel? She flipped the Ethanol thing back down, and put the pump gun back in its holder. The guy in the kiosk looked out at her, more with annoyance than readiness to provide assistance.

She took a coin out of her pocket and flipped it.

A few minutes later, gas tank full, she drove back across the road to the grocery store parking lot, and saw Dylan standing there, looking somewhat forlorn, clutching several items to his chest. Several more items lay on the ground around him. And behind him in a trail back to the door, like Hansel and Gretel's bread crumbs.

"She said 'paper or plastic' and—it's all so confusing now. You've made it all so—" he waved a box of Froot Loops, "difficult."

She picked up the items that had fallen around him—a package of donuts, two bags of Doritos, a six-pack of Red Bull—then followed the trail leading back to the grocery store, picking up as she went.

He shoved the items he had hung onto into the back seat of their car, and called out. "There's more inside!"

She returned to the car, passed off her load to him, and went inside the store. She followed the trail to the only cashier on shift, who was eyeing her like she was some crazy. Rev picked up three deli containers—three cheese tortellini, she read as she picked up the first one, cranberries and wild rice, and chicken salad—and a loaf of whole grain bread, a couple containers of yogurt, and a box of Smarties. Dylan met her half way and took what he could.

"Did you see the cashier?" he asked.

"Yes. She looked—intrigued."

"She looked like she was going to call 911."

"Hm. I wonder if she was going to ask for the police or an ambulance."

THEY'D SWITCHED AGAIN, and Dylan was behind the wheel. Rev had settled comfortably into the passenger seat with the box of Smarties.

"Okay, so if it's the same with capitalism and communism," Rev picked up from a couple hours ago, as she handed Dylan a Smartie, "it's not the system."

"I want a red one," he said.

"But I want the red ones."

"There's more than one red one," he pointed out.

"Okay," she said grudgingly as she rooted around in the box and picked out a red one. "So—what was I saying?"

"That it's not the system."

"Right. So it's the people. The individual people. They make those choices. That makes sense," she said, thinking it through. "If you've got a lot of money, it's probably because you've used your money for yourself. If you give it away as you go, you don't get rich. So those in power, that is, those with lots of money, have a tendency to be selfish. It's a self-selection thing. Positions of power attract those who want power. And since power is having lots of money, positions of power attract those who want lots of money. For themselves. So power attracts those who are selfish—who make self-interested choices. Not choices for the greater good."

"So we're all going to die because the people in power are selfish. Okay, so why are they selfish? What is it about our society that makes them so selfish?"

"They're men."

"What?" Dylan looked over at her.

"Well, look at the numbers. The overwhelming majority of people in power are men. So we need to ask what is it about our society that makes men so selfish?"

"Oh come on. Surely women in power would be just as self-interested."

"Well, I wonder about that. I mean look at the way we socialize girls and boys. Girls are supposed to be nice, they're supposed to help others, they're cooperative. Boys are supposed to win, they're supposed to beat others, they're competitive.

"And," she continued, "who is it who doesn't clean up their own messes? Men. Maybe that's why the whole accounting externalities thing doesn't seem wrong to them. They've been 'externalizing' their whole life. It's always the women who clean up."

"What?"

"My brother never did his own laundry. He never did the dusting or the vacuuming."

"I bet he took out the garbage."

"Yeah, like it was a weight lifting thing. But he didn't pick up shit off the floor and scrape off plates and put all the garbage in the garbage in the first place. I swear, if we were ever able to do a study, I bet we'd find that well over 90% of the litter would be due to men. Somehow I just can't see women tossing their beer cans—or empty bottles of Crystal Light—out the car window and throwing their fast food containers onto the grass in the park."

"But men are janitors."

"And women are cleaning ladies. And paid a lot less, I might add."

"Men are garbage collectors."

"Which means they do it only if they get paid. So yeah, they'll run the dumps and the sanitation companies, but when cleaning up is just part of whatever else they're doing, they don't do it."

"Hm."

"And what if it's not just nurture," Rev said. "What if it's nature? I mean what if it's the Y chromosome or testosterone that makes males so driven for self, and it's estrogen or whatever that makes females other-oriented."

"We're fucked," Dylan said ambiguously.

"Well, Koestler thought so."

"*The Callgirls*? I read that too!"

Rev reached into the back seat and grabbed a couple cans of Red Bull.

"You've had this stuff before?" She tried in vain to read the label.

"Yeah. It's just like triple Pepsi. Lots of caffeine. Thought we should have it. You know, driving all night. And being old."

"Right." She opened a can, passed it to him, then opened another, and took a slug.

"Good?" He asked her.

"It's okay," she said. And took another slug. "Hate the aluminum aftertaste though."

"Yeah, they didn't have it in bottles."

"Oh, wait a minute." She opened the glove compartment and rooted around. "Thought I had some straws in here. Looks like not."

"You up to putting together a couple sandwiches? We should eat some real food. At some point in time."

"Yeah." She reached into the back and pulled the loaf of bread and container of chicken salad toward her.

"Oh," he said then, "you're vegetarian, aren't you."

"Well, yeah. Except when I'm not."

He looked at her inquiringly.

She sighed. "It started out simply enough, because I couldn't afford meat. Then I read about all the health stuff, you know, nitrates in hot dogs, and all the shit that goes into the animals, the growth hormones—"

"But shit goes into vegetables too, pesticides—"

"Yeah. But then there's the way they live—and die. It's cruel. Painful."

"Well, you can eat eggs from happy chickens."

"I do."

"And chicken salad from ex-happy chickens."

"Yeah, but how do I know? Truthfully, and inconsistently," she conceded, "the more recognizable it is—I have more trouble with fish, say, than fish sticks."

"So when they point to the lobster tank and ask which one—"

"Right." She shuddered. "You know, speaking of being consistent, they should trot out all the little lambs. Let them frolic among the dinner tables and then ask you which one. Do you know what veal—"

"Yes."

"It's little babies kept in a cage so small they can't even turn around—"

"Stop it."

"Because that way their muscle doesn't develop which means it stays tender—"

"I don't eat veal."

"Not anymore," she grinned to herself. "Then there's the relative inefficiency of food production per acre," she trailed off as she made a sandwich.

"Here," she passed it to him.

He looked at it rather helplessly.

"Oh wait, sorry." She took it back and cut it in two.

"Here," she passed him a half he could manage with one hand on the steering wheel. And reached for the container of triple cheese tortellini.

"Do you know what cheese is?" he asked smugly.

"Yes."

"It's made from milk from cows they keep always pregnant so they keep producing milk—"

"Stop it."

"And then because half of them have mastitis, pus gets into the milk which gets into the cheese."

"I don't eat cheese. Anymore." She closed the container, turned to toss it into the back seat, and grabbed the yogurt instead. Half way around, she tossed that as well and grabbed the rice and cranberries.

"Shut up," she said as she opened the container, unwrapped one of the spoons she'd found in her glove compartment, and started eating.

"But it's the self-selecting that really dooms us," Dylan said after he'd finished his sandwich. "So what if positions of power didn't go to the ones who wanted them?"

Rev laughed. "Right. 'A prerequisite for this job is that you don't want it.'"

"Exactly."

"Well, I've always thought the best president would be the guy who doesn't want the job. The one who sees the responsibility instead of the power. After all, who in their right mind would *want* the job?"

"So, what," she said then, "we'd appoint them instead? Surely someone *forced* to fill a position would be worse than someone who—isn't." She paused then. "And the other option is?"

"Right," Dylan conceded. "Okay, so maybe *that's* the problem. It shouldn't be a single position. There shouldn't be a president. Power should be distributed among a committee, a network."

"But someone has to be in charge," Rev said. Then added, "I can't believe I just said that."

"What if everyone had to serve their time on the council, the committee, or whatever. You know, like it's your civic duty. Like jury duty."

"Yeah look how well that works."

Dylan looked over at her and waited for the elaboration he just knew was coming. Then changed his mind.

"Let me guess," he beat her to it. "You were on jury duty. And they very nearly lynched you."

"How—" she opened her mouth.

"Because you kept insisting on evidence. *Relevant* evidence. Because you kept asking 'But *on what basis* do you say you know that X?' and they got more and more pissed off at you because they didn't *have* any basis. Most people use 'I know' as a synonym for 'I hope.'"

She closed her mouth. He was absolutely right. Most people *do* use 'I know that' when all they really mean is 'I hope that.'

"You hung the jury, didn't you," Dylan said. "After a week of—deliberations, they all voted guilty and you still maintained you couldn't possibly know for sure.

"But," Dylan continued, "you didn't have to *know*. Don't they just ask for *reasonable doubt*?"

"Yeah," she sulked. "But—"

"Ah." Enlightenment dawned. "It was the *judge* who got pissed off. You asked him to define 'reasonable.'"

"He thought I was nitpicking," she burst out. "Nitpicking!! People have written entire books trying to define 'reasonable' and I was expected to figure out which one to use—in a week, with everyone jabbering on—I kept having to—it was like trying to teach an entire Critical Thinking course in one week."

"Bet they liked it when you did that," Dylan said dryly.

"Did what?"

"Tried to teach them—"

Rev sizzled for a few minutes.

"They threw their donuts at me," she confessed. "Which brings up the matter of qualification," she resumed their main discussion. "I mean I didn't even run for town council because I thought what the hell do I know about road maintenance, tax administration and—"

"And I bet the council is made up of—"

"The mayor is a plumber." She waited a moment. "Why is it that men never seem to doubt their capability to—"

Dylan made strangling sounds.

"No, really, I read that somewhere."

"Oh well then."

"Some journalist—you're probably familiar with this study—whenever she called some expert to interview, men never declined, but women often did, saying they really didn't know enough to comment. Why is it men always think they're qualified," she asked.

"I think it's more that they won't admit to *not* being qualified."

"Hm."

"So where does all that leave us," Dylan asked after a while.

"Fiddling while Rome burns."

"I THINK WE'RE LOST," Dylan said after a while.

"Well duh."

"No I mean now. Here. Get out the map."

"How can we be lost? We just had to stay on Highway 11 until Huntsville."

"Yeah, and I turned off at Huntsville. But this doesn't look like a highway."

She looked out at the streetlights, the sidewalks, and the quiet houses. The tricycle at the curb gave it away. "You're right. This is not a highway."

"Shouldn't we be on a highway?"

"Yeah. Hang on." She rustled the map and tried to find where they were. Or at least where they were not. "Pull over. I'm getting nauseous trying to read the map."

Dylan pulled over. He peered out at the dark. "We're on Center Street. Look for Center Street."

"This is a road map. Not a street map."

"Streets are roads."

"Yeah but. Are we *in* Huntsville?"

"How would we know?"

"Well, let's drive around, see if there are any other signs."

They drove around for a while and were completely unable to determine whether they were in Huntsville. They saw a Pizza Pizza, a Staples, a Canadian Tire, a Shoppers' Drug Mart—all of which were in every town and city in the country.

"Aha!" Rev cried out. "The *Huntsville* Public Library! Okay, wait a minute." She looked at the map. "Oh. There were four turn offs at Huntsville. The one we wanted—"

"Was not the one that got us to Center Street."

"No, we wanted the one to Highway 60."

"Okay, so, how do we get—do we have to back to Highway 11?"

"I don't know. I don't have a Huntsville street map. And it doesn't look like anything's open. There's no one around we can ask—yeah, let's just go back to the highway."

"And that'd be—which way?"

"Um, back the way you came?"

"And that'd be—which way?"

"Shit, you're worse than I am. Well, let's drive around—want to switch while we're stopped?"

"Yeah."

They switched places and Rev drove around for a while, trying to find a way back to the highway.

"There! Dylan pointed to a sign. That way to Highway 11."

"Ah. Good. Okay." Rev turned in the direction indicated by the sign and very quickly they came to Highway 11.

"Okay," she said, mostly to herself, "the exit to 60 was above the exit to Center Street, so..." She took the north exit, and soon after they saw the sign indicating the exit to Highway 60. She turned off 11 onto 60, and once they'd passed the outskirts of Huntsville with its many turn off options and were clearly still on Highway 60, she resumed.

"But it's not even just the big money. Or the big decisions. I mean, if everyone did X, we wouldn't need a law saying we had to do X. Didn't the whole recycling thing take off without there being a law saying you had to recycle?"

"Yeah, but didn't municipalities start providing those blue boxes first? With 'We Recycle' on the side?"

"Oh, right. Apparently very few people figured out they could just put their recycled stuff in an ordinary box."

"And paint it whatever color they wanted."

"And spray cans had to be not made," she sighed. "Remember the CFC thing and people kept using their hair spray and spray deodorants until the government prohibited their manufacture. That was how it happened, wasn't it?"

"Yeah, and people are still driving cars."

"Actually, they're not," Rev cursed as she pulled out to pass. "They're driving these goddamned mini vans. And pick-up trucks. I swear accidents must be increasing because people can't see ahead on the road anymore."

"Not that you can see the road ahead in any case," he peered out at the black.

"No, but."

They drove in silence for a while.

"You know, what with the road work and getting lost—"

"Yeah," Dylan reached into the backseat for his laptop.

"Cool," he said after a while.

"What?"

"They've suggested we meet them at the airport instead of at the house. So that gives us until 8 instead of 7. Plus the airport is a little closer. Save us Montreal morning rush hour traffic."

"Brilliant. Are these people rocket scientists or what."

"Yeah."

She looked over at him. "What?"

"He teaches astrophysics at McGill and she's in engineering." He shrugged.

"Wow. I wonder what their house looks like."

"What, you think it looks like a rocket?"

"Could," she said defensively.

"They'll have the keys with them," he continued reading their message, "and they've left a bunch of notes at the house. About the cats and plants and stuff. We can read, right?" he said to Rev. "I mean, we're not rocket scientists, but we can read the notes they left. Right?"

THEY DROVE ON INTO THE NIGHT. After about half an hour, Rev picked up where she had left off.

"Plus," she said, "I just don't care anymore. I mean fuck it. Twenty some years I've been frugal with electricity, and rationing my car trips, and not subscribing to newspapers because it takes 75,000 trees for just one day's edition, and not eating meat because an acre of grain produces five times the protein as an acre of beef, and meanwhile my neighbour drives a gas-guzzling mini-van that seats eight into town every other day because she's bored. And companies leave their lights on all night and they have displays that are backlit and advertising signs in blinking neon. And California is getting water all the way from Canada—do you know how expensive that is? Not only in terms of money and time and labor but in terms of ecosystem damage?—they're getting water all the way from Canada to fill their swimming pools."

"Okaaay," Dylan roused himself from a half-nap at this outburst.

"I'm not doing any of it anymore unless everyone does it. Because unless a lot of people do the right thing, it's not the right thing."

"You didn't get an A in Ethics, did you."

"No, listen. Taking more than you need is wrong only if it deprives someone else of what they need. Taking more apples than I need because otherwise they'll just rot on the ground, what's wrong with that?"

"Okay…so you're a consequentialist."

"Right, and if I'm the only one who does something, there is no consequence to speak of. My using less fossil fuel will have no consequence whatsoever unless a lot of other people also use less fossil fuel. So my action isn't right—or wrong—unless a significant number of others do the same action."

"Wow. Morality by majority. Scary."

"And apparently that's not going to happen until they pass laws. Which isn't going to happen because 'they' eat meat—"

"—in their swimming pools."

"And raising prices doesn't do it because the banks are all too happy to lend into oblivion—"

"—at which point they can claim bankruptcy—"

"—so even when gas goes up to two bucks a litre, people can keep driving their pickups. Because my truck is my penis."

"And I have a right to my penis."

"Well?" she said after a moment.

"Well, what."

"You're not rebutting."

"There's nothing to rebut. You're right. It's hopeless. We're all going to die."

DYLAN NODDED OFF AGAIN, but then awoke a little while later when he felt the car slow down.

"We're about to enter Algonquin Park," she announced, nodding at the dimly lit entrance kiosk ahead.

"Yeah?" He sat up. "I've never actually seen Algonquin Park before. And I'm not about to see it now either," he added, looking out at the pitch black.

"Really? You grew up in Ontario and you've never been in Algonquin Park?"

"No, I just went to teacher's college in Ontario. I grew up in B.C."

"Oh, I didn't know that." She paused. "Did I?"

"I don't know. Did you? We should stop here on the way back."

Rev looked over at him. "The way back? Stop here?"

"Yeah. Let's go hiking or canoeing or whatever in Algonquin Park for a week. After our month in Montreal. It'll be fun."

"Okaaay…" she said.

He smiled out the window.

"Want to switch?" she asked then. "I'm tired."

"Yeah, let's. I had a nap. Sort of."

She pulled over and they got out, stretched a bit, then got back in.

"Want another Red Bull?" She reached into the back.

"Yeah, good idea. Wake me up a bit."

She opened a can, passed it to him, and opened another one for herself.

"You know, every time I hear someone on TV talk all serious about how now is the time to start recycling or cutting back or—well, fuck, we said all that in the 70s!! 'The time for action is past.'"

"'Now is the time for senseless bickering.'"

She chuckled. "You got the t-shirt too? Isn't that a great site?"

"'It's always darkest just before it goes pitch black.'" Dylan giggled.

"'Until you spread your little penguin wings,'" Rev sputtered, "'you'll have no idea how far you can walk.'"

"It's just PR anyway," Rev continued a while later. "The grocery store is finally, or again, charging 5 cents for plastic bags. But only so people buy *their* reusable bags. I remember not too long ago, I walked into a grocery store with my own reusable bags and I was told I had to leave them at the check-out while I shopped. They were afraid I was just going to fill them as I walked through the store, then walk out without paying."

"Really?"

"I kid you not. 'Course it didn't help that I *did* fill them as I walked through the store."

He stared at her.

"Well, taking one of those wire baskets would be redundant, wouldn't it, if you've got a handful of bags."

"But *now*," she said, "now that they've figured out how to *make money* from the idea, *now* it's okay. And yet, they serve salads in containers that use probably a hundred times the plastic a bag uses," she reached into the back for cheese tortellini. "If they were serious about it and it wasn't just a marketing ploy to get more customers, more money—"

"So why don't you take the containers back to reuse?"

I tried that. "They wouldn't use my brought-back containers."

"Really? Why not?"

"They said something about their hygiene policy, and I finally figured out that they were afraid that I might not have washed them out well and if I got sick I'd sue them for selling expired potato salad or something."

"But this is Canada. We don't know how to sue people. Even when we spill hot coffee on ourselves."

Rev grinned. "That's because we're always blaming ourselves. We say sorry when someone else steps on our toes."

"Which makes you so very Canadian."

She looked over at him, puzzled.

"You're blaming yourself for not—for the world."

"Hm."

"So there's another reason," she said after a while.

It was his turn to be puzzled.

"The people who *are* to blame, the country that's caused most of the damage, they're the ones so quick to point the finger at other people—to sue."

"Be interesting to see what China does."

"What do you mean?"

"Well, if they follow in the States' footsteps, they're going to be leaving an even bigger footprint—" he smiled—then laughed. "A Godzilla footprint. No, wait a minute," he muttered to himself, "that was the Japanese."

"What was the Japanese?"

"Godzilla."

"Godzilla was Japanese?"

"Yeah, don't you know your comic books?"

"Godzilla was a comic book?"

"Well it was a film first, but *my* Godzilla experience was comic books."

"Hm. No. I don't know comic books," she answered his question. "I'm a girl. *Was* a girl."

"No you weren't," Dylan said grinning at her.

"No, I wasn't," she happily agreed. "Still, I wasn't into comic books. Why is it that comic books are such a boy thing?"

"It's the leotards. We all secretly want to wear leotards."

Rev burst out laughing.

"The bulging muscles, of course, and saving the world!"

"And yet..."

"Yeah."

"So if you weren't into comic books," he said after a minute, "and you weren't into dolls—that's a given—" he anticipated her. "what were you into?"

"Actually, I did play with dolls." She tried to think back. "Sort of."

He glanced over at her, waiting for her to confess to chopping off Barbie heads.

"I remember liking...oh my god—their clothes. My mom used to sew all these little outfits for my dolls. I don't remember carrying them around or anything though. Mostly I think I just dressed them and then sat them somewhere."

"You would've made such a good mom."

She snort-laughed.

"And I was into those kids' puzzle books. And reading. *That's* what I did with my dolls," she suddenly remembered then. "I read to them!"

"Now *that* sounds right."

"It does, doesn't it. God we are so—what we are."

"Well, not completely."

"What, you played with dolls too?"

"No, I played with guns."

"No!"

"Cowboys and Indians." He laughed then.

"Sober Indians?" she asked.

"Dead Indians," he replied.

"Hm."

"Time for some music," she reached under the passenger seat and dragged out flat box full of CDs.

"You've got music? You've had music all this time?"

"Yeah. Of course," she said lightly, grinning at him. "She flipped through the CDs, selected one, and popped it into the player. Offspring's 'Get a Job' started playing. She turned up the volume and sang along. Loudly. "'My friend's got a girlfriend and he hates that bitch...'" Dylan winced.

Halfway through, she started playing pattycake—on the dashboard. "'I won't pay, I won't pay ya, no way...'" Then she started embellishing. Enthusiastically.

She'd set the player on single repeat, so the song started again. She turned it up and sang along again. "'My friend's got a girlfriend...'" More loudly. And with great abandon. Dylan looked over at her in amazement. "'I won't pay, I won't pay ya, no way...'"

"Wanna switch?" she shouted as it started on its third time.

"No, you're—how many Red Bulls have you had?"

She looked in the back seat. "Oh. Four?"

"Right. I'll keep driving. You'll kill every bullwinkle we see."

"You can see now?"

Offspring started again. "'My friend's got a girlfriend...'" She starting adding a few elbows, and head bobs, to her elaborate patty-caking. When she started adding her feet, whipping them up to bang on the dashboard, Dylan became alarmed.

"Ow ow!" she suddenly shrieked. "Pull over!"

"What? What's wrong?"

"My calf muscle has seized!" She had her ankle in her hands and was trying to flex it.

He pulled off the road and skidded to a stop. "What should I do?"

"I have to move my ankle. That'll move my calf muscle. The ankle's connected to the—shit!"

He reached over with his right hand to flex her ankle. She tried to sit sideways so she could straighten her leg.

"Holy shit. This thing is like iron." He grabbed it with both hands. "A chunk of iron all welded together."

"Tell me about it," she gasped. "Cement and iron. I'm a hard hard person. It hurts."

He tried to move it, applying more pressure. "I'm afraid I'll break it."

"Just—shit!" She was kneading her calf muscle, and trying to go limp in the presence of that clutching pain, and he was trying to get the moveable part of her ankle to move. Suddenly it loosened.

"Ah," she cried out in relief. Then pointed her toe up and down a few times, relaxing the muscle.

"Wow," he said, sinking back into his seat. "Does that happen often?"

"No. It used to. Back when we were kids. My sister and me. We used to wake up in the middle of the night like that. But it hasn't happened lately. Maybe it's because I've been in the car for so long."

"Right. Had nothing to do with playing pattycake with your feet on the dashboard. At—your age."

"What—oh. Yeah. It's a good song."

"Pick another one," he said, as he started the car and pulled back onto the road.

"Wanna switch? I wanna switch. Wanna switch?"

He looked over at her. "Not yet." He looked down at her leg. "What if that thing seizes again when it's on the gas pedal?"

"Good point. Though that's never happened. Not to say that it couldn't. Cuz it could. All things are possible. With God. Which isn't to say there is a god. Let alone *the* god. The one with the capital G. But it's—"

He'd put in Meatloaf and her meth-like babbling stopped instantly when 'On a Hot Summer's Night' began. She waited, a broad smile on her face. She waited, waited through the question-and-answer, started giggling at the 'Again?' then positively exploded at 'I bet you say that to all the boys.' Dylan lost it too, though partly because she was so gone.

When 'Paradise by the Dashboard Light' started, she immediately began singing along. "'Well I remember every little thing as if happened only yesterday…'" He joined her. At the 'I couldn't take it any longer—Lord!' scream, they both threw up their hands, realized it, then laughed delightedly.

In the silence that followed the end of the song, Rev said, "You know, that's really such a sad song."

"It is, isn't it."

They giggled. Just a bit.

"Eyes!" she suddenly shouted.

"I see them!" Dylan said, somewhat less frantically, slowing down as a pair of eyes gleamed at them from the edge of the road. He cast a quick look in the mirror to confirm he wouldn't be rear-ended, then stopped altogether as the eyes moved toward the center of the road. It was a wolf.

"Cool," Rev said.

"Indeed," Dylan agreed.

Then ever so timidly, three little wolves stepped out of the forest onto the road. The adult wolf remained in the center of the road, staring at their car, as the three little ones crossed the road behind it. Once they were safely to the other side, it trotted after them.

"Wow," she said. "A wolf crosswalk."

ABOUT HALF AN HOUR LATER, they passed through the exit kiosk.

"Okay," Rev said," Ottawa should be soon."

"Soon?"

"Well, not soon, no. We stay on 60," she grabbed the map and turned on the light. "We stay on 60 until we come to 17. That takes us to Ottawa."

"Switch?"

"Yeah, you need a break."

Dylan slowed and pulled off the road. Rev opened her door and—fell out.

"Careful," Dylan couldn't resist saying. It would never get old.

"Oh shut up." Rev picked herself up, reached down to touch her toes, which was never gonna happen, then walked around the car. She met Dylan behind the car. They smiled at each other.

"What," Rev said.

"Nothing," Dylan smiled more broadly.

Rev smiled back. More broadly. And got into the driver's seat as

Dylan got into the passenger seat.

He reached into the back seat to see what was left of their stash.

"Donut?" he said, holding out one of the two remaining donuts.

"Sure," she said, taking the glazed buttermilk concoction of sugar and fat from his outstretched hand.

They munched on their donuts, staring out at the still black night. Then Dylan grabbed the last bag of Doritos, opened it, and offered it to her. She took a handful, as did he.

"So whose fault it is," he tried to summarize to this point, "is complicated. But it's not your fault. And it's not my fault. We don't have enough power to be at fault, to be held responsible."

"And we can't be faulted for not trying to gain power?"

"You tried. So did I. Though not nearly as hard, it seems. I write articles, sure, but the only people who read them are the ones who don't need to. The magazines that need to print them won't. So I'm preaching to the converted. You heard about the Adbusters thing?" he asked.

"Their attempt to place ads in mainstream media, you mean?"

"Yeah. They discovered, no surprise, that magazines won't accept any ads that challenge the ads of their largest sponsors. Same goes for articles. So if a car company buys an ad in a magazine, you can kiss goodbye any other ad or any article that addresses the evils of cars. Same goes for—everything."

"What about public service ads, like on TV?"

"TV stations are owned by car companies. Or what have you."

"Hm. Still," Rev continued, "maybe we gave up too soon. The internet has bust the world wide open. Blogs, podcasts, guerrilla reporting... Everyone, anyone, can take a picture with their ever present cellphone and post it on YouTube or whatever and it's there for everyone to see. Blogs are full of eye-witness accounts. Sometimes even arguments. There's no gatekeepers. No one to say

'No, the car companies won't like that so we won't print it.'"

"But no one will believe any of it," Dylan said. "Because there *aren't* gatekeepers. Who knows which photos are fudged—well, besides the ones with Roseanne's head on—anyone else's body.

"And," he continued, "there's so bloody much of it. Have you actually *read* any of those blogs? Most of them are full of sheer drivel. Proust would've loved to blog."

"They're not investigative reports," he continued, "they're just diaries. No one's walking around with their little cellphones asking the right questions."

"And if they are," Rev conceded, "no one's giving them the real answers."

REV SNOOZED FOR A BIT then as Dylan drove. When she woke up, she saw that it was getting light.

"Should it be getting light already?" she asked as she looked out.

"What do you mean, 'already'? It gets dark then it gets light. This I know," he added proudly.

"But we're not at Ottawa yet."

"We're almost there."

"Which means we might almost make it."

Dylan glanced at the back seat. "We need to make another pit stop," he said. "Should be a 24-hour something or other near here, yeah?"

"I should think so," Rev said absently. "And a gas station. We need gas?" She leaned over to look at the gauge.

"Yeah."

"And a washroom. We need—*I* need a washroom."

"I should think so. You've had four cans of Red Bull."

A few minutes later, Dylan pulled into a convenience store with gas pumps and a public washroom. "How cool is this," he said.

"Very cool. Take my string bag this time." She twisted around and rummaged behind the passenger seat. "It's back here somewhere, probably under—"

Dylan reached over, and under, and pulled out a mess of purple rope. He shook it and untangled it and it eventually looked like a bag.

"It's got holes in it," he announced. "This is a bag with holes in it. That won't work," he added helpfully.

"Sure it will. Just don't put anything in it that's smaller than the holes."

"Hm."

She got out and headed for the washroom. "Get some more Red Bull," she called back. "We've got a few hours yet, yeah?"

When she came out of the washroom, he was already back at the car, leaning against it with a bottle of water in his hand.

"That's a disgusting washroom," she said. "Why are gas station washrooms always so disgusting?"

"Because it's up to the gas station *guy* to keep it clean?"

She grinned. "I was going to splash a little cold water on my face to wake up, but—it was so disgusting."

He uncapped his bottle of water and tossed half of it into her face. "There. Awake?" He laughed. Sort of.

She spluttered. "I can't believe you did that!"

"Actually, neither can I. Was it okay? To do that?"

She took the bottle from his hand and splashed the other half into his face. "Yeah."

"WELL, WE TIMED THIS RIGHT," Rev said, as they drove quickly around Ottawa, having gotten there just before rush hour. They'd switched again, and she was at the wheel. "Which means," she said, "that we get to the airport and Montreal—not at the right time."

"Hm."

"You don't seem to care."

"I'm too tired to care."

She glanced over. "You don't want to come across like that at the meet. Maybe you should have a Red Bull."

"Okay, but we're not putting Offspring on again." He reached into the back.

"Here." He handed her a banana.

"You think I need—" she held up the banana suggestively, "a banana?"

He laughed. "I don't know, do you?" He smiled devilishly. Then said, "You need potassium. Good for muscle cramps."

"Oh yeah? I didn't know that. Really?" She gripped the steering wheel with her elbow for a second in order to peel it—he put his Red Bull into the cup holder, reached over, took the banana, got it started, then gave it back.

"So bananas have potassium?" she asked before she took a bite.

"That's what makes them yellow."

She looked over at him dubiously. "No, it's not."

"Okay then what makes them yellow?"

"Beta-carotene?"

"That should make them orange."

"Hm."

"I think of potassium as white," she said a while later. "And magnesium is white, and calcium is—actually, come to think of it, I think of all the—no, no I don't. Iron is grey. Though that's in the white family, isn't it. And silver is—copper is green," she burst out. Then when he looked over at her to object, she added, "well, it is when it oxidizes. So that makes it green. In my mind. But iron is still grey, not orange," she anticipated him. "Gold is yellow," she said cheerfully. "Maybe bananas have gold in them." She put the banana peel in their garbage bag. "Pass me a Red Bull," she said then.

"No," he said, uncapping a bottle of water and handing it to her. "No more Red Bull for you."

"I wonder why they think of it as red," she said without missing a beat. "Aluminum is silver." She raised the bottle to her lips. "And water is—"

Dylan looked over. She was stumped.

"Okay, your turn," she said after a few moments.

He looked over at her. "My turn?"

"Where did we go wrong."

All that up to now had been *her* turn?

"Okaaay..." he thought for a bit. He took a slug of Red Bull. Then he thought for a bit longer.

"What you said," he finally said.

Rev burst out laughing. And snorted just once.

"Except for the 'men are scum' bits."

"Men aren't scum?"

"They are, some of them. A lot of them." He looked over. "Most of them," he slumped. "But so are most women."

"Explain."

"Okay, remember how you said men use kids as an excuse—'I have three kids to support'—and that keeps them in evil jobs—"

"I think my point was more that it gets them high-paying jobs."

"Okay, right, but it's also an excuse to hang onto a job, and do things that they might not otherwise do—because otherwise they'll get fired and, well, they've got three kids to support. But women use kids as an excuse too."

"Explain."

"It's like they think once they're pregnant, they're god's gift to the world. I know," he rushed on, "it's a demanding job. It's 24/7, exhausting as hell, and the guy—some of the guys—many of the guys—the guy comes home and just sits in front of the TV. I get that.

"And," he continued, "our society isn't set up for a person to raise a kid *and* have a job, so yeah, for fifteen years someone else has to pay rent, buy food and clothes, not only for the baby, but also for her—I get that. Though I don't get why *I* should be the one to pay."

Rev looked over.

"I mean I don't think the government, I as a taxpayer, should pay her for raising kids. Why should I pay some woman to have a kid and not pay you to publish your book?"

"Hm. Good point. *Very* good point."

"If the guy—the kid's father—wants to pay her, indirectly, by paying rent for the three of them and buying the food and what have you, that's completely different. That's a partnership, an arrangement between the two of them. But my point is—what was my point?"

"Something about fifteen years."

"Oh, right. If she gets pregnant—if she chooses to have and raise a kid—that accounts for having to be dependent on someone else for roughly fifteen years. Once the kid is fifteen, it can be home alone, it can feed itself—"

She looked over.

"Unless it's a boy. Granted. Though *I've* been ordering out for pizza since I was ten."

She smiled.

"But that's only one-third of her adult life. She's got another 30 years." Dylan looked over at Rev. "You yourself pointed out, with no great affection, all these 'kept' women, acting so entitled—"

"Yeah. But it's not that easy," she said, "if you've been out of the workforce for fifteen years. It's not like they keep your job for you."

"No, but if I understand correctly, *you* started over from scratch at thirty-something. Having found yourself without a career. And with a criminal record," he grinned. "*You're* paying your own way. And will do until you can't anymore. Right?"

"Right."

"So why shouldn't they? I mean what's so god-damned special—it's like you say you're a 'mother' and automatically you've got this halo—"

"That's so very—insightful."

"I have my moments," he grinned again.

"I heard this one woman," he continued, "she said she *got* pregnant because she thought the judge would be more lenient with her sentence."

"Really? Wow. Talk about *using* someone."

*"Making* someone—*to* use."

"OKAY, SO WE'RE NOT PART of the solution," Dylan said a while later. "But we're not part of the problem either. Isn't that good enough?"

"Well, we are driving a car. And eating pepperoni pizza."

"But, as you said, until a lot more people don't drive cars and don't eat pepperoni, our actions have no consequence whatsoever. Which means they're *amoral.* Not good, but not bad either."

"But the principle of the—"

"Is just a warm and fuzzy. Or notice to a god that doesn't exist."

"Hm."

Dylan opened their last can of Red Bull.

"MAYBE IT'S JUST AS WELL we don't survive," Dylan said quite a while later as he munched on Froot Loops. "Maybe it's just as well we blow ourselves up, make the planet uninhabitable. Give it to the cockroaches. The aliens probably have us cordoned off anyway. 'Sickness here, stay away.'"

"Still," she added, not entirely convinced. "Bach takes my breath away."

"Yeah but for every Bach, there's thousands of—"

"No, Bach was an asshole too," she admitted. "I mean the guy had twenty kids. And probably didn't give any of them the time of day. Let alone a diaper change. Left it all to his wife. Wives. How irresponsible is that. To have created all those human beings. Who would then use resources—there oughtta be a crime for that," she said. And pondered it a bit. "What's the term for crimes when you fail to foresee something or don't take consequences into consideration?"

"I don't know. Irresponsible?"

"No, I mean the legal term."

"Oh." He thought for a moment. "Negligence? Reckless endangerment?"

"Yeah, we could call it 'negligent reproduction.' Or 'reckless replication.' We could say you had to have a license before you become a parent."

"Well, we already sort of say that," he said. "At least for people who want to adopt. Don't they have to pass a test? Prove they know that babies aren't born knowing how to speak English?"

"That's right! So why don't we do that for everyone? Why should being biologically related to the kids you want to raise exempt you from meeting some standard of—"

He rooted around in the Froot Loops.

"What are you doing?"

"Looking for the toy."

"Didn't they stop putting them in? Afraid the kids would eat them."

"Oh, right."

"The kids," she clarified, "whose parents need to be told that babies aren't born speaking English."

"The ones replicating without a license," he added.

"You did say the aliens had quarantined us, didn't you?" she asked.

"'Cuz maybe we should let them know. We are too stupid to visit."

THEY HAD SWITCHED ONE MORE TIME, and Dylan was behind the wheel as they approached the airport at Dorval.

"Okay, exit in two kilometers," he said out loud, energized by the second Red Bull he'd had. "Approaching lift-off!" He giggled.

He changed lanes, then changed lanes again, and a few minutes later, he entered the maze that was the airport.

"Okay, we've got," he glanced at his watch, "shit! Five minutes to find them!"

"This is an airport," Rev said. "You'd need five days to find someone!" She looked with dismay at all the signs, all the exit lanes and ramps—

"There!" he shouted and pointed. "Terminal One! That's what we need, right? Even though it's not really a terminal, since it's a point intended to connect people to another point."

He swerved into the lane for Terminal One and stopped behind a row of taxis.

"They should call them connections, not—no, wait—" he twisted to look up out the window, "this is Arrivals. We need Departures." He paused for a microsecond.

"It'll have to do." He was already unbuckling his seat belt. "I just go down once I get in, right? Or up. One of the two," he concluded. With great perspicuity.

"Wait a minute!" Rev said. He was already out of the car. We can't park here.

"Right," he said, processing that obvious fact. He got back into the car. "We need to park—not here. But we don't have time to park. Why don't—" he looked over at her. "It's probably better that you don't come in anyway. They're expecting just me. Some people are really strict about no parties, no friends over, etc." He got out of the car again.

"What are they, your parents?"

"No, but—"

"You're right," she said then. "They ask me my name, do a background check, and find out—"

"You showed a bunch of teenage boys how to put on a condom."

"Well I think it'll just say corrupting minors—"

"Which sounds worse."

"— or misdemeanour. Or maybe mischief. Causing a disturbance?"

*"All* of which doesn't sound like a housesitter who will leave your house in one piece."

"Agreed."

Dylan opened his door and scrambled out of the car again, as Rev scooted over into the driver's seat. He took off at a jog, looking wildly about for a rocket scientist and an engineer. He found the Departures floor—it was up, which was not the direction he tried first—then ran past a line of people snaking around velveteen ropes on metal stands. He dodged in and out of clumps of people who were, like him, trying to figure out where to go or what to do, then he saw the signs for Domestic Departures and International Departures. He started heading for the latter when it suddenly occurred to him to stop and read one of the Departure schedule pixel signs that was constantly updating departure times and gates.

The flight to Oregon left from Gate #17. In three minutes.

He considered hijacking one of several nearby motorized contraptions, but then decided he'd actually get there faster if he just ran. Which is what he did. Fortunately, the first gate he found was #8 and not #58. Fortunately as well, they seemed to be arranged in numerical order. Ascending numerical order if he kept running forward. Which he decided to do.

He got to Gate #17 in two minutes—though it wasn't a gate at all, of course, but a counter with a bunch of chairs in front of it and a door behind it. All of the chairs were empty, and one last man and woman were being shepherded through the door by the airline attendant—

"Rocket engineer!" Dylan shouted.

They turned.

Dylan rushed up. "Sorry, I all driving been night. 've."

"Wow, that's the best split contraction I've ever heard," the man said.

"There's no such thing as a split contraction," the woman objected. "There's just split infinitives. Right?" She looked at the attendant for support.

"I don't know. There's split planes—" she tried to get them moving again.

"Jack and Diane?"

They stared at him.

"Kazam?" He added helpfully.

"Poof!" the man said. Then laughed. "It's Kazeem, actually," he said then, reaching out his hand. "Though I like Kazam much better."

"Me too," the woman said, reaching out to shake Dylan's hand as well. "Maybe we should change our name," she said to the man.

"Something to consider," the attendant said, "once you're on the plane—" She tried to get them moving again.

"Dylan O'Toole, I presume?"

"Yes," Dylan said, and reached out his hand to shake Jack's hand again. "Pleased to meet you."

"You're a journalist, you said?" Diane asked.

The attendant looked like she was about to explode.

"Um," Jack caught the signs of incipient combustion, "we don't have time to interview him now—"

"Oh, right, of course—" she hesitated.

"It'll be fine," he said to no one in particular, as the attendant continued to move them into the hallway that led from the door. To Dylan he said, "We've left notes at the house. About—everything."

"And here are directions," Diane reached out to hand him a piece of paper, as she was moved along. "From here."

"Ah, good. Thanks."

"All right then. Take care of our house—and we'll see you at the end of the month."

The attendant had managed to—push—them halfway down the hall.

"You've got our email addresses," Diane called out, "and our cell numbers—"

"I do," Dylan called back in confirmation.

"Splitting—" the attendant interjected as she tried to get them to turn the corner at the end of the hall.

"Thank you!" they called back.

"Thank *you*!" Dylan called ahead, as they turned out of sight.

"Oh wait!" He ran down the short hall. "The key!"

An object landed on the floor where the hall turned the corner. He bent down to pick it up, seeing Diane see that he did so. It looked like a Rubik's Cube. But it was a sphere.

He stood up, looking at it dumbly. "All set then," he muttered to himself and walked back to the counter and chairs, where he turned—which direction had he come from?

"UH-OH," REV SAID TO HERSELF half an hour later. She'd forgotten where exactly Dylan had gotten out. And she assumed—a likely to be true assumption, she thought, when she thought about it—that that was where he'd expect her to be to pick him up. All the drop-off spots—or was she at the pick-up spots?—looked the same. A couple of glass doors, then building, then a couple of glass doors, then building. A bunch of taxis and a bunch of weary people with way too many suitcases were parked in front of each one. Which couple of glass doors had they stopped at before?

Oh sure, there were identifying numbers on the concrete pillars in front of each set of doors. Huge numbers in fresh red paint. But who noticed them?

She drove by slowly, looking for Dylan. He was nowhere in sight. She followed the road, circled around, and drove by again. Still no Dylan. She followed it again, this time splitting off to check the row of doors on the upper level, and—oops. She was halfway to Montreal before she realized she wasn't on the ring road anymore.

"UH-OH," DYLAN WAS SAYING TO HIMSELF at about the same time. He'd forgotten where exactly he'd entered the faux-terminal. There were lots of counters on his left, lots of people in the middle, and lots of doors on his right. And every one of them said 'Exit.'

He went out the next one he came to, and looked up and down the row of waiting cars. No Rev. A few small black cars, but none spattered with globs of pine tar.

He walked along the building to the next collection of waiting cars. No Rev. He walked all the way to the end. No Rev. And back again. Still no Rev.

Ah! He was on the wrong level. He went back inside, found an escalator, and rode to the next level. Again, there were doors the length of the building. He checked each one before he decided he must've somehow gotten to the wrong terminal. Or maybe Rev was at the wrong terminal. He decided to catch the terminal shuttle bus, and—oops. He was halfway to Montreal before he realized he wasn't on the shuttle bus.

So he stood up and approached the driver.

"Excuse me, could you please let me out? I need to go back to the airport."

The driver shook his head.

"S'il vous-plaît, j'en ai besoin de retourner à l'aéroport," Dylan tried.

The driver shook his head again.

"Hae shuutei? Touhou futsutsuka."

"Ah," the driver smiled. Then said something, in Japanese, that Dylan had no hope of understanding. He sat heavily in the seat nearest the door.

Fifteen minutes later, the bus stopped and the driver looked at Dylan. He pointed out the door. Dylan looked out the door and saw a bunch of people standing at a bus stop in a maze of underpasses and overpasses.

"Airport," the driver said.

Ah. Dylan got up, nodded his thanks, and got off the bus. He joined the people waiting, he hoped, for a bus that would take them to the airport.

Meanwhile, Rev had taken the next exit and was on her way, she hoped, back to the airport. The congested traffic slowed to a stop at one point, and as she glanced idly out her side window, she thought she saw Dylan. Standing at a bus stop. No. How could he be standing at a bus stop halfway to Montreal when he was at the airport waiting for her to pick him up? Traffic started moving again, and she had no choice but to move along with it.

As he stood there, he looked idly up and out at the highway above him. He thought he saw Rev's spattered black car in the distance, several lanes over. No. How could she be way out here when she was back at the airport picking him up? Before it occurred to him to wave, the car moved on.

"So," Dylan said, an hour later as Rev pulled up to stop in front of him at the pillar marked #1076-Q, "shall I drive this last bit?"

"Yeah, sure," she said. "'Cuz I already did," she muttered to herself.

"What?"

"Sounds good," she said, as she got out and walked around to the passenger side of the car.

"Here's the key," he said, handing the sphere to her, as he got into the driver's seat and pulled away from the long line of drop-off—or pick-up—spots.

"The key to their house? It doesn't look like a key." She got into the passenger seat and studied the sphere.

"No, it doesn't, does it. I think we have to figure it out."

She started fiddling with it.

He slowed down at an Escher-like intersection of several roads.

"That way," Rev said, pointing, barely looking up.

"Are you sure? Doesn't that just go back to the airport—like a ring road?"

"Nope," she said. "Trust me. That way."

Dylan took the road she had pointed to.

"So, what, this is a test?" She turned the sphere around in her hand, methodically pressing each bit, trying to open it. Nothing.

"Not exactly. It must be an engineering puzzle. Diane tossed it to me."

Rev had gone onto pulling each bit. Nothing.

"Okaaay..." She shook it and heard the key inside. She was getting a little frustrated. "What kind of engineer is she?"

"The—weird kind?"

"No, I mean, well, if she's a chemical engineer, this will open when it senses the salt in the sweat from my skin..." Rev gripped it tightly. Nothing happened.

"And if she's an electrical engineer, it'll plug in—" she turned it in her hand again, looking for some sort of plug or socket.

"And if she's a mechanical engineer—" she smashed it onto the dashboard. Dylan looked over, horrified.

"Gear humor," she said, laughing uproariously.

Dylan looked mystified. And glanced in the back expecting to see a new stash of Red Bull cans. Emptied.

"I went to the University in Waterloo," she explained. "Huge engineering school. Lots of gears there."

Dylan continued to look confused.

"The mechanical engineers were called 'gears,'" she said.

"Ah. And what were the electrical engineers called?"

"'Superior,'" she said and snort-laughed.

Rev considered the sphere again.

"And if she's a Star Trek engineer," she said, "there will be a hole in the space-time continuum where there's a door into which this will fit, and it'll make a sizzling sound as it bends the continuum and unlocks the door, and it'll then transform itself into—"

"Or it would do if you hadn't broken it."

"—dilithium," she finished.

She fiddled with it while Dylan moved in and out of the slow, dense traffic that was moving toward Montreal. Despite their hour at, roughly speaking, the airport, they still hadn't quite missed the morning commute congestion.

"Okay," she said finally, with great frustration, "I've pushed, and pulled, and twisted—what else is there?"

"More than one of the above?" Dylan suggested. "You know, like those child-proof bottles. Maybe you have to push and twist at the same time. Then pull," he added helpfully.

Rev pushed and twisted, then pulled. The sphere fell open and a key fell out. She slumped in—disappointment.

"Geordi would be proud," Dylan assured her.

"OKAY, SO LOOK FOR NUMBER 29," Dylan said as they turned onto Ellesmere Street. "No...no...no...," Rev said at each house as they crawled down the street and she peered out the window trying to locate the house numbers. "Wait, I can't—no... Yes! This one!" Rev called out excitedly, and consulted the sheet of directions Dylan had given her to navigate them to this very spot. "'Dark grey stone,'" she read aloud, "'flower beds along the front, black porch'—that's a bit weird. But I actually like it."

"The flowerbeds?"

"God no. The black porch."

"Of course you do," Dylan mumbled as he pulled the car into the driveway.

"They have a garage," Rev said.

"Expect furniture too. We'll have to put most of it away," he added.

"Why?"

"It's a rule of mine. I put all the good stuff away as soon as I arrive."

"That doesn't sound like fun."

He grinned. "And if I can't put it away," he said as he got out of the car—then peered down at Rev, sprawled on the pavement, "I cover it up." Then he burst out laughing. "I'm sorry—it just—"

"Oh shut up," she said as she got up.

They gathered up their stuff from the back seat.

"One time, there was this little mat by the sliding glass door that led to the balcony off the bedroom. And I kept carefully wiping my feet on it whenever I came in from the balcony so I didn't get this woman's white carpet dirty, and one day it occurred to me that it would be much better if the mat were outside the door instead of inside, so that's where I put it. It got rained on and sunned on, as things outside tend to do, and, anyway, turned out it was a priceless antique," she said. "An antique wool rug. Being wool, it had faded and shrunk, of course—and she wanted a couple hundred dollars reimbursement."

"A couple hundred dollars for a doormat?"

"A couple hundred dollars for a priceless antique."

"Well if it was so priceless, why didn't she put it in a closet before she left? Or under the bed."

"Exactly what I said!" They walked to the front door. "But, well, one bad reference and there goes my gig. So, from then on, I walk around the house when I arrive—"

"And put everything away. Makes sense. We'll do that."

They stood at the front door. Rev held up the key triumphantly as she put it into the lock and turned it.

"Are we still here?" Dylan asked, looking around. "Have the aliens come through from the other side? Dad?" he said plaintively.

"Give it up. He's not coming back."

"You're so cruel."

"Wow," Rev said, as she walked in. "Look at this place." They set their bags down and just stared. "It's all nice and—rich."

The floors were polished wood, and there was a little table by the door that looked like, well, a priceless antique. As did the ornate mirror hanging above it. And the pedestal thing beside it, on which there was a—crystal model of the universe? They wandered in. The hall led to a huge kitchen that was full of—kitchen things.

"They're our age, aren't they," Rev said. "And they have all this. And we have—"

"Don't go there."

"But—"

"They each have a career. A job they have to go to every day, all day. The same jobs they've had for the last twenty years. And now, finally, after those twenty years, they get a month or two off each year. Just a month to do—whatever. In between, they probably don't get home until six or seven, and then he has papers to grade, and she has project deadlines to meet—"

"Still. I've got deadlines to meet. And—I'm nowhere near this."

"They have to deal with the same people every day. At least one of which is sure to be an asshole in some really, really irritating way. An asshole who will never get transferred to another department and who certainly won't quit and who is nowhere near retirement. An asshole who refuses to have a fatal car accident on the way to work. An asshole who—"

She stared at him.

"—is the price of this priceless antique," he summarized, nodding at the little table.

"Okay," she said, "I'll stick with door number one. The one with the milk crates and the brick and board bookshelves. And no career."

Dylan noticed the note on the stove then, and picked it up. It was a lengthy list of instructions for care.

"Oh, this is one of those ceramic stovetop things. You ever use one?" Dylan asked.

"I don't have a stove."

"How can you not—"

"I have a hotplate. And a toaster oven."

"But how can you prepare meals?"

"Prepare meals?" She looked at him as if he was nuts.

"Right," he said.

"A neighbour gave me their old microwave a few years ago. That enlarged my cuisine considerably," she bragged.

She stood beside him then and looked at the stove. "Have *you* ever used one?"

"No. One place had a gas stove and I had to light the flame thing. Scared the heebee-jeebees outta me."

"You had the BeeGees inside of you? How many of them?"

"Not the heebee-beegees, he said, the heebee-*jeebees*."

"Ah. Good. Because the BeeGees are, um, dead. Or should be," she corrected.

"Right," he said. "Okay, so..." he looked around, "they've got a microwave," he pointed. "And a toaster oven. We'll be fine."

"What's that?" She pointed to—a kitchen machine.

"I don't know."

"Espresso coffee maker?"

He stepped up to look more closely at it. "Maybe it's a transporter. To go with the dilithium key thing."

"Did they leave instructions for it?" she looked around.

"If not, don't try to figure it out—like you did with the dilithium key thing."

"'Kay," she said grudgingly. She had wandered into the dining room and found a another sheet of paper on the dining room table. "Here," she handed it to Dylan. "More notes."

"Plumbing emergencies," Dylan read, "call Jake Barrow. 724-yada yada. Furnace emergencies, call The Furnace Guy 726-yada yada."

"Bet he gets a lot of business."

"Electrical emergencies, call an electrician."

"Funny guy. No yada yada?"

"No yada yada. There'll be a phone book somewhere. We'll find it later."

They moved from the kitchen to the living room. There were two leather couches—that didn't really look all that comfortable. There was a state of the art home entertainment system—that would take them a day to figure out. Even with the five sheets of instructions that lay nearby. And there were lots of hanging plants. Dylan picked up another sheet of paper that was on the coffee table. The antique coffee table.

"Plant care instructions?"

"Yup."

"You be in charge of that."

"Okay." He scanned the sheet and put it back down by the plants.

She wandered downstairs then, while he wandered upstairs.

After a minute or so, Dylan called out. "Hey Rev, you gotta see this."

She jogged up the stairs and followed his voice. Into the master bedroom. It had walk-in closets, a couple very large dressers, two adjoining bathrooms. Very nice. But not what she herself—

"Check out the view," Dylan said from the almost-wall-to-wall glass doors that led out to a balcony.

She went toward him as he opened the door, then she quickly took a step back.

"Not good with heights," she said.

"But isn't it—" he stepped out onto the balcony. "Look how far you can see!"

"Yeah. Too far. Down. And—out. It's too—" she tried to explain her discomfort, "—much. Tell you what," she said from the doorway to which she had retreated. "You can have this room. I found a cozy den downstairs. All dark and woodsy. A patio door that opens onto—ground. It's got a desk. And the couch is a foldout. That can be my room."

"Okay," he said agreeably. "Let's go check it out," he said as he threw his bags onto the floor beside the bed.

"You've got a TV," he said, as he stood in the den she'd found.

"You can come watch it if you like," she said.

"I intend to," he smiled. "And you've got a fireplace." He stepped toward the fireplace and picked up the note.

"Instructions for using the fireplace," he read aloud. "Step one—You don't need a fire in July!! Funny guy," he said.

"Okay," Dylan said, "so we need to find you some bedding."

"Got some. Out in the car. The dorm was bring your own."

"Right. Would be."

"Okay, then," he said, "that's all settled. Let's find a room we're not going to use and move the priceless antiques into it..."

"Or maybe just a corner, on each floor—"

"Yeah," he looked around. "It'd be stupid to start moving stuff up and down stairs. I'll do the upstairs, you do this floor—"

"There must be a linen closet somewhere with towels—I'd like to cover up that little table at the front door—"

"Good idea. And that pedestal thing—with that crystal primum mobile thing on it—let's put that away somewhere—"

So they went about Rev-and-Dylan-proofing the house and bringing in the rest of their stuff from the car.

"OKAY," DYLAN SAID A LITTLE WHILE LATER, as they stood by the front door. "Just this part of the house left, yeah?" He picked up the note that was on the little table—the one note they hadn't read yet.

"The cats' names are Fish 'n' Chips," he read from the note.

"Fish 'n' Chips? That's good," Rev laughed. "I'd like to meet these people. I wonder which is which," she added.

"Cat emergencies," Dylan continued reading, "call Dr. Genereau, yada yada. Empty the litter box, yada. Food is in the cupboard, yada. Note: Fish 'n' Chips are indoor cats. DO NOT LET THEM OUTSIDE UNDER ANY CONDITION."

There was just the smallest moment of silence.

"Oops."

Dylan looked at Rev.

"They were at the door," she protested. "I thought they wanted to go out. I told you, I don't know cats," she said as she followed Dylan downstairs. "Who ever heard of indoor cats?" She started babbling. "They'll be okay. The yard's all fenced in, I checked fir— Oh."

"Okay, we've got to find them. This was just, what, a few minutes ago?"

"Well, more like—half an hour."

"Shit. Okay, your car is still in the drive?"

"Yeah," she reached into her pocket for the keys. "No, wait. I have this vague idea that cats don't do good in cars."

"Right. Probably not a good way to find them anyway. Bikes. We need to just bike around the neighbourhood."

They ran back upstairs, out the front door, to the garage. And realized they hadn't yet figured out how to open it.

"Downstairs," Rev said. "There's gotta be a door to the garage from the downstairs."

They ran back inside and downstairs. "That's a washroom," she pointed to one door. "This one." She opened the door on the other side of the room, and they saw that it did indeed lead into the garage. She reached around for a light switch. Found it.

"Aha," Dylan cried. "*Two* bikes!" They started wheeling them toward the garage door, where Dylan started randomly pushing buttons on a panel he hoped wasn't the fusebox. Or the transporter. Eventually, a motor engaged and the garage door starting rising.

"Okay," Dylan said, when they were outside. "You go that way," he nodded to his left, "and I'll go this way." He started to get on his bike.

"Wait," she said. "We didn't lock the inside door."

"Right." He started to get off his bike.

"Actually, we should just close *this* door instead," she looked around to all the stuff in the garage. All the nice, rich stuff in the garage. She wheeled back to push a button.

"No!" he cried out. "We don't know how to open it yet from the outside."

"Oh. Right." They stood there.

"Okay, I'll go back inside," Rev said after a moment, "and close it from the inside, then I'll go through the downstairs door and come out the front door."

"That'll work."

Rev leaned her bike against her car and went back inside. Dylan watched as the garage door closed. A few seconds later, she appeared at the front door. Just as it was about to shut, Dylan cried out, "Wait!" She caught the door as he leaned his bike against the car too.

"I don't have the key," he said, checking his pockets as he walked toward her.

She went back inside and returned almost immediately, holding the key aloft.

Dylan went back inside then as well and grabbed the note about the cats. And a pen that had been lying beside it. He turned the sheet over and scribbled something onto it.

"What are you doing?"

"Making a list of to do's."

"Get an extra key made. Good idea."

"Get *two* extra keys made," he corrected, shoving the note, and the pen, into his pocket. "One for you, one for me, and one for when we both forget to take our keys."

"Brilliant."

"Okay," he said as they both got onto the bikes, "you go that way and I'll go this way—and we'll call each other if we find—"

"Wait. I don't have a cellphone."

"You don't have a cellphone?" He was stunned. "How can you not have a cellphone?"

"No service where I live. No point."

"Right." He pulled out his list. "Get Rev a cellphone," he said aloud. "Okay, you go that way and—"

"Maybe we should leave the back door open in case they come back?"

"Good idea." He got off his bike again, leaned it against the car, and headed back to the front door, reaching into his pocket—"No! Bad idea!" He spun around and headed back to his bike. "The thieves'll come!"

"Right. Okay, so one of us stay here. I'll stay here—"

"But you're the one—"

"I'll get lost," she explained. "And I don't have a cellphone anyway."

"Right. Okay, you stay here—and call me if they come back."

"Right. Good. Okay."

Dylan got back on his bike and—

"Wait! I need the key."

"Right." He reached into his pocket, gave her the key, then took off on the bike, calling out for the cats as he went. Rev watched as he turned the corner at the end of the street, then went back inside, downstairs, and opened the sliding glass door to the yard. She looked anxiously outside. No cats. She went upstairs, found their food and water dishes, and their bag of food. She took the bag downstairs and out onto the patio. She shook the bag several times, clattered their dishes unnecessarily, and as noisily as possible, filled the dishes. No cats. Bob would've come running at warp speed, she thought. From the Laurentians.

Meanwhile, Dylan biked up one street, and down another, calling out as he went, "Fish 'n' Chips!" He didn't see any cats. Which was probably a good thing since he'd forgotten to ask Rev what they looked like. What if he brought home the wrong cats? No, that was as likely as bringing home the right cats, he thought. Still, he reached into his pocket to call her to ask what they looked like. Then realized he didn't know the number. He pulled out his to do list. Memorize the house phone number, he added.

He started biking again, and resumed calling, though with decidedly less enthusiasm. "Fish 'n' Chips. Fish 'n' Chips."

Three teenagers standing at the corner flagged him down.

Dylan slowed to a stop beside them, hopeful.

"I'll have a couple," one of them said.

"A couple what?"

"A couple fish and chips," he said, reaching into his baggy pants.

Dylan stared at him. "Do I look like I'm selling fish and chips?"

"Well that's what you were calling out," the kid said, a ten dollar bill in hand. "Thought you were a fish and chips guy. You know, like the ice cream truck and the hot dog wagon."

Dylan pointedly looked at his bike and then at the kid. "Do I *look* like a truck or a wagon?"

"Well, what the fuck are you shouting Fish 'n' Chips for then?" He shoved his money back into his pocket.

"Because," Dylan said, "I'm looking for a couple cats. Their names are Fish 'n' Chips."

The kid looked at him. Scornfully. "Cats don't come when they're called," he stated the obvious.

"They don't?" Dylan said. Dumbly. He realized then that he didn't know cats either. "So how do I find them?"

"They find you. Just go back home. They'll show up eventually."

"They won't get hit by a car or something?"

"Well not if they're outdoor cats. Outdoor cats are—" he broke off as he saw Dylan's expression. "They're *indoor* cats? You let *indoor* cats outside? You better find them, man. Indoor cats don't know shit about being outside."

So Dylan carried on, becoming more and more frantic. At some point, he realized he was lost. So he stopped the next people he saw and—realized he didn't know where he lived. He pulled out his notepad again. Then he pulled out his cellphone again. Rev could jog to the corner and see what street they were on. Or could if he knew the house's phone number. "I need a Red Bull," he said to himself. An hour later, he showed up at the house.

"Where have you been?" Rev was standing anxiously at the front door.

"I got lost."

"But—"

"And I forgot the address. I remembered what the house looked like but I didn't know what street it was on."

"Why didn't you call me?" she asked the obvious.

"Because I didn't know the house's phone number!"

"Oh. Right. Well, um, the cats came back. Um. A few minutes after you left."

"Then why didn't *you* call *me*??" he asked with exasperation.

"Because I didn't know *your* number!"

"Oh. Right." He pulled out his to do list.

"What are you writing down? Little bells for the cats?"

"No. They don't need little bells. Because we're not letting them outside again. Ever."

"Well—I might—"

"Never ever."

"Little bells for us?"

"We'll put a big sign on the door. On every door. 'DO NOT LET THE CATS OUT!'" He wrote that down on his to do list.

"*Big* bells for us?"

"ID cards. For us," he clarified. "Put our phone numbers and our address on it."

"Better put our names on it too. We'll be forgetting those next. Seeing as we're so old..." she trailed off. "We can tie them to our mittens."

"It's July. We don't need mittens in July. Besides, we didn't forget so much as not know," Dylan said defensively.

"Well, we forgot to know."

He stared at her. “Forgot to know?”

“Okay,” she ignored his look, “so the cats are here. The doors are closed. Locked ev— Uh-oh,” she said then. “You’ve got the key, right?” she said to Dylan. “You took the key with you, right? You’ve got it?”

“No, I thought—” he reached into his pocket. “Didn’t I give the key to you? So you could get back inside?”

“Oh yeah.”

They stood there. Rather stupidly, they both realized.

“The patio door!” Dylan cried out. “When you let the cats back in, did you lock the patio door?”

“No, just the—” she ran around to the back yard. And appeared at the front door in a moment, beaming.

“We better do the to do’s tomorrow,” she said. “First thing.”

Dylan pulled out his list and wrote that down.

“SO,” SHE SAID, ONCE THEY WERE INSIDE. And had put Dylan’s bike, and Rev’s car, after unloading the rest of their stuff, into the garage.

“I’m hungry,” Dylan announced.

“We don’t have much left—”

“Let’s have fish and chips.”

She was horrified. “But—they have faces.”

“No, I want some fish and chips. After bloody yelling it for the last hour—We can order out,” he said.

“This is so cool,” she said, as they sat at the kitchen table with the yellow pages open at the restaurants.

“Ordering out—is so cool? Surely you’ve—”

“Not in the last—decade,” she realized dully. “No one delivers where I live. Not that there’s anything to deliver anyway. There’s one pizza place and one Chinese place in town, and neither of them deliver past the town limits.”

"Oh wow," she said, flipping through the pages. "There's *way* more than one pizza and one Chinese place in Montreal. There's—a cheesecake place? I can order out for cheesecake??" She sounded like the proverbial kid in a candy shop.

Dylan looked over her shoulder. "'54 varieties of cheesecake in a quaint little café'—let's just go there instead. Tomorrow."

"We can do that?"

"Of course we can. Why can't we," he added suspiciously.

"It's just—I think I'm going to like living in the city for a month."

"But you've lived in a city before—"

"Yeah but before, I couldn't afford to just go to a café for cheesecake. No full-time job, remember? You know what substitute teaching pays. A couple hundred here and a couple hundred there. And I was saving every little extra for the down payment. For when I found my cabin."

"But you can now? Afford to just go to a café for cheesecake?"

She thought about this. "Yeah. I can. Now that I'm no longer supporting Greenpeace, Sierra, disarmament, protests at nuclear power plants—"

"Or feeding the hungry."

That made her pause. "Yeah," she said wavering. Then rallied, "Let them eat—"

"Cheesecake when they've had their vasectomies."

"Right. Okay," she continued scanning the pages, "so we've got The Brit's Fish and Chips—"

"Which is probably run by a Jamaican—"

Rev looked at him.

"—or some other non-Brit—"

"—or Simon's Fish and Chips."

"That sounds good." He went to the little table where the phone was, now covered with a towel—the table, not the phone—and dialed the number Rev called out to him.

"Hi, could we have two orders of fish and chips." He paused. "Delivery." He paused again. "I'll call you back."

He hung up the phone and turned to Rev.

"29…" Rev said. "29…shit. Just a minute." She went out the front door and took off at a jog. Dylan started looking for the piece of paper Diane had given him, with the directions to their house on it. Must be still in the car, he realized just as Rev returned.

"You ran to the corner and back? Already?"

"Yeah," she said, a little insulted by his surprise.

"And you're not even out of breath?"

"No," she said with some indignation. "But I have to sit down," she conceded, pulling out one the chairs at the kitchen table. "And in ten minutes, you can watch me fall down when I try to get up."

"Okay. Looking forward to it," he grinned. "So where do we live?"

Pause. "Shit!" Then just as she began to get up again, it popped into her head. "Ellesmere!"

"Ellesmere," he said.

"Yes!"

"We live at 29 Ellesmere…what?"

"Ch," she said.

"What?"

"Ch. That's what the sign says. Ellesmere Ch. Oh," she suddenly remembered, "that's short for chemin!"

"Okay, is that road or street or—?"

"I don't know…" she tried to remember her high school French. Dylan pulled out his to do list and added 'Get a French-English dictionary.'

"Rue is street," Rev had remembered that much. "Chemin is—Way? We live at 29 Ellesmere Way?"

Dylan dialed Simon's Fish and Chips again. "Hi, it's me again. Two orders of fish and chips. 29 Ellesmere. Ch." There was a long pause, then "Yes. No. Yes. No. Yes. Good, thanks." He hung up.

"So what'd you get?"

"I don't know."

"But you said—"

"It was yes-no's turn."

She waited.

"When I order out, sometimes I answer all their questions with 'no' and sometimes I answer them all with 'yes' and—"

"Sometimes you alternate. But how do you—"

"It works, you'll see."

"Okay. As long as you didn't get us fried octopus legs."

That stopped him.

"They fry octopus legs?"

"Well, I'm sure they batter them first."

"What, to make them all soft?" he giggled.

She snorted. "No, I think they're already soft."

"SO," DYLAN SAID, AS THEY SAT ON THE COUCH downstairs. They'd started a joint and were munching on the fish and chips they'd spread out on the table they'd covered with a towel. "What *do* the cats look like?" he looked around. "I haven't seen them yet."

"What do you think they look like?"

He thought a long moment. "Furry," he finally said.

"You're absolutely right!" Rev said. "Wow, you must be psychic! What else?"

"Um…they're smaller than a bear and bigger than a mouse. Because—because—" he couldn't wait to explain his reasoning—"they're food for the one and the other is food for them."

Rev thought about that as she took the proffered joint. "Do bears eat cats?" she finally said. "I thought they ate berries."

"Grizzly bears do. Or would if they could. They eat everything."

"So they also eat mice."

"Yes." Then he asked, "How does that change what size cats are?"

"Well, it—doesn't."

"So it's irrelevant."

"Yes, (B): The diet of grizzly bears is irrelevant to the size of Fish 'n' Chips," Rev stated with enthusiasm. She'd nailed that one! Wait 'till she emails the LSAT people.

After a while, she moved their conversation forward. 'Forward' defined in the broadest way possible. "And not only are cats in between in size, they're in between in alphabet."

"What?"

"'C' is between 'B' and 'M.'"

Dylan pondered that. "The LSAT people—they *do* buy your questions from time to time?"

"They *do*."

"Amazing."

"So—oh yeah—what *color* are the cats? *That's* what I meant. I remember what I meant!" she said happily.

"Oh. Okay. Let me see. One's silver-grey and one's golden-yellow."

"Silver-grey?"

"Fish are silver-grey. Well, they're rainbow too, if they're trout, but cats don't come in rainbow. Do they?" he said after a moment.

"I don't think so. But Dalmatians come in Smarties," she said.

"I saw that picture too! But that was a made-up Dalmatian."

"Really? I didn't notice any make-up."

"Not made-up. Made-up!"

"Oh. But it looked like a real Dalmatian."

"It was—it was just—the *spots* were made-up. Perspicuity," he said then and took a long draw on their joint.

"Palomino!" Rev shouted. "Palominos have spots too! Don't they?

But probably not Smarties spots."

Eventually she remembered that they were talking about Fish 'n' Chips. "Okay, but when fish are turned into fish and chips, they're not silver-grey anymore." She held up her fork. Dylan studied the piece of fish on the end of it.

"Right. So one's white, and," he looked at the chips in the carton, "one's golden-yellow. No, that's mixing up inside and outside. Bad things happen when you mix up what's inside and what's outside," he shuddered.

"Yeah," Rev agreed. "That's almost as bad as mixing up upside-down and downside-up. Wait, that makes me dizzy." She leaned back into the couch for a moment. And took another draw on their joint.

"Okay, so," he continued, "they're either white and white—hey, both fish and chips are white inside! What are the odds of that?" He paused to consider the odds. "Or, they're gold and gold," he said. It took him a minute, but he got there: "Hey, both fish and chips are—"

"Close," Rev interrupted, because she couldn't wait. She whistled. And two furry black heads popped out from behind the TV.

"No," he groaned loudly with despair and tossed his knife and fork onto his plate in disgust. "They come when you whistle for them?"

"Oh," she said, having just realized that's what she'd done. "Guess so."

After a moment, Dylan said, "Bob used to do that." Happy at the memory, he picked up his fork again and resumed eating his fish 'n' chips.

"Okay, but that's not the point. The point is—what is the point?"

"They're both black," he said easily. "Oh." His fork stopped midway to his mouth. "That doesn't make sense." Undismayed, his fork finished its journey.

One of the cats approached Dylan.

"I wonder if cats like fish." He cut off a piece of fish—"I'm making it mouse-sized"—he explained—to himself—then speared it with his fork and held it out to the cat.

"Of course cats like—"

The cat swatted viciously at the piece of fish, sending it clear across the room where it went splat against the wall.

"Wow," Dylan said, belatedly following the trajectory of the fish from the fork to the wall. "Bob never did *that*." He loaded his fork again. And giggled as another chunk of fish shot across the room.

"Do you think it's possible they're not Fish 'n' Chips?" Dylan asked a bit later. When he'd run out of fish.

"Well they came right up and helped themselves to the kibble I'd put in their dishes."

He gave her a look.

"Oh. Right. Okay, they walked right in and immediately found the spots in the sun. Oh. Right." She paused, trying to think of something that would count as convincing evidence. "Why don't we just email Jack and Diane and ask?"

"Right. 'The house is fine, what do your cats look like?'"

"Oh. Right."

"I know!" he said suddenly. "There's got to be pictures! We look for pictures!"

"Yes!! There was a picture on the desk—" she got up and opened the drawer—"I put it away for safekeeping," she said with an inordinate amount of pride.

"Oh." She brought it back to the couch and showed Dylan. It was a picture of two people, presumably Jack and Diane, with two cats—one black and one white.

"Okay that's not right," Dylan said, taking the picture.

"Maybe the black one is Fish, or Chips, and the white one died, and they bought another one."

"Maybe. They look younger. Jack and Diane. In the picture," he said. "Not now," he clarified.

"No, they couldn't look younger now," she understood. That would be inside out.

"'Course," he turned the photograph over, "if you name a pair of black and white cats Salt 'n' Pepper you probably wouldn't name a pair of black cats Fish 'n' Chips."

"They named them Salt 'n' Pepper?" she reached for the photograph.

"I don't know," he said, as she saw that the back of the picture was blank. "I'm just saying."

"Oh. So if the black one is Fish, or Chips, what's the other one's name? The one that has ceased to be. That's expired. Demised. The ex-cat."

They thought about it, each taking one last draw on their joint.

"Fish and sticks!" Dylan suddenly cried out triumphantly.

"No it's 'fish sticks.' There's no 'and.'"

"Poker sticks!" He waved the joint at the fireplace.

"But if they're poker sticks, they're not fish or chips."

"Right. I went in the completely wrong direction there, didn't I." He slumped back in defeat. Then rallied immediately. "Go Fish!"

She looked at him sadly.

"Chippendale!"

"HEY," REV SAID AS SHE wandered into the kitchen the next morning.

"Hey yourself," Dylan said. "I made some coffee." He leaned against the oven, smiling.

"Excellent. Thanks." She poured herself a cup and inhaled. "Mandatory, first thing in the morning."

"Or the afternoon."

"Is it afternoon?" She vaguely looked around as if that might tell her. "Didn't we go to bed in the afternoon?"

"Yup."

"Well," she said, digesting this, "we needed the sleep."

"Because we're so old."

"Oh shut up."

"So I'm thinking we should go shopping today," Dylan said. "Get some stuff, do our to do's."

"Then we can say ta-dah." It was lame, but hey, it was early in the afternoon.

"But first I have to clean the fish off the walls," Dylan said.

"You threw the cat against the wall?" she asked, horrified, looking around again.

"Not *Fish, the* fish."

"Oh." Then a moment later, "Do we have to feed them?"

"There aren't any fish to feed." Dylan looked around vaguely. "Are there?"

"Not *the* fish, *Fish*. And Chips."

"Oh. Right."

"We're still a little stoned, aren't we," she said.

"Or still a little tired," he suggested.

"We're so old," she said with disgust.

Dylan reached to the stove top, picked up several notes, and looked for the one about the cats.

"Okay," he said, reading through the note, "it doesn't look like they're on any sort of schedule."

"That's good."

"We just have to keep their food and water dishes full. And if they're empty, apparently they'll let us know."

"How?"

"Well, Bob—"

"—'s a dog."

"Right."

"Maybe they'll sit at their little dishes and meow politely," she suggested.

"Or come flying out of nowhere to land on our heads."

"That'd work."

She finished her coffee, then said, "Okay, you clean the fish off the walls, I'll see to their little dishes."

AN HOUR LATER—NEITHER WAS a morning, or an early afternoon, person—they were both at the front door, ready to go.

"Where's your shape-shifter bag?" Dylan asked.

"My what?"

"Your shape-shifter bag. The one I used the other day. I put a bag of chips into it and it became the shape of a bag of chips. I put a box of cookies into it and it took the shape of the box. It's a shape-shifter bag. We should take it with us."

"Okaaaay." She went to get her shape-shifter bag.

"You have the key?" She asked, as she opened the door.

"Yes," he said, checking his pocket, bumping into her as she'd stopped.

"You know where we live?" She stopped again.

"Yes," he said, bumping into her again. "Here." He grinned.

"Right. Good. That'll work."

"Oh shut up."

THEY DISCOVERED THEY WERE JUST A FEW BLOCKS from Maisonneuve, on which they found a small hardware store, at which they had two copies of the house key made.

Next stop was a grocery store. Rev wandered up and the aisles slowly, looking at all the food.

Dylan stared at her. "You've never been in a grocery store before?"

"Of course I have," she continued looking carefully up and down the shelves, "but it's always been the same one. Where I live, there are two grocery stores within a half hour's drive, but they're both Foodlands. So they both carry the very same things. The very same, very boring things. What kind of stupidity is that?" she said as she idly picked up a tin of lychee fruit.

"Stupidity driven by the greed and ego of the owner who wants a monopoly," Dylan answered.

"Right. Variety and the pleasure of choice for the rest of us be damned." She stared at a box of smarties-colored pasta. "There's another five grocery stores within an hour's drive—three one way and two the other—"

"But they're also Foodlands." Dylan scanned the shelves of cereal.

"Well, four of them are, yeah."

"And I bet they don't carry Cinnamon-Sprinkled Froot Loops," he said, taking a box off the shelf.

"They don't. And you know," she added, "until now, that wasn't a problem."

"Wow," she stopped halfway down the juice aisle. "See this is what I'm talking about. Back home, I can have orange juice or apple juice. Here..."

"You can have pomegranate," Dylan reached out for a bottle of pomegranate juice.

"Or pineapple coconut," Rev chose a bottle of pineapple coconut.

A few aisles later, she found sugar pie. "And this," she held it aloft, "you can get *only* in Quebec."

"Let's take two then," Dylan said.

Outside the store, their juice, Froot Loops, and sugar pie safely in their shape-shifter bag, Dylan consulted his list and looked up and down the street. "I think we're going to have to venture further from home to find a cellphone store."

"Well, that's not quite as urgent as the keys—"

"Or the sugar pie—"

"So let's make that another trip," she said. "'Cuz look what's over there," she pointed.

"Ah. The Cheesecake Café!"

They crossed the street.

Rev pressed her nose to the window. Well, not literally. But almost. "I think they really have 54 varieties," she said.

"In we go, Dylan said, opening the door.

It was a nice little place, rather like a cross between a Baskin Robbins and a European tea room. They cruised along the display cases, looking at all the different kinds of cheesecake.

"Half of them are variations on chocolate," Dylan said.

"You say that as if it's a bad thing," Rev responded. In an oddly threatening tone.

"No, I was just—no. You're the kind of woman who can't get enough chocolate, aren't you," he said warily. And smiling to himself.

After a while, a long while, until Dylan pointed out they could come back, every day if they liked, she chose a caramel chocolate pecan affair and he chose coconut lime.

They headed to a little table by the window.

"Watch," Dylan said, as he slowly put down the bag. "It's going to take the shape of the floor."

"Wow," Rev said, with exaggerated amazement. Then went back to the counter for their cheesecake.

"And two cups of coffee," Dylan said to the counterperson, following Rev back to their table with said coffee.

"Oh," she moaned after her first bite, "this is good." She moaned with her second bite as well.

"Oh get a room," he grinned at her. She grinned back.

They continued to eat their cheesecake, and drink their coffee, looking idly out the window as people walked by.

"This is nice," she said after a few moments, smiling.

"What, exactly?"

"Sitting with you eating caramel chocolate pecan cheesecake in a café in Montreal."

Dylan smiled. "It is, isn't it. Not sitting with me," he clarified. "That would make me just a little bit full of myself—or beside myself." He paused a moment to wonder which, then said, "I meant sitting with you eating lime coconut cheesecake in a café in Montreal. Is nice."

"You know," she said, thoroughly licking her fork after each bite, "if I have only one piece a day, there aren't enough days to try them all."

"Let's switch then, seeing as we're each half way through." He started to move their plates around. "This way, you get to try two a day, and then there *will* be enough—" he broke off his merry explanation, having suddenly noticed her eyes narrow and her nostrils inflate. "That is—if you—tell you what," he said, wisely making a sharp right turn. "You can have the rest of my coconut lime cheesecake," he pushed his plate toward her, "*and* the rest of your chocolate caramel pecan," he pushed her plate back toward her. He made much to do about arranging them very nicely right in front of her. Then pushed them a little closer to her.

And reached over for the newspaper that had been left on the adjacent now-empty table.

"Oh look," he said, after a few moments of shuffling through it. "We should take this home." He cautiously met her eyes. The murderous intent had subsided. "It's got one of those 'What to do where to go tonight' sections."

"Oh—" she said suddenly, "what day is it today?"

He looked at the front of the newspaper. "Tuesday. If this is today's paper."

"Oh, good."

"You like Tuesdays?"

"No, yes, I don't know—sometimes—it depends—" he furrowed his eyebrow at her. "It means we didn't miss the fireworks. They're Wednesdays and Saturdays."

"Ah. So tomorrow night we go see the fireworks. Let's see what we do tonight."

"Okay, but at some point in time I have to do some work."

"At some point in time," he agreed.

"Hey, look at this," he said a few minutes later. "They've got a daily contest for an under-ten-words summary of your life so far. 'Looked for love in all the wrong places,'" he read one of the winning entries. "'School, marriage, kids, career, not necessarily in that order.' Hm."

"So what would yours be?" Dylan put the paper down and took a swallow of his coffee. Seeing as he didn't have any more cheesecake.

Rev thought for a moment. "Failed miserably, slit my wrists, missed the arteries."

Dylan's hand stopped half way to his mouth. "Are you still flogging yourself for not changing the world??"

She avoided his eyes.

"No offence, and I'm the last pot to call the kettle black, but a few years of smashing your head against the brick walls of various boards of education and one unpublished book doesn't exactly warrant—" he broke off, then tried again. "It's not as if you've spent your whole life trying to—" he broke off again, suddenly realizing—"you wrote more than one book, didn't you."

"Yes."

"How many more?"

"Nine."

"You wrote nine books?"

"Nine more. That makes ten," she said helpfully.

"You've written ten books?" He put his fork down. "And *none* of them have been—"

"And a couple hundred op-ed pieces."

"A couple hun—I didn't know you had a col—ah."

"Anything else?" he said after a while.

"Well..."

"You said your teaching certificate was revoked so you can't have—"

"Go figure," she said, "but universities don't require their instructors to have any teaching credentials."

He was momentarily distracted by that. Then—"You taught at university too?"

She nodded. Forlornly. "Theories of Justice. Business Ethics. Environmental Ethics. And my favourite, Class, Race, and Gender for Rich White Men."

He was silent for some time. "And you *missed* the arteries, yeah?"

ON THE WAY HOME, she said, not really out of nowhere, "Why do they fill our heads with such dreams...we can change the world, we can grow up and be anything we want..."

"Would you rather they told you you couldn't?"

"I'd rather they told us how."

"Maybe 'they' didn't know. Either. Does *anyone* know how to get from—here to—there? I mean," he continued, "when the guy who spent years picking things up and then just putting them back down again ends up being the Governor of California...who could've seen that coming?"

"And when the guy who starred in a B-movie with a monkey becomes the most powerful person on the planet—"

"So shall we take the bikes to the fireworks tonight?" Dylan asked the next afternoon.

"Sounds good."

"They start at—"

"Dark."

"Right. So let's leave—"

"Before dark."

"Excellent."

Dylan took the one he'd ridden before, a blue one, and Rev took the green one.

"Wait a minute," he said once they'd wheeled them out of the garage. "We may need to lock them up. Do they have locks?"

"Better question," she said, "do we have keys?"

They established that the bikes did indeed have locks. And that they did not indeed have keys.

"So we stop at that hardware store on the way, buy a chain big enough to circle both of them, and a lock, yeah?"

They biked to the hardware store they'd found the other day, and found a suitable chain and lock. Though deciding whether to get a lock that required them to remember keys or one that required them to remember numbers took some time. Once they'd made the decision—keys, which they'd keep on the handlebars—Dylan started wandering around the store a bit.

"Whatcha lookin' for?" Rev asked, happily following him.

"Something to clean the stickies off your car."

"But—" she stopped in the middle of the aisle, "that's my anti-theft device!"

"Have you checked out the competition lately?"

She didn't understand.

"Who would steal a '99 Saturn when they have so many new SUVs to take instead?"

"Ah. Okay, true. But without the stickies my car will suffer an identity crisis. Irreparable damage to its psyche."

He narrowed his eyes at her. "You have trouble with change, don't you."

"Yes," she freely admitted.

"Odd for someone who wants to change the world."

"Yeah—oh wow, what an interesting insight."

"Okay, just the stickies on the sides," Dylan said. "Where one might lean. And the ones by the door handles and the trunk. I'll leave all the stickies on the hood and roof," he promised.

"Okay," she agreed reluctantly. "Did you lean against it and get the stuff on your jeans?"

"Yes."

"Did you get the stuff off your jeans?"

"Yes. Still."

"Still," she agreed. "But you'll leave the hood and roof? You're not likely to lean on the hood or the roof, are you?"

"Not unless gravity changes its orientation."

"Okay then."

Standing outside the hardware store, Rev saw the cheesecake café and decided they had time. She had a slice of Orange Cinnamon and he tried the Pure Buttercream. Half way through, they switched.

"Oh my," she said, taking a bite of the Pure Buttercream. "I wonder if they sell whole cheesecakes. I wonder if they freeze well."

"Would they make the trip back? In August?"

"Hm. Probably not."

They carried on their way then, biking down to St. Catherine toward La Ronde, where the fireworks were going to be. But they quickly realized St. Catherine wasn't a good street for bikes, so they turned up and went along Ontario. But that proved to be rather boring.

"We should find out what streets the bike paths are on," Dylan called out.

"Good idea. I hear Montreal's full of them."

"Fifteen minutes later," Dylan stopped and walked his bike onto the sidewalk. Rev followed.

"What's here?" she asked as he looked for a place to chain their bikes.

Dylan pointed. "Cellphones."

"Ah. Is it really worth buying a cellphone for just one month?"

"You could use—is this the only time you're going to leave your cabin? For the rest of your life?"

"Well—no, probably not."

"And what about just driving," he continued. "Haven't you ever gotten a flat tire or something and you needed to call a tow truck and you're in the middle of god knows where and it's night and even if you walked to the next town there wouldn't be a phone booth there and even if there was it wouldn't have a phone book and it's not like you've got the phone numbers of tow truck places memorized or the phone would have been pulled out of its thing by someone whose girlfriend just broke up with him on a payphone for gods sake or Bell would have disconnected it because no one uses payphones anymore because everyone has a cellphone—"

"Yes," she put him out of his misery. "I had a flat tire once."

So they went in and bought her a cellphone. A glow-in-the-dark cellphone. She liked it.

"Wait," he said, as she started to get on his bike. "We should put your new number in my phone and vice versa."

"We can do that?"

"What do you mean, 'We can do that?' Don't you have speed dial on your home phone?"

"No. I have slow dial. The numbers go round and round—"

"You don't have touch tone?" He was amazed.

"I like that the numbers go round and round," she said. "Actually, they don't so much go round and round," she considered, "as go part-way-round and back. I think that's what I like. A place for everything and everything in its place. Things go somewhere but they come back. To where they're supposed to be."

"How very eighteenth-century of you."

"And yet it was the Romantics I liked best."

"So you have an eighteenth-century mind and a nineteenth-century heart. That—explains stuff."

"Especially since I live in the twentieth-century."

"Twenty-first. The numbers go part-way-into-space and bounce off a satellite now."

"And then do they come back?"

Dylan was stumped.

"And if not, where do they go?"

THE CLOSER THEY GOT TO LA RONDE, the more congested the pedestrian traffic became, and they finally decided to park their bikes some distance away, on one of the side streets now lined with cars, and walk the rest.

"Where should we go?" Dylan asked once they'd arrived. Tons of people were standing, or sitting, as many had brought collapsible chairs, all along the water's edge, extending a good half mile up. And a steady stream was walking across the bridge, claiming spots along the way. Others looked like they were heading clear across the bridge to the other side.

"I don't know. I think across the bridge is where you have to pay. But—"

"Apparently the view from here is good too. Otherwise there wouldn't be so many people here, right?"

"Right. sh why don't we stay here this time. Next time, we'll come a little earlier and walk across, or at least onto, the bridge."

"Okay. *Right* here?" Dylan said, looking around. "I wonder where exactly the fireworks will be. We don't want that lightpost to be in the way. For example."

"Or the hydro lines. Let's try and get closer?"

"Okay."

They made their way among the throngs, and vendors of hot dogs and pogo sticks, ice cream, and bottled water and pop—

"What is this need to have food and drink ever present? Can't people can't walk half a mile without getting so dehydrated they need a drink?"

"No, it's the entertainment thing. You know, like the concession booth at a movie or a baseball game."

"Yeah, well, I've never understood that either. It's not like people have gone without dinner when they go to a movie. That's why we are the most obese nation—"

Dylan veered off and quickly bought an over-priced Haagen-Daaz ice cream bar.

"Here. Eat it. It's chocolate."

She grinned as she unwrapped the bar, took a bite, then held it out to him. He took a bite as well.

They wandered a bit more and in a few minutes decided to stay put. Until it became clear that the person next to them was going to talk on her cellphone the whole time.

"Hey Lu, yeah, I'm at the fireworks. Yeah. No. Not yet. I'm waiting. Yeah. Lots of people. Yeah."

They moved away before Rev shot her.

"I talk therefore I am, "she said wryly.

As they wandered around looking for another spot, she said, "The problem with people for whom thoughts don't exist unless they say them out loud—I wonder if she can read without moving her lips—" she interjected, "is that they can't deliberate."

"Maybe they're just not conscious. You've read *The Bicameral*

*Mind*?"

"Yeah. Wow. So you're saying there are humans among us who haven't yet achieved consciousness? Who exist at the level of—Bob? Just doing—what they do? That would explain—a lot."

"Or maybe they're just *less* conscious," Dylan suggested.

"Hm. Most theories of personhood consider consciousness to be one of the criteria, but come to think of it, it's always assumed to be an on-off quality. What you're suggesting certainly fits my experience of the world better. That it's a matter of degree. That some of us are more conscious, more aware, than others."

They steered themselves among the crowds.

"So would that mean some of us are more a person than others?" Rev stopped. Dylan bumped into her.

"Sorry," she said. "And so would rights, and responsibilities, accrue accordingly? Wow."

"But—"

"You're familiar with Nagel's bat?" she asked him. "How would we know whether someone else is more or less conscious? I mean, I've often wondered whether other people's brains are as—"

"Busy?" He asked, bumping into her again.

"Exactly. I was going to say 'loud' but 'busy' is better. I wonder if, for example, I suddenly had, say, Pat's brain—"

"Who's Pat?"

"One of my neighbours back home. I've often—well, not often, actually—but I've wondered—at least once—if I woke up one day—you've read the brain exchange thought experiments? Williams, Shoemaker, Parfit? What if I woke up one day with Pat's brain? Would it be—quiet? Would I have whole stretches of time with—nothing?"

"You live in a cabin on a lake in a forest. Don't you already have whole stretches of time with nothing?"

"On the outside, yeah."

He suddenly understood. Why she lived where she lived. Why she lived how she lived. Still.

They settled then on a spot some distance from the main crowd, but nevertheless, they hoped, with a good view.

"Well, if I woke up one day with Bob's brain—" Dylan started giggling.

"But he needs it right away! Well if you can't do it, see Jack. He'll know. No!"

"Shit!" Rev said, staring at the man standing a few feet away who could be heard a mile away.

"Maybe he'll put it away when it starts."

She considered that, studying him. "I don't think so," she finally said, as she watched him pace back and forth, all the while speaking with great urgency to whoever was on the other end.

They moved away again. And again. Finally finding a cellphone-free area.

A vendor pushed a cart along the curb selling—sparkly things.

"Hey look," Dylan said, as he picked up a bracelet that seemed to be its own little fireworks show.

"How much are these?" he asked the man.

"Three bucks."

"Really? I'll take two." He chose a yellow sparkling one for himself and a purple one for Rev.

An explosion suddenly burst into the night. Everyone seemed to—prepare themselves.

"Was that the five-minutes-to-curtain announcement?" Dylan wondered aloud.

"Guess so."

"Cool."

And indeed five minutes later, the fireworks began. They didn't say a word for the next half hour. They watched rainbow starbursts, shooting fuchsia comets, bursting weeping willow trees gold against the black sky, shimmering silver curtains like moonlight on water, and sparkly trails of—sparkles. Gold and green, silver and blue, pink and purple, gold and purple. Taking the eye this way, then that. It was to painting what dance was to sculpture. It was like—seeing music.

"LET'S GO ON A WALKABOUT," Dylan said the next day.

"A walkabout?"

"Yeah, we just go outside and—walk about. See what there is to see. Do whatever there is to do."

"I don't think I've ever done that."

"What do you mean?"

"Well, I go for long walks in the forest—and I see what there is to see—which is always pretty much the same thing—the same beautiful thing," she qualified, " and—"

"Don't you ever go into town?"

"Yeah, but I only go when I need to get something. I go in, get it, and come back."

"There's no adventure in that!"

"None whatsoever."

"I think you've been living in the forest for too long."

She considered that. "I think you're right."

They made sure the cats had food and water, they made sure they had their keys to the house, Rev grabbed her knapsack, in case, preferring to have her hands free if they decided to get anything while they were walking about, and Dylan did the same.

Once out the door, they turned in the direction they had not yet taken. It was a beautiful day for walking about. Sunny and warm. Not hot. Not humid.

They passed a park, which, at the far end, turned into a sculpture park. The best piece, Dylan said, was the pigeons perched on the head of some military dignitary—sculpted pigeons.

A few blocks later they were on a side street that looked like it was leading to a downtown street. It had a couple used bookshops, and they spent nearly an hour in each.

Once they reached the main street, they turned—left. Dylan had spotted a store that sold weird stuff. That's what its sign said: 'We sell weird stuff.' They went inside and wandered around. Dylan bought a Star Trek hologram postcard for Rev and a little bottle of bubbles for himself.

They found a chandelier store.

"I didn't know chandeliers came in colors," Rev wandered around in awe. "Look at this one, she pointed up to a glorious arrangement of glittering ruby raindrops."

"And this one," Dylan pointed at one with alternating yellow and clear icicles that had a gold and silver effect.

"Cool."

They had tea and croissants at a café that had really good tea and croissants.

They came to an art gallery and decided to go in and look around. They came to a used record store and did likewise. And a Harley Davidson shop. When they came to another park, they decided to just sit for a while.

"So what would your less-than-ten-words be?" Rev asked him, as he blew bubbles.

He thought for the briefest of moments, then blew another bubble. "Turns out I *don't* have a lot of potential."

"HEY REV, COME HERE," Dylan called out later that night. She ran up the stairs into his room.

"Look at this," he said, and pushed a button. The ceiling retracted.

"Wow. Oh wow," she said, as she saw the stars. She lay down on the bed and just stared. He joined her. And they just stared at the stars.

IT RAINED THE NEXT DAY. Rev loved the rain and was curled up on the chair in the den she'd appropriated as her room, staring out through the screen door at the downpour. Huge drops were splashing up from the patio stones. The noise was almost deafening. She had a cup of coffee in one hand, and one of the books she'd bought at the used bookstore in the other.

"No walkabout today," Dylan said, as he came down the stairs.

"Just as well," Rev said, looking out at the rain. "I have to get some questions done."

"Yeah, I haven't written up my article on the debt demonstration yet either. Sounds nice, doesn't it," he said as he stood there for a few moments.

"It does."

"It looks cool from upstairs too. Mist in the distance."

"Maybe I'll come up and look at it later. From a distance."

"HAVE YOU EVER HAD THAI FOOD?" he called down to Rev a while later.

"No," she said, coming upstairs to the kitchen, where Dylan sat at the table, looking through the yellow pages that were permanently open to the restaurants section.

"Wanna try it?"

"Sure. What have they got?"

"There's no menu. No problem," he said, reaching for the phone and dialing the number.

"Hi, can we have dinner for two, both half-vegetarian, under $30, delivery. Surprise us. 29 Ellesmere. Thanks." He hung up.

She stared at him.

"What?"

"It's just—I've never—I wouldn't've even ever thought to—What if—"

She stopped.

"So what if what if?" he asked.

THEIR FOOD ARRIVED ABOUT HALF AN HOUR LATER, and they took it downstairs to her room. She had the only TV. Except for the expensive entertainment system in the main living room with the leather couches. Which they hadn't gotten around to figuring out yet.

"Good?" Dylan asked as Rev tried a bit of this and a bit of that.

"Yeah," she said, "pretty much. Let's order out that way again."

"Okay. We can do Portuguese next. Or Polish."

"And French. We have to eat at least one crepe while we're here."

"Or we could go out for raclette. Or poutine."

"Or all of the above."

"Agreed."

"UM, DYLAN!" REV CALLED OUT some time during the next afternoon.

"Yeah?" he said, thumping down the stairs as she opened the patio door. A pair of cats sauntered in like they owned the place. One was sort of grey and one was sort of gold and white. And grey.

He stopped in the doorway. "Well that's more—likely."

"Still." She watched as they leapt onto the chair in the corner.

"Yeah. We need to think about this." He held up his baggie at Rev in question. "I was on my way down anyway—"

"Good idea." They settled onto the couch-bed.

"Fish and Chips are indoor cats, right?" Rev said, having thought about it. "So wouldn't they be de-clawed?"

"Would they? Be?" he drew in, then passed the joint over to her.

"Well, if you've got antique tables and leather couches—" she drew in and passed it back.

"And that." he waved the joint at the scratching post in the corner.

"Oh, right." She was momentarily deflated. "Okay maybe declawed cats still feel the need to scratch. You know, like neutered dogs still feel the need to hump."

"Being neutered doesn't take away your need to—just because you can't actually reproduce doesn't mean you don't want to—hump," he finished lamely.

"Hm." She considered that. "Okay, so maybe declawed cats scratching are like female dogs humping."

He tried to think that one through. "Do—Why would—" And gave up.

"We could just check," he said a moment later. Rather astutely, he thought. He handed her the joint, grabbed a cat that was walking across the bed at that moment, and turned it over.

"Um, their claws are on their paws, not their—"

"I know that. I just figured—" he fingered the cat's paw, "I don't feel any claws."

"Yeah, but don't they retract? Don't you have to—" she grabbed another cat.

"OW!" Dylan cried out as the cat righted itself and proceeded to paw his thigh right through the denim. "Okay, this one has claws." He put it down. Quickly.

Rev squeezed the pad of the paw of the one she had. No claws came out. "And this one doesn't."

They checked the other two. One had claws and one didn't.

"Okay, so one of the black ones and the grey one is declawed. That doesn't make sense. If they're Fish and Chips—"

"They've each found a new friend."

They pondered that possibility for a while. A longer while than they would otherwise need to.

"I know! We send them an email—"

"The cats have an email address?" Dylan was surprised. Understandably.

"Not the cats. Jack and Diane."

"Oh right. Yeah. We can send *them* an email. And say what?"

"'By the way, which one's Fish and which one's Chips?'"

"Brilliant." Dylan went upstairs and sent off the query.

"Rev—" he called out a few minutes later.

"Yeah?" She went up into his room.

"Jack was online."

"Geez, doesn't the guy ever take some time off?"

"He says 'Chips is the golden one. Duh. Hah hah.'"

"Okay, so that makes the grey one Fish? But it's the gold-ish one that has claws."

"I thought it was the grey one," Dylan said.

"And the black one."

"Yeah but not the one black one, the other black one."

They went back downstairs to figure it out. After they took a couple more tokes.

Dylan reached out to a cat, but then quickly changed his mind. "Can we figure it out without touching them?"

"I don't know, can we?"

They thought about that for a while.

"I know! We throw something and when they reach out for it, we see if they've got claws. On their paws." He reconsidered then. "*In* their paws?"

"No I think it would be *on* their paws. If their paws are, like, their feet. And their toes. So they'd have claws *on* their toes, not *in* their toes."

"But aren't they *in* their toes when they're retracted? Then they come *out*. *Out* of their toes."

They stared at the four cats pacing the room. After a moment, Dylan said, "What were we going to do?"

"I can't remember. Oh yeah. Throw something at them."

"Oh yeah." He tore a piece of paper from the notepad on the table, bunched it up, and threw it at one of the cats. It hit him on the head.

"And why were we going to do that?" Dylan asked.

"I can't remember. Oh yeah. It was supposed to reach out for it and we were going to see if it had claws."

"Oh, right. Okay so maybe the trick isn't to throw something *at* them, but to throw it *near* them. So they'll swat at it."

"Right. Can you do that?" Rev asked.

Dylan bunched up another piece of paper and threw it in front of the cats. All four of them pounced on it. Making a four-cat-sized blur of black and white and grey and gold.

"Did that work? As planned?" he asked.

"Not exactly."

They stared at the cats again.

"We need to think about this a bit more," she added.

"Back in a minute," he said, as he left the room and went upstairs. He returned, in a minute, as promised, with his little bottle of bubbles. He settled himself back on the bed with Rev, opened it up, and reached in for the little stick with the circle on the end.

"I think better with bubbles," he explained, and blew a bubble.

The cat sitting nearest them reached out a paw and touched it. It popped into nonexistence. Dylan giggled. Even though it was the bubble and not the cat that had popped into nonexistence. He blew another bubble. The cat reached out touched it again. Though this time it had gotten up and it was more of a swipe than a touch. Dylan giggled again. He blew another bubble—

"Hey!! Good idea!!"

"What?" Dylan said. "I haven't thought of anything yet."

"When the cat reaches out for the bubble, we can see if it has claws."

"We can? Cool. Okay, wait." Dylan reached in the bottle with the stick and blew a stream of bubbles.

The other three cats came flying at them from across the room. At supersonic speed. They ducked. Unfortunately, not in time.

"OW!" Dylan cried out. "Okay, one of them had claws."

"Which one?"

"The one that hit my head."

"And which one was that?"

"The one with claws."

"Okay, that kind of thinking isn't working. Try a different kind," she suggested.

He blew some more bubbles. They were almost seriously maimed.

Rev grabbed his bubble stick.

"What?" he said. "Oh."

He sulked for a moment. "Okay, what if we test one cat at a time. Can I have my bubble stick back then? We sit one cat down and I blow a slow bubble. So we can see it reach out—"

Rev got up and went to the bathroom door. "Okay, come here, you three. In you go."

The cats stared at her.

She whistled encouragingly.

The cats stared at her.

She motioned with her arms.

The cats stared at her.

"Here," Dylan handed her his bubbles. "Blow a stream of bubbles into the bathroom."

"Brilliant." She blew a stream of bubbles into the bathroom. A blur of black, white, grey, and gold followed, and she quickly closed the door.

"We did it!" she said triumphantly and did a little happy dance.

"We rule!" Dylan agreed as they high-fived each other when she came back to the bed.

"Okay now what," he said.

"I forget," she confessed.

"Oh yeah," she said in a moment. "Now you blow a slow bubble."

He did so. They watched as the bubble formed, then grew fat, then slowly, lazily, drifted to the ground.

"That was so cool. Blow another one."

Dylan blew another big, fat, slow bubble.

They giggled.

"Here, let me try." Rev blew a bubble. It burst immediately. She tried again. It held, but it wasn't as big as Dylan's.

"Here," she handed the bubbles back to him. "You do it."

He blew another one. It was huge.

"Okay, is this working?" he asked.

"Is what working?"

"Aren't we supposed to be—doing something?"

"Oh yeah. When the cat—" she looked around. "Where's the cat?"

"In the bathroom."

"Oh yeah. Oh. That's the problem," she said.

"What?"

"Only three cats were supposed to go into the bathroom," Rev said.

"Oh. Right. Okay so now what."

"If I open the door, do you think just one cat will come out?"

Dylan gave that some thought. "No."

"If *you* open the door, do you think just one cat will come out?"

He gave *that* some thought. "No."

"So what, we just blow some more bubbles?"

"Yeah," he giggled. "Let's just blow some more bubbles."

"You know what?" Dylan said, half an hour later. When there were no bubbles left.

"I know dick," she replied dispiritedly. "I don't know what. Do you?"

"Do I what?"

"Not 'Do you what,' 'Do you *know* what.' You missed a word."

"Especially words like perspicuity. I miss words like that."

"Yeah," Rev said dreamily. "I miss perspicuity too."

"You know," Dylan said a moment later, "I've been thinking." He took a moment to bask in that announcement. "Jack said 'Chips is the golden one. Duh. Hah hah.' That 'Duh. Hah hah.' Jack's a funny guy, remember? Instructions for the fireplace were we don't need a fire. Told us if there was an electrical problem to call an electrician. I think *both* Fish and Chips are golden."

"You mean—" she worked it through, "you mean—we have four cats—*none of which* is Fish and—or—Chips?"

IT RAINED AGAIN THE NEXT DAY.

"Let's do a subway tour," Dylan said as they sat in the den with their morning coffee. Well, their first coffee. Since it was one o'clock.

"A subway tour?"

"Yeah, you spend a day on the subway. Well, not the whole day *on* the subway. You pick a color, buy a ticket for that line, get on, then get off at every stop. Walk about, see what there is to see, then get back on. As long as you keep going in the same direction, it doesn't cost any more. Then at the end, you just buy a ticket to get back."

"Isn't there just subway tracks and garbage cans and dripping concrete walls to see?"

"No! There's a whole underground city in the subway. Well, at some places. At some places, yeah, there's just the—what you said—but—actually—I don't know," he concluded. "I've never done a subway tour in Montreal. That might be all there is. But it might not be. We'll find out."

So an hour later, they headed out the door. The neighbours on the other side were coming in as they were going out. Dylan nodded at them.

"Hi, how's it going?"

"Good. You're friends?" The man gestured vaguely at the house.

"Yeah, we're staying at Jack and Diane's for the month. Looking after their cats."

"Oh yeah? I didn't know they had cats. Must be indoor cats."

"Nice try," she said when they were out of ear shot.

"Okay, so we find people they've had over. Like for dinner or something."

"That might work."

They decided to take the green line since that's what was closest. And sure enough, there was a whole underground city. 'Bazaar' was more like it. Mostly there were small shops and kiosks selling all sorts of things. Books and newspapers, pretzels and cinnamon buns, drinks, tshirts and baseball caps, knick-knacks and bric-a-bracs, trinkets of all kinds, and baubles, and—

"Hey look!" Dylan said, pointing to a kiosk. "Dilithium Key Holder Spheres!"

A COUPLE DAYS LATER, Dylan lounged in the doorway of Rev's den. "You need anything?"

She looked up from her laptop. "That's a pretty broad question."

"I meant," he grinned, "I'm going out. To the weird store."

"So do I need anything weird? Is that the more specific version of the question?"

"Well, I pass the grocery store on the way."

"And the cheesecake place."

An hour later, he returned and called out to her. "Cake break!"

She ran up the stairs. He was lifting four slices of cheesecake out of a pastry box. "I got Minty Mint, Buttered Cashew, Mango, and—a pink one. Raspberry?" He couldn't remember.

"Maybe it's Candy Floss."

He looked at her. "Only you would think of Candy Floss Cheesecake."

She dipped a fork into the corner of it and tasted. "It *is* candy floss! I was just kidding. Wow. So which one do you want now," she asked.

"Well, all of them of course. This is an all-you-can-eat cheesecake buffet," he said. "Your mother let you have only one cookie for a bedtime snack, didn't she," he said after a moment.

"Yes." She dug into the cheesecake.

"It's true," she said later, as they had almost finished the cheesecake. "We spend our whole lives recovering from our childhoods."

"I can't believe you never snuck back into the kitchen to get another one."

Rev's fork stopped midway to her mouth.

"What?"

"I can't believe that never even occurred to me."

LATER DYLAN CALLED REV UP to his bedroom again. "Check this out," he said. He was lying on the bed wearing silly Groucho Marx glasses with a big nose.

"Check what out, exactly?"

He handed her a pair of glasses from the pile on the bed beside her. He had fitted each pair with a differently colored filter.

"I'm looking at the stars through rose-colored glasses," he said. And giggled.

She chose a pair with yellow filters and put them on. "Oh wow. It's like the stars are gold!" She lay back on the bed.

"Try the purple ones."

She did.

"It's like—frozen fireworks!"

"Yeah," Dylan said, grinning at her.

"Too bad it's not like this all the time."

"Well, there's nothing stopping you from wearing the glasses all the time."

She looked at him.

"You can take off the nose," he pointed out. "Or," he sighed, "you can just imagine it that way from now on. When I look at the clouds, that's what I do. I imagine them in all different colors."

"Really?"

"Really."

"And the rain," Rev said. "It should rain in rainbow."

"That'd be cool."

SEVERAL DAYS AND NIGHTS LATER, during which they did another couple walkabouts and subway tours of the orange and blue lines, ordered out for Mexican, Caribbean, Swiss, Russian, and Swahili, saw fireworks, watched TV, figured out how to work the entertainment system, and sampled Jack and Diane's music collection, Dylan went downstairs to visit Rev.

"I feel the need to do something meaningful," he said leaning against the doorway, blowing bubbles.

"Why?"

He didn't have an answer, so he just turned and left.

A few minutes later he returned.

"Because."

"Works for me," she said cheerfully, and closed her laptop.

Dylan looked at her with suspicion.

"Your work's not going well, is it."

"Nope."

"Did you get *any* questions done?"

"Nope. Let's go on a walkabout and see if we can find something important for you to report about."

"Does it have to be important?"

"No. *You* were the one craving meaningful."

"Oh yeah."

THEY DECIDED TO BIKE to a different part of the city and start their walkabout there. As they were locking their bikes to a light post, Dylan noticed a sign pasted to the post.

"This looks interesting," he said.

"What," Rev came to stand beside him.

"Dancing Through the Streets," he read, "a modern dance troupe moves through the city of Montreal and dances with it—come follow us."

"Hey it's now. Well, today, at 2:00. What time is it now?"

They asked a passerby for the time. Quarter to.

They looked at the notice again and realized that it showed the troupe's route. People could join it at any spot and just follow them for as long as they wanted. They got their bearings, walked a few blocks east, and waited. Sure enough, in a few minutes, a group of black-clad dancers appeared from around the corner. Dylan and Rev watched them run up and down the stairs leading up to some office building, then leap back and forth over the rail in the middle. They moved on, pausing at a monument two buildings up, draping themselves around it. Then they did a series of jazz ballet movements to get from the monument to the next—

"Stop that." A voice boomed from above, thundering through the city noise. "You look ridiculous."

Dylan and Rev burst out laughing, then tried to stop, since the dancers did not look amused. They were not entirely successful, so they turned away and scanned the surrounding office buildings, looking for someone with a megaphone. Failing that, God. They finally spotted someone at a sixth floor window.

The dancers ignored the voice and moved onto the next site of interaction, a wall.

"Oh no, the wall," the megaphone voice deadpanned.

Dylan couldn't help himself, and burst out giggling.

"Not the wall." The voice had dropped an octave.

Rev was somewhat beyond giggling. A snort escaped.

The dancers valiantly carried on with their serious art, doing jetés to move from the wall to the next site.

"Run away! Run away!" the voice then mimicked, and both Dylan and Rev lost it.

"Okay," that wasn't exactly meaningful, he said as they watched the dancers disappear.

"DYLAN, DID YOU LET IN another pair of cats?" Rev asked lazily a couple days later as they were enjoying another joint in the den.

"No, why—"

Then he saw why. *Six* cats were lying in the sun. "Okay. We can figure this out."

Rev looked at him dubiously.

"We have six cats. We let in four. So that means two were already here."

"Ah. Brilliant," she said. "Where," she asked then.

"Right there!" he pointed at them.

"No, I mean where were they? All this time."

"In a box?" Dylan suggested.

"No, that's Jack. Jack's-in-a-box. Cats are—"

"In a hat!"

"With eggs and ham!"

"Unless it's Jack," Dylan said. "If the cat's name is Jack—"

"But it wouldn't be Jack. Because Jack's name is Jack. You wouldn't name your cat after yourself. Would you?"

"No, but if its name *is* Jack, it wouldn't be Jack's cat."

"Right. Because Jack's cats are Fish 'n' Chips."

"So...if its name were Jack, its name wouldn't be Fish. Or Chips! We'd've solved—nothing."

"Let's go back. We have six cats. We let in four."

"Yes! Yes! So we just have to figure out which two were already here—that'd be Fish 'n' Chips."

"Except that I'm positive the ones I let out when we first arrived were both black," Rev said. "And if I let them out, they were already here," she added. Just in case.

"Okay maybe Fish 'n' Chips already had their friends over, two of their friends, when Jack and Diane left."

"And they didn't know?"

"Or forgot to tell us. So, if that's the case," Dylan continued, "then we can eliminate at least two. The two you let in later that first week, right?"

"Right. And which two would they be?"

"You don't remember?"

"Not exactly. Grey-gold. -white. -ish."

"That sort of describes all of them."

"Not the black ones!" she said defensively.

"Yeah but they're already eliminated."

"From what?"

"From—I forget." He drew in and held the smoke. "From consideration!" he said triumphantly, as he exhaled.

"Consideration for what?"

"I don't know," he confessed. "Okay," he grabbed a grey-whitish one. More whitish than greyish. "This one's declawed. So's this one." He'd grabbed a mostly gold one. "Wasn't only one of the two you let in declawed?"

"Yes!" she said happily.

"Which one? Right," he said, seeing her slump.

"Well," she rallied, "if the gold—the gold-*ish* one is Chips, okay, that fits, so then Fish would have to be the white-ish one."

*"Is* there such a thing as whitefish?" he asked.

"Not whitefish. White-ish. But yeah, there *is* such a thing as whitefish. There's also bluefish."

"And cod."

Rev nodded in sage agreement.

"Okay, so—" Dylan tried to catch his thought. The one that was long gone. "If Fish and Chips are indoor cats and they've been outside for two weeks, free at last, shouldn't they look—"

"A little less coiffured," she agreed.

"So that means—"

"They're *not* the ones you let in."

"Did the ones I let in look un-coiffured?"

"I don't know. Which ones did you let in again?"

"I don't know."

"Oh yeah."

"Or—or—I have no idea if this (a) supports or (b) undermines what you said, because," Rev confessed, "I can't remember what you said—but maybe someone's been looking after them. While we've been looking after—"

"That's it!" he said.

"What's it?"

"We look around the neighbourhood for signs about lost cats."

"Hm. Why didn't we think of this earlier?" she said.

"Because we're old," he said as he reached for the joint, "and our brains are turning to oatmeal?"

"Right. *That's* why our brains are turning to oatmeal," she said, taking the joint back.

"We can't keep them all for the whole month," Rev said a bit later. "People will be worried."

"They *will*!" Dylan seemed inordinately happy about that. "So *we* put up signs about lost cats. We say we found two cats and we wait for people to call and then we ask them to describe their missing cats. If they say they've lost a pair of black cats—"

"Then we know there are at least *two* pair of black cats living in the neighbourhood."

"Oh. Right."

"Plus," Rev said, another long while later, "if four of them are outdoor cats, we can't just keep them indoors for a couple weeks. They'll wreck the place."

"So we get another scratching post. And we cover up the couch. And *all* of the tables."

"And what about fleas and stuff they might pass on to the real Fish 'n' Chips."

"So we give 'em all a bath. Piece of cake."

So when Rev picked Dylan up from Emerg, various parts of him stitched back together, they went to a pet store and picked up another scratching post. And a lot more cat kibble.

The neighbour on the other side happened to be out when they returned.

"Hi," Dylan nodded, "how's it going?"

"Good. You're housesitting?"

"Yeah, and looking after their cats."

"Oh yeah? I didn't know they had cats. What'd you do," he looked at Dylan's bandaged arms, "try to give 'em a bath?" He laughed. The neighbour. Not Dylan.

They installed the new scratching post in the upstairs living room, and covered up the rest of the furniture with sheets they found in the linen closet.

"Looks a little like Miss Havisham's place, doesn't it," Rev said when they were done.

"Which reminds me, we should vacuum or dust at some point in time."

"At some point in time," Rev agreed.

They put out an extra two dishes for kibble. Making six. Then heard a knock at the door.

"Not two more," Dylan groaned. Rev jabbed him.

"Hi!" It was the neighbour on the other side. "Kelly says to ask you two over for dinner. Is tomorrow good?"

Dylan and Rev looked at each other.

"Tomorrow's fine," Dylan said. "Thanks!"

"Did she say what time?"

"Oh, any time—six-ish?"

"Sounds good. See you then!" They closed the door.

SO, NEXT DAY AT SIX-ISH, Dylan and Rev went next door for dinner. They rang the bell, heard the TV blaring as they stood on the step, and wondered if they should ring the bell again. But the door opened just as they were about to do so.

"Hey, glad you could come! I'm Josh, by the way," their neighbour said, almost shouting, and reached out to shake Dylan's hand. "Come in!"

"Hi there," a woman came from around the corner, wiping her hands on a dishtowel, "I'm Kelly."

"Kevin, turn that down!" Josh said as they moved toward the living room.

Kevin looked to be about fifteen and was stretched out on the living room couch, feet up on the coffee table, watching a large-screen—a very large-screen—TV, remote in hand.

"Kevin! We have guests!"

Kevin didn't care.

"Perhaps you could watch TV in your room," Kelly tried a gentler tone.

"Well if I had a large-screen TV," he said, clearly indicating that he was entitled to one, two maybe, "I would." He otherwise ignored his parents' request. In fact, he turned the volume up even higher.

"Kevin!" Josh said sharply.

"I was here first," he complained. Not moving.

"Now!"

Kevin threw the remote onto the table, then very slowly got up off the couch, and very slowly left the room, intentionally bumping into Dylan and Rev on the way out.

"Sorry about that," Kelly said with some embarrassment.

"Kid's got balls!" Josh said proudly, laughing.

"You say that as if it were a good thing," Rev commented. Dylan jabbed her.

"So," Kelly said cheerily, "I thought we'd have some hors-d'oeuvres in here before we—have a seat, please," she gestured.

Dylan and Rev sat on the couch Kevin had vacated. It was beige leather. The coffee table was glass and chrome. There were some abstract paintings on the walls. Probably commissioned to match the furniture. Kelly sat in one of the two chairs that faced the couch from across the table. Also beige leather.

"Care for a drink?" Josh asked.

"Sure," Dylan said.

"What'll it be—rum and coke okay?"

"Sounds good."

Rev nodded agreement.

Josh went into the kitchen, returning in a minute with two rum-and-cokes, which he handed to Dylan and Rev.

"Honey, you want the same?" he asked from the kitchen.

"Sure," she replied, and he returned bearing another two rum-and-cokes. He handed one to her, then sat in the other chair.

"So—" he began, but Kelly interrupted. "Josh, would you please get the hors-d'oeuvres?"

He got up and went out to the kitchen yet again.

"Where are they?" he called back.

"On the counter," she called back sweetly. "See the platter?"

"Oh yeah." He brought the platter into the living room, set it on the coffee table, and sat down again.

"We need napkins, dear."

Josh got up again and went into the kitchen.

"Where do we keep the napkins?" he called back.

"Where we always keep them," Kelly called back sweetly. "In the cupboard above the fridge?"

"Oh yeah. Got 'em," he said, returning to the living room with a handful of napkins, which he put on the coffee table. He sat down again.

Kelly stared at the huge chunk of cheese sitting on the platter amid little finger foods.

"We'll need a knife for the cheese, dear."

Josh got up and went back into the kitchen.

"Where do we keep the knives?" he called back. Rev was wondering the same thing by this point.

"So," he said, sitting down again, "you two ever hear of Blow Systems?"

Dylan and Rev shook their heads.

"I'm Senior Project Manager there," he said.

"I've always wondered," Rev said, taking a cracker and slicing some cheese onto it. "What exactly does a project manager do?"

"Well, I manage projects." He astutely realized that more should be said. "Essentially, I make sure everything gets done, when it's supposed to get done."

"So you—organize—things," she said. With some disbelief.

"Well, yeah, but there's more to it than that." She'd made it sound so—simple. "The company depends on me to avoid cost overruns. So I'm sort of an efficiency expert as well."

"I see." Her gaze went from the living room to the kitchen and back. And back again. She couldn't help it.

"And how exactly do you make sure things get done in time?" she asked. "I mean, what if something just takes longer than whoever drew up the schedule thought it would take?"

"Oh, well, everyone has their price," he smiled.

Her cheese and cracker stopped halfway to her mouth. "You mean you offer people overtime to get the job done on schedule?"

"Well, that wouldn't be very cost-effective. Usually specs can be changed."

"You cut corners?"

"Oh I wouldn't put it that way."

"No I bet you wouldn't."

Dylan grinned. At his rum-and-coke.

"I'm good with people," Josh said, oblivious to—well, oblivious. "Usually I can find a way—people just need a little motivation from time to time. To get them working to their max."

"And it pays well, I take it?" Rev looked around at their stuff.

"Well, Senior put me close to the quarter mark, so yeah, we do okay," he grinned at Kelly.

Close to the quarter mark? It took Rev a moment to realize he meant that he made close to $250,000 a year. To organize stuff.

"What about you," Josh asked Dylan.

"Oh, I'm in maintenance," Dylan replied.

John looked like he didn't understand.

"I clean up other people's messes."

"Oh," he chuckled, "I got you. Yeah, we had a guy in just last month, did all the damage control, after the restructuring—so you've got your own consulting company then?"

"I've got my own mop."

Josh burst out laughing again. Then suddenly stopped, seeing that Dylan wasn't even smiling.

"Oh—I'm sorry—I thought—you seem—"

"More cheese?" Kelly held the platter out to Dylan. He took a very large piece. Seeing as it was very expensive cheese.

"I just assumed you were college graduates."

"We are," Dylan said. "I've got a Ph.D. in History."

Rev smiled. At her rum-and-coke.

"But—" Now Josh really didn't understand. "Then why—"

"When's the last time you saw a job ad for a historian?"

Josh laughed. "Good point!" Though of course he had no idea what point Dylan had just made.

"So how does one become a project manager?" Rev asked. "It's not like you can get a degree in organization…"

"Of course you can."

"You can?"

"Sure. Organizational Management. It's a major in Business."

Rev looked a little stunned. She could have majored in organization and been making a quarter of a million dollars by now?

A teenaged girl came in the back door then.

"Hi dear," Kelly called out, "come and meet our company!"

The girl sauntered through the living, said a desultory "Hi" to

Dylan and Rev, then headed upstairs.

"'Course that's not the best way to—" Josh continued, "most of the guys I know who are Project Managers just sort of—"

"Worked their way up?" Dylan suggested.

"God no. That'd take too long. You've got to present the right resume."

"The right resume?" Rev repeated. "What do you mean?"

"Well, you know, you gotta figure out what they need. And whatever they need," he laughed, "you've got!"

"Gee. Maybe *we* should start lying," Dylan deadpanned to Rev.

"More cheese?" Kelly offered the platter again.

"So you're saying you got your current position by—"

"You see that something that needs to be done, you prepare a proposal, you sell it to upper management—"

"Hm, last time *I* prepared a proposal for upper management, I got fired."

"Well, you gotta sell yourself. Tell 'em you've got the skills."

"Hm. What if you don't?"

"Don't what?"

"Have the skills?"

Josh laughed.

Everyone was quiet for a moment.

"More cheese?"

"Aren't you going to ask what I do?" Rev said in the lengthening silence.

"Well, I—"

"Kelly, what about you?"

"Oh, you know, the kids."

"But they're what—fifteen, sixteen now?"

"Yes," she said proudly. As if she'd had something to do with that.

"Oh," she caught Rev's waiting look then, "I was going to go back to work. You know, do something meaningful with my life," she chuckled. "But then I realized, I *have*! I've raised two wonderful kids," she beamed at Josh, who beamed back.

"*I* don't think they're so wonderful," Rev said.

A little bell in the kitchen rang just then, and Kelly popped up. "Dinner's ready!" She gestured toward the dining room. "Shall we?"

"MAYBE," DYLAN SAID THE NEXT DAY, leaning in the doorway to Rev's den, "I'll write a piece on yuckies."

"Yuckies?"

"'The truth about yuppies.'"

She laughed. "You'd have to interview a bunch of them," she pointed out. "Can I come?" she added after a moment.

"Wouldn't have it any other way," Dylan said, grinning. "In the meantime, feel like another walkabout?"

"Or we could go down to the water."

"Right. I keep forgetting Montreal is actually an island."

"I wonder if there's a water tour boat or something. Tomorrow's another fireworks. Maybe we could plan to end up there."

So Dylan went back up to his room and did some surfing. Fifteen minutes later, he called out to Rev.

"What'd you find?" she asked as she entered his room.

"I found a Montreal morning cruise, and it actually starts and ends at La Ronde. Which is where the fireworks are, right? So we could do that."

Rev snorted. "A *morning* cruise?"

"Right. That's what I thought. So I also found a sunset cruise, but it goes to a different place."

"Well, why don't we do the sunset one tonight and do the fireworks tomorrow like usual."

"Sounds good to me. I'll make the reservations."

So later that day, they were on their way to the waterfront to where the sunset cruise left.

"Hey," Dylan pointed, "one of those living sculpture things!"

"What?"

A young man, heavily made up to look like stone and similarly costumed, was holding a pose on a pedestal. He did indeed look exactly like a sculpture. A sculpture made out of cement.

"You'd be good at that," Dylan said to Rev after he'd tossed some coins into the hat on the ground.

A little further on, they came to a trio of street musicians. Dylan picked up a tambourine from the open instrument case and joined in. They grinned at him in delight until he broke into the Hare Krishna riff. At which point they all stopped playing. Dylan had a solo.

"Krishna, Hare Krishna," Dylan chanted tonelessly as he jingled and jangled and jerked through the bunny hop. "Jeremiah was a bullfrog," he segued, seamlessly, though still tonelessly. "A hairy bullfrog," he improvised, then gave it up. Only Rev was amused.

Eventually, they arrived at the waterfront. But when they saw the crowd waiting to get onto the boat, full of cellphones and screaming kids, they decided, in the interests of crime prevention, to inquire about a refund. Since there was actually a waiting list, the tour clerk gladly agreed.

"Why don't we just walk along here," Dylan said. "Don't know how far the boardwalk goes, but we can find out."

"Okay," she said.

"Actually," he said, as she turned to the left, "the sun sets—to the right. So why don't we go that way?"

"'Sun sets to the right,'" she muttered, making a 180. "If they'd told me that when I was a kid instead of 'sun sets in the west'..."

A COUPLE DAYS LATER, Rev had actually finished a set of questions, and

Dylan had actually written up his article on the debt demonstration, so they decided to celebrate with pizza and a movie. And a little baggie.

They stared at the six cats, who were, just then, sitting in a nice little row. Much like a police line-up.

"I think it's those two," Rev said, pointing at the mostly-white one and the mostly-grey one.

"Why?"

"They look smug."

"They all look smug."

"You're right. They do."

He passed her the joint.

"I think it's those two," he pointed at the two licking their butts.

"Why?"

"Well, if you're an indoor cat you must spend a lot of time bored. So you probably—"

Two of the others started licking their butts.

"Bloody hell!" he cried out, giving up yet again.

They continued to stare at the row of cats. The cats stared back through their beady little eyes.

"In a minute, they're going to hold up little cards with—"

"'2' and '3' on them."

"Well," Dylan said, "I was going to give us at least a '6.'"

SOMETIME DURING THEIR LAST week at the house, two more cats arrived. Both were gold and white striped.

"Oh for the love of—!" Dylan cried out. "This makes eight!"

"You know, it makes *most* sense that these last two are Fish 'n' Chips. They're gold *and* white."

"Except that Jack said Chips was 'the gold one.'"

"Oh yeah."

"So we know for sure these are *not* Fish 'n' Chips—so we can toss 'em back onto the street."

"No, we just know for sure that *one* of them isn't Chips," Rev said.

"Oh right. You're good."

ON THE MORNING, GIVE OR TAKE, of Jack and Diane's scheduled return, Rev and Dylan packed up all of their stuff and put it into the car, which they moved onto the street so Jack and Diane could pull into their driveway. They went through the house then, moving stuff back to where it had been when they arrived. However, since the cats—eight of them and holding—were still inside, they left much of it covered. They dusted, they vacuumed, they cleaned the kitchen, they cleaned the bathrooms. Then they sat on the front porch, the black front porch, and waited for their arrival.

"Oh," Rev said then, "what are you going to tell them about me?"

"What do you—oh. Right. Um, you're a friend?" He paused, as if waiting for confirmation. She grinned.

"They won't know you've been here the whole time," he said, "your stuff's in the car, right? So they can think you're just here now, and for some reason, I'm driving you somewhere."

"Okay, so when we leave, *you* get in the driver's seat," she said, getting her car keys out of her pocket and handing them to him.

"Good thinking."

"Do you think *they* remember where they live?" Rev said idly, as they waited.

ABOUT TEN MINUTES LATER, Jack and Diane pulled into their driveway.

"Hi, how was your trip?" Dylan said as they got out of their car.

"Fantastic, thanks," Jack said coming around to the porch. "And how was your stay? Any problems with the house?"

"No problems whatsoever," he said as Diane joined them. "And you've got a lovely house," he added. "Oh, this is Rev," Dylan introduced Rev.

"Hi Rev," Jack said, Diane echoing him.

"You live here in Montreal?"

"Yeah," she improvised. "Just moved here. Discovered Dylan was housesitting, so I dropped by."

"By the way," Dylan interjected, "some friends of Fish 'n' Chips came by, so we—I just let them in. Hope that's okay," he said as casually as possible as they followed Jack and Diane into the house.

"Sure," Diane said, as she put her house keys onto the little table. She called out 'Fish 'n' Chips!' and Dylan and Rev watched, absolutely stunned, as two cats sauntered into the room. Both were solid gold. Not grey-ish, not white-ish, not mostly-gold, not grey-gold-and-white-ish, not gold-and-white striped. And not black. Solid gold.

"Hey you," Diane stooped down to scratch their ears. "Did you miss us?" She picked up the one cat, and Jack picked up the other.

"I think they've lost a bit of weight," Jack said.

"Well," Dylan sputtered, "I kept their dishes full, as you said to do in your note. They probably just missed you and weren't eating as much," he suggested. "Their color's good though." Rev jabbed him.

"SO," DYLAN SAID, IN THE DRIVER'S SEAT. "Where to?"

"The cheesecake place," Rev said without a moment's hesitation.

"Right. Silly me."

They had two last pieces. Dylan chose one called Nutty, which had, surprise, all kinds of nuts in it. Rev chose a slice of Brown Sugar Cheesecake.

"Isn't that sort of defeating the purpose," Rev asked. "Putting a bunch of little hard things in cheesecake?"

"Oh shut up. Cheesecake doesn't have a purpose."

"The hell it doesn't," Rev said, licking her fork with what can only be described as intense gratification.

"Okay," he conceded. "But it doesn't so much defeat the purpose, as accentuate it," he said. "By contrast. The nuts make the creaminess seem that much more—creamy."

"Hm," Rev replied.

When they'd finished their two last pieces, they decided to buy four more for the road. Well, Rev decided to buy four more for the road.

"OKAY, SO NOW WHERE TO?" Dylan asked as he pulled away from the cheesecake place.

Rev looked over at him. "Were you serious about wanting to spend a week in Algonquin Park?"

"I was," he said. Then looked over at her. "I am."

"Okay..." she said, thinking it through, "we'll have to rent stuff though. I've got a tent at home, but—"

"So we rent a tent," Dylan said happily. "And whatever. There'll be a—tent-rental store there somewhere, yeah?"

"Yeah. Okay," she pulled out a map, "so do we want to take the same route back or go a different way?"

"Is there a different way?"

"There's always a different way. Actually," she unfolded the map, "I've always wanted to see the Kawartha region. Why don't we sort of detour—it would add a day or two—"

"Fine with me."

"Okay, so we go back the way we came, to Ottawa, then we head south and pick up Highway 7. West. Right."

"Right."

"No I mean we turn right on Highway 7."

"West."

"Okay."

"AND THE THING IS," she resumed the conversation they were apparently still having, "I can't even blame it on having had to raise or support a family."

"'It' being your utter failure to achieve any of your noble goals."

She looked over at him. "Yeah."

Then she continued. "It's amazing really. How a little 'selfish gene' manages to derail over ninety percent of the human species."

"And a hundred percent of the rest."

"Yeah, but we're supposed to be the most intelligent ones. And yet everyone gets suckered in. Just as they're starting their lives, they get—used—by a microscopic bit of—stuff—as a replication machine. So suddenly they've got a two-year-old they have to watch night and day or a full-time job to find and keep."

"But surely some of them want that," he said, concentrating on the traffic, which was merging from four lanes to two as they left Montreal behind.

"I don't know...they *say* it was a choice and try to convince themselves it's noble and worthwhile—I mean look at Kelly—that's denial if I ever saw it. Two wonderful kids, my ass. They're going to grow up to be just like their parents."

"Most kids do."

"Exactly," she looked out the window.

"Exactly!" she said a minute later. "It's another one of those president things!"

"President things?"

"The people who *should* have kids are exactly the ones who don't."

"Ah."

"But I think that's just—what is that?" she asked. "Not sour grapes, that's when you don't get what you want, so you tell yourself you didn't want it anyway. What is it when you get what you don't want, and you tell yourself you do want it. After all."

"Sweet grapes?" Dylan changed lanes to pass—a minivan.

"No that wouldn't make sense. Sweet...the second part has to be bad."

"Sweet brussels sprouts?"

Rev laughed. "That'll do."

"Must be hard," he said, "to admit you let your life get hijacked by a microscopic bit of stuff that isn't even conscious."

"No doubt. But—and this is, was, my point—it's hard to change the world when you're changing diapers all the time or out making the money to buy the diapers—but I don't have that excuse."

"SO WHY," DYLAN ASKED quite a while later, "if you wanted to change the world and all—why did you pick such a conservative field?"

"What do you mean?"

"Well, teaching. Everyone knows teachers are the most conservative—"

"What?" She was stunned. Had to rethink.

"*I* didn't know that," she said finally. "I've *never* thought of teachers, or teaching, as conservative. I've always thought of it, them, as *radical*." She looked out the window, remembering her own experience of high school. "Teachers opened my mind."

She turned to face Dylan, still not quite believing what he'd said. "Really? *Everyone* thinks that? And it's *true*? That would explain a lot."

"A lot of what?"

"Well, my frustration for starters. I kept assuming I was dealing with like minds, so every time I met resistance, it caught me *so* by surprise. If I'd just expected it, if I'd known from the start that I had to make my case to someone who was *not* on the same page—if I'd know I had to make my case—Why is it that I never seem to know what everyone knows?"

"Because you're so socially unconnected."

"Is that another way of saying I don't have any friends?"

"Yeah." He quickly glanced over and back. "Do you?"

"Do I what?"

"Have any friends."

"No," she admitted. "Which has been a real mystery, given I was Miss Congeniality."

Dylan took his eyes off the road to stare at her. "You were—? You were not!" He turned back to the road, then back to Rev again. "You didn't—did you?" He turned back to the road. "I can't believe you even *entered* a beauty pageant."

"I didn't."

Dylan looked at her again. She was grinning from ear to ear.

"I entered the arm wrestling contest instead."

"And won, no doubt," he muttered.

"Yeah," she said smoothly, "but only because I have wrists of steel. All those years of practising the piano."

"I didn't know you played the piano!"

"Almost as well as you play the tambourine," she said.

He giggled.

"Okay, so why is it?" Dylan asked a moment later.

"Why is it what?"

"Why don't you have any friends?"

"Oh. It's because I'm terribly shy."

Dylan snorted.

"It's true! It takes a lot for me to just walk into a room, a party, a bar, whatever, where I don't know anyone."

"Well it'd take a lot for anyone to do that. Most people who go to parties *know* someone there. *And* they go *with* someone they know."

"So that makes it a vicious circle. If you're shy, you don't know anyone, so the social thing is extra hard, so you become even shyer. More shy. Do *you* have any friends?"

"Not so much now, no."

"What do you mean 'not so much now'?"

"Well, when I was with Ani, yeah, I did. But it turned out everyone was *her* friend, not mine. And there's that whole couple thing. You know that dinner with Josh and Kelly? That was the first time in ten years I'd been invited over to dinner."

"First time ever for me," Rev said. With a I'm-such-a-loser tone.

"It's because we were a couple. Or at least perceived to be a couple," Dylan skirted over the issue. "It seems perfectly normal for one couple to have another couple over for dinner, but for some reason it's weird for them to invite just one person."

"You're right! Unless they're inviting *two* singles, hoping they'll become a couple. Why does everyone want everyone else to become a couple?"

"Sour grapes and sweet brussel sprouts?" Dylan giggled after a moment.

"I was going to suggest envy-resentment-and-pure-malice, but sour grapes and sweet brussel sprouts works."

He changed lanes to pass another—minivan.

"And when I had a regular job," he continued then, "I had friends. Me and the guys—"

"See, there's that too—"

"What."

"The 'guys' don't—a woman can't go out with 'the guys.' I remember back in university, in the cafeteria, all the philosophy students would sit around and—whenever I tried to join them, well, the silence was deafening."

"I take it all the philosophy students were guys."

"Yeah."

"So why didn't you hang out with the girls?"

"Because I wasn't a girl either. And they weren't talking philosophy."

"Neither were the guys probably."

That stopped her. "Oh," she finally said.

She watched as the industrial areas gave way to agricultural areas.

"I did have a few women friends," she continued, "but as soon as they got married—well it's like you said. That whole couple thing. And as soon as they had kids, it was like they turned into someone I didn't know. And, frankly, didn't want to know."

"You'd think they'd want to keep a few friends from before they got swallowed up by the Mom thing—"

"You'd think. God knows I'd want to. But even if they didn't have kids—and this was the most obnoxious, and hurtful, thing—as soon as they got married, hell, as soon as they got a boyfriend, I got dumped. Like what am I, a piece of shit? Like they've got a *man* now, so he automatically takes priority, he's so much better than me.

"And even *before* they got a boyfriend," she continued, "all the girls, all the women, I knew seemed to be focused, one way or another, on getting one. On 'finding someone.'"

"You didn't want to find someone."

"Sure I did. Me." She grinned at him.

They drove on in silence for a bit.

"What's worse," she said after a long while, "not ever figuring out who you are, or figuring it out and then realizing twenty years later you were wrong. Been wrong for your whole life."

"PLUS," SHE WENT BACK A FEW STEPS, "I kept refusing to align myself by gender. You know, years later when I was teaching at that university? I walked into the faculty lounge and there were clumps of male profs sitting together and clumps of female profs sitting together. Just like—not just like when I was in university, but like when I was in high school! I swear I stood there for a whole minute before I turned and walked out. Next time I pulled up a chair at the men's table, just to make a point, and—"

"The silence was deafening. Same thing happened when I'd sit with the women."

"Yeah? You did that?"

"Yeah. Do you have any idea how utterly boring men are when they sit in a clump?"

"Hm."

"Why is it," she said a little while later, "if men and women dislike each other so much, or live in such separate worlds, or have so little in common, why is it they get married?"

"Well, you said it yourself. They get hijacked. Look at how many get divorced once the spawning is all done."

"That's probably why they stopped asking you to teach courses, by the way," Dylan said after a moment.

"What?" She struggled to catch up. "But—they said they'd decided not to offer applied ethics anymore."

"Did you ever check?"

"No, I—They *lied* to me? But—"

"You made them uncomfortable. Someone in the faculty lounge probably mentioned it to someone they played golf with and, well, next time around—"

"So *that's* why I lost the—that's why I couldn't change the world? Because I sat at the men's table?"

"PIT STOP?" DYLAN ASKED AN HOUR LATER, as they approached a town on the outskirts of Ottawa.

"Good idea. And we can switch if you like, you've been driving since we left Montreal."

"Yeah, let's." He slowed down at a gas pump—convenience store—public washroom place. He filled the tank, while Rev hit the washroom. They met up in the store.

"Pepsi?" Rev said as she opened the drinks fridge door.

"Sounds good. And we've got cheesecake, don't for—of course you haven't forgotten." He wandered to the readi-made sandwiches, then changed his mind, and grabbed a bag of nuts and raisins instead.

"I WANT A DO OVER," Rev said once they were on the road again.

"My god, woman, we're not dead yet."

"Yeah, but still. All those years."

"Yeah, still." He munched the nuts and raisins pensively.

Rev waited.

"You regret giving up too late, and I regret giving up too soon," he held the open bag out to her.

"Yeah, what happened with that? You never really said. You got that job up on some reserve and—"

"Well, it became quite clear quite early that no self-respecting Native person was going to be taught anything by a white man."

"Ah."

"Least of all history."

She laughed, then stopped. "But you'd never use 'Columbus' and 'discover' in the same sentence," she said.

"No I wouldn't. But 'Which of the following assumptions is most likely to be made if…'"

"Ah."

"You talk about being caught by surprise, well, me too. I mean I didn't, I don't, identify myself as a white man. Most days I have trouble identifying myself as Dylan."

She grinned.

"So when it became clear they—well it wasn't even resistance, really, it was just—they couldn't care less about me, or what I was doing or wanted to do or was trying to do. And, so, I quit. I too know when I'm not wanted. And you're right, it's not particularly fun to be where you're not wanted. But at least that prepared me for now," he added.

"What do you mean? You're not where you're not wanted."

He looked sideways at her. Then grinned. "Good to know. What I meant was that that was the first time I realized that people respond to me according to what I look like to them, not according to what I am. When we're young, most of the time the two match, I think. And then, suddenly—"

"People start calling you ma'am."

"Or Mr. O'Toole. And you want to say, 'No, Mr. O'Toole is my father.'"

"And then you look in the mirror."

"Well, not if you can help it. But yeah. I look like a middle-aged man now. I don't look like this cool young guy anymore. And people, strangers, who don't know I'm still a cool young guy, they treat me like a middle-aged man. But it doesn't catch me by surprise."

"That's weird."

"What."

"When I look at you, I don't see the middle-aged man. I see the cool young guy."

Dylan grinned. "Maybe that's because that's what you saw when we first met?"

"Maybe," Rev grinned back.

"That would explain what I see when I look at you."

"What, a young cool guy?"

He giggled.

"Maybe that's why people keep the friends they had when they were twenty," Rev said. "Because those people see you for who you are. Assuming you stay what you were back then. Some people are middle-aged in their twenties, and so for them it's not a big thing. But for those of us who are—"

"Eighteen 'till we die—"

"Yeah. It's like—gradually having to live in a body that doesn't look—it's like having a body image dysfunction. You know those people who are really thin, but when they look in the mirror, they see a fat person?"

"Or those people who want to cut off their hand because it doesn't belong to them."

"Yeah. But how do you cut off your whole body when it turns forty?" she said.

"Hm."

"And then?" Rev asked. "After you quit?"

"Well, that's when I went on tour with a Bunch of Drunken Indians."

"And after that?"

"Well, like you said, it was the eighties, there weren't any other teaching jobs except the teach-English-in-Japan ones."

"Which you did?"

"I did. Ani had gone back home to Japan, so..."

"But that didn't work out as planned."

"No. So after a year, I came back. And did...whatever. Here and there. This and that. I tried—you remember the newspaper job I mentioned. I did try—I was willing to pay my dues until—until I saw that the guys who got anywhere weren't the ones who'd paid *their* dues."

"Guys like Josh."

"Guys like Josh. So suddenly writing obits for five years until I got promoted to writing about village council meetings didn't seem—"

"Worthwhile?"

"I was going to say fun, but worthwhile works. Anyway," he continued, "in the meantime, I realized I didn't need a quarter of a million dollars. Didn't need a quarter of a quarter million. I realized I'd much rather have time and freedom than money. So I just carried on with the here and there, this and that thing.

"Which doesn't," he continued, "seem to put one in a position of power. As you pointed out. So while you regret a life without fun, I regret a life without significance."

"But don't you see? My life hasn't had significance either."

"Well, mine—"

"Hasn't had fun?" She found that hard to believe.

"It's hard to have fun by yourself."

Rev looked over at him and narrowed her eyes.

He giggled.

THEY'D LONG PASSED OTTAWA, and had switched and switched again, and were somewhere on Highway 7. Trees, fields, meadows, rivers. There was the occasional side-road leading off into forest, and every now and then they saw a cluster of houses.

"I hate that," she said seemingly out of nowhere.

After a puzzled moment, Dylan agreed. "Me too."

She laughed, then gestured out the window. "Billboards in general, but ones like that in particular."

Dylan turned in his seat. "My x-ray vision seems to have shut down. What did it say?"

"'Thou shalt not kill. Exodus 20:13.' With a picture of a fetus. That had Bambi's eyes and ET's head."

"Would you rather it had Hitler's mustache?" He giggled. "And ET's head?"

While Rev considered the implications of that, he rushed on in excitement, "Oh, oh, remember those things you got in cereal boxes, cardboard folding cut-out flipping things, and you could—"

"Mix and match one person's legs with another person's middle—" she joined in.

"And a third person's head!" He was laughing. "I used to make my own—"

She looked over at him sharply.

"What?" he said.

You had such initiative."

"You didn't?" He was puzzled.

"No, I was more the 'Don't do anything unless you're told' kid. I didn't even look ahead in my textbooks. At the beginning of the year, when we got new books, I didn't turn the page until I was told to."

"Wow," he said, considering. "Such self-discipline. You must have the delayed gratification thing down pat."

"Not really. It simply never *occurred* me to look ahead. I've got the no imagination thing down pat."

"And yet look how you turned out. Initiative *and* imagination."

"Hm," she said uncertainly.

"We should go back and add Hitler's mustache," he said. "And tone down ET so the right message—"

She looked over at him, eyes glittering. "I've got a better idea. We should add 'Blessed are they who basheth their babies' brains against the stone.' Psalms something or other."

"It really says that? In *The Bible*?"

"Look it up."

He did. He snagged his knapsack from the back seat and took out his laptop.

"Well bloody hell. Psalms 137:9. 'Blessed are they that taketh and dasheth thy little ones against the stone.'"

"Okay," he said then. "So what we need is a can of spray paint and a ladder. And a flashlight."

She looked over at him. "I've got a flashlight. Under your seat," she said.

Dylan reached under the seat and pulled out a flashlight. He flicked the switch on the side.

"Okay, so what we need is a can of spray paint and a ladder and new batteries."

"Next town."

"How do you know?"

"It's part of the rule. Every town has a gas station, a beer store, a corner store, a motel, and a hardware store."

"A hardware store before a grocery store and a drugstore?" he asked doubtfully.

"Well certainly before a clothing store. Men have to have their power tools."

"Right. Vroom vroom," he said.

They drove for a while, no town in sight.

"So why do you dislike billboards in general?"

"What gives anyone the right to impose their opinion on me? I get so sick and tired of seeing 'Buy my stuff—make me rich' signs all over the place."

"So it's just advertising billboards you dislike."

"Well that's most of them, isn't it. And *especially* on the roads, especially the ones with blinking lights and moving pixels or whatever. They're *intentionally* trying to take our attention of the road. They oughta be illegal. Conspiracy to cause an accident or something. And if you ignore the sign, if you intentionally don't pay attention to it, well it might be an important one. Like construction ahead or something."

"That happened once." He just knew it.

"It did. I missed a change in the maximum speed limit sign. The cop said 'Didn't you see the sign?' I said no, there's so many fucking signs on the highway these days, every hundred yards there's a sign. McDonalds in 5 km, visitor info center ahead, Tim Horton's in 10 km, divided highway ends, Paula's Pottery next left, no U turns, moose crossing go slow, school crossing go fast, turn back for Santa's Village, littering fine $1,000, McDonalds 3 km ahead, turnaround ahead, 90 kmh, hospital, McDonalds 1 km ahead. If I read every one, I'll cause an accident."

"School crossing go fast?"

"*And*," she wasn't finished, "especially in the country—what gives them the right to scar the landscape? It's the same as graffiti. It ruins the beauty, other people's appreciation of the beauty. And *graffiti's* illegal.

"The companies that put up their billboards are ruining my pleasure," she went on, "with their greed. With their pleasure. Why does their pleasure trump mine? My god, I get ads in my mailbox, on my answering machine, in my email, on my radio, on my TV. Know why door to door salesmen don't exist anymore?"

"Because you killed them all."

That stopped her. For just a moment. She grinned, then carried on. "I can't do anything in public, not even take a walk, not *especially* take a walk, even in the privacy of my own home—"

"You take walks in your home? How big is this cabin of yours?"

"—without someone clamouring for me to buy their shit.

"It's especially annoying," she still wasn't finished, "because there's so little evidence that billboards actually make any difference. I mean when was the last time you bought something because you saw it on a billboard. Or in an ad. And yet, when you accuse business of making unnecessary products, they say 'Oh no, we're just making what people want.' Well if that were the case, why do they have to advertise? Why do they have to make people want what they make if they want it already?"

"Good question."

"Do you know how much money companies spend on advertising??"

"No."

"Over 400 billion. Pharmaceutical companies spend twice as much on advertising as they do on research and development. Fast food spends 3 billion a year. That would feed about 10% of the world's hungry. Not that I think we should feed the hungry instead."

"Certainly not."

"Because—"

"Town ahead. See the sign?"

"Oh shut up," she laughed.

SURE ENOUGH, THERE WAS A HARDWARE store in town. Not a mom and pop hardware store of course, but a huge Home Depot or Home Hardware or Home Hardware Depot.

They got out of the car—Rev ever so carefully—stretched a bit, then headed inside. They found the paint aisle and spent some time trying to decide whether they wanted glossy black or matte black.

"Let's ask," she said, taking a can of the glossy from the shelf.

"Ask what—which kind is better for defacing private property?"

"Well," she conceded, "not in so many words. We could ask which kind is better for redressing the imbalance of opinion in the public forum." She put the glossy back on the shelf and picked up the matte.

"Tricky thing, isn't it."

"What, asking a question?"

"Private property in the public forum."

"Worse when you consider not just what we can see—" she put the matte back, right beside the glossy, and studied them, " I mean, smell and sound crosses property lines a lot more than sight. Whenever my neighbour cuts his grass, he imposes his noise and his gasoline fumes on me. I can't help but hear it, and if the wind is blowing my way, I can't help but smell it. Unless I leave home."

"Does that happen a lot?"

"Oh yeah. Almost every day in the summer. If it's not one person, it's another. And when you live on a lake, the sound travels wonderfully well. I didn't think of that back when."

Dylan put a can of semi-glossy beside the two cans Rev had arranged.

"And I've never understood why people who live in the forest *must* have a lawn," she continued. "It's just a knee jerk thing. I don't believe for a minute they really want it, really *enjoy* having a lawn. They never feast their eyes on it, they never roll around on it. I wouldn't mind so much if it's my passion versus theirs. I'd understand we'd have to compromise or take turns or something. What makes me angry is that what I really really enjoy, what I *do* feast on, bask in—the silence, the stillness, the stunning beauty of it all—is taken away by what other people don't even really care about. They cut their grass just because. They do it without thinking. I hate that I suffer because other people don't think.

"And men like to make noise," she said, changing the order of their three cans so the glossy was right beside the semi-glossy. "Notice it's always men who do it. They're the ones who buy power lawn mowers and weed whackers and—"

"Having a lawn gives them something to do."

"Which makes it even worse. My life is hell because men can't find anything else to do?

"And my god they have to be doing something," she put the semi-glossy back beside the matte. "They've bought into the whole Puritan ethic thing. You ever notice how they use 'Well I've got work to do' as an all-purpose excuse to walk away from—whatever? As if 'work' has some moral status that puts it above everything else. Again, it's only because they haven't stopped to think about it—I mean look at this place!" she gestured to the whole store. "Do we have whole box stores full of just kitchen tools and vacuum cleaners?"

"Can I help you?" a clerk approached them. Warily.

"I doubt it," Dylan said. "She's beyond help," he added.

The clerk scuttled away.

"Why don't we take one of each," Dylan suggested. "We actually don't know how much it'll take—do we?"

"No, but if we take one of each, it won't—match."

"Okay, glossy. It might reflect headlights and stand out more."

"Yeah, good point." Rev took two cans of glossy.

"Glossy," Dylan said again, and giggled. "Perspicuity."

"What's next?"

"Batteries." They wandered around until they found the batteries. Dylan picked out a four-pack of D batteries.

"Ladders," he said then. "If you were a ladder, where would you be?"

"Outside."

"Good, yes." They headed outside and found several ladders.

"They're big."

"And expensive."

"Maybe we can stand on the roof of your car."

"Possible," she said. "Grappling hook and rope?"

"You've been watching too much *Mission Impossible*," he said. "And a harness," he added.

They went back inside and asked the cashier, "Do you sell grappling hooks here?"

"Grappling hooks? I don't think so."

Rev waited a minute, during which nothing happened. "Well, could you find out? That's kind of your job," she added.

Dylan jabbed her.

"What? That *isn't* her job?"

"Probably not. She's a specialist. She's only trained to do the cashier thing. Someone else is trained to do the look-up-in-the-inventory thing."

"Oh, right. Yeah."

"Manager to check-out, manager to check-out," she spoke into the intercom phone. The cashier, not Rev.

"Now you've done it, she's called the manager."

"Do you think he knows how to look something up in inventory?"

"Probably not."

A pot-bellied man sauntered over to the check-out. Didn't deign to speak. 'Can I help you' would be too—servile.

"We're wondering if you sell grappling hooks here," Dylan said. In the silence.

"Grappling hooks? What do you need a grappling hook for?"

"None of your business," Rev replied.

Dylan jabbed her again. "We're buying props for a performance of *Mission Impossible*," he improvised.

"Oh. Well, let me see," he scratched his jowls. "I can sell you an anchor and some rope. Will that do?"

"Might do. Where are the anchors?"

"Aisle 5. Rope's in 6. I like *Mission Impossible*. Did you see they're coming out with another one?"

"No, I didn't. Thanks for that."

They went to aisle 5. Dylan hefted an anchor. "Cool. It's even shaped like—an anchor. I like it," he said, taking it and moving on to aisle 6. They decided on a prepackaged length of thick rope they could tie knots in for footholds.

On their way back to the cashier, Dylan starting humming the *Mission Impossible* theme.

"Okay," Rev said, when they were back in the car and heading out of the parking lot, "now what? When does it get dark?"

"At night usually," he said. "Though there are several notable exceptions."

"Supper time then?"

"Supper time," he agreed.

THEY DROVE AROUND, LOOKING FOR THE RESTAURANT. It was beside the motel. Across from the corner store. Just up from the gas station and beer store. And it was called Molly's Restaurant.

They walked in, a bell on a string in the doorway jingling as they did so, then took seats at a small table by the window. A young woman came out from the kitchen, and approached their table.

"Hi, what can I get for you?"

Rev took the plastic-covered menus from their holder and started to look through.

"What have you got for dessert?" Dylan asked. They'd finished their cheesecake within two hours of leaving Montreal. That is, Rev had finished their cheesecake within two hours of leaving Montreal.

The woman paused a moment, then pointed to a mound of plastic-wrapped brownies on a plate by the cashier.

"Molly made some butter tarts, but they're all gone."

"Ah. Too bad."

"I'll have the French toast," Rev said, putting the men back in its holder. Only at places like this could you get what's traditionally a breakfast item for supper.

"Sounds good," Dylan said. "You've got maple syrup?"

The woman nodded at the sticky jug on the table.

"And coffee, please," said Rev.

The woman looked at Dylan, pen poised. "Make that two coffees."

While they waited, they looked around. A fish mounted on a plaque was on the one wall. Moose antlers were on the other.

“They should mount the whole moose,” Dylan said. “I mean, they mount the whole fish.”

“Hm. What they should mount is a pair of chipmunk ears,” Rev said.

He raised his eyebrows.

“Anyone can shoot a moose that’s just standing there,” she explained. “If you really want something to brag about, try shooting a chipmunk from fifty feet.”

“Good point. Though I like chipmunks.”

“Well so do I. I was just saying.”

The woman soon arrived with two plates of limp French toast. Dylan slathered his with maple syrup, then took a bite.

“Oh, wow.” He looked closely at the jug and saw that it had a handwritten label on it. Frank’s Maple Syrup. “This is really good.”

Rev reached over and forked a soggy piece.

“Hey! This is *my* French toast!”

“I’m not a fan of maple syrup,” Rev said as she took a bite, “but it does taste—true.”

“Good thing the cats aren’t here to swat pieces of this across the room,” Dylan commented.

“Think they could?” She took another soggy forkful, as Dylan looked on with exaggerated indignation. “It’s not quite as aerodynamic as chunks of fish.”

“Well, there’s one way to find out.” He cut himself a large piece of *his* French toast.

“Don’t you dare!” Rev said quickly.

“What? Of course I’m not going to drive all the way back to Montreal to get the cats!” he grinned.

They finished their meal in comfortable silence.

“So…” he said, looking out the window. “Want to check in to that motel while we’re waiting? I mean, we’re staying here, right? After?”

"Unless you want to drive."

"Could do. But is a motel down the road a few hours likely to be open? In a few hours? We're still quite a ways from—wherever it is we're going."

"Right. Good point." They paid for their meal, then headed out to the parking lot. And walked across it to the motel.

BY THE TIME THEY'D REGISTERED, it was dark, so they headed back to the billboard. And couldn't find it.

"I know what the problem is," Dylan said. "We have to be driving in the other direction."

"Riiight." Rev turned at the next turning place.

"You do know that was for emergency vehicles only."

"Oh was it? I didn't see the sign."

"You didn't *read* the sign."

"See?"

"Okay, now don't go so fast…McDonalds, The Comfort Inn, Casey's, maximum speed 90 kmh, Paula's Pottery…my god but there are a lot of signs, aren't there. Oh, oh, there it is. Thou shalt not kill. Bambi meets ET."

Rev pulled onto the shoulder and turned off her lights.

"Okay you get the anchor and rope, I'll get the spray paint and the flashlight. And quit humming 'Mission Impossible.'"

He was silent for a moment.

"And 'I'm a Little Teapot' isn't even remotely relevant," she said after another moment.

"This is rather high off the ground isn't it," he said when they had reached the billboard. "I've never been to a billboard close-up."

"Hm. So you've tied the rope to the anchor?"

"Well, give me a minute." He fumbled for a few minutes. "Give me some light. I didn't learn knots in Boy Scouts."

"What *did* you learn in Boy Scouts?" She turned on the flashlight.

"Do you really want to know?"

"No, probably not," she sighed while he tied the rope to the anchor.

"Okay, the rope is tied to the anchor."

"Okay, throw it over the billboard."

He looked up, hefted the anchor in his hand, executed a few warm-up swings, then let it fly. It hit the billboard a full three feet above his head and bounced back, landing heavily at his feet with a dull thud.

Rev collapsed in laughter.

"Jesus Christ," he said, "I almost got hit in the head with an anchor! How would I have explained *that* to—anyone who wanted to know. And you're laughing!"

"I'm sorry," she said, "it's just—can I see that again?"

"No!" Dylan picked up the anchor.

"Okay, so you have to throw it higher." She stifled a snort.

"Thank you very much Einstein." He stood back a bit, then heaved it with a grunt. It went up, and up, and over the billboard, the rope trailing up, and up—and over the billboard.

"Okay, I guess one of us should have held onto the end of the rope."

"You think?" He went around behind the billboard to retrieve the anchor.

"Here, you try. I think I've got only the two throws in me."

Rev took the anchor, hefted it experimentally, then flung it at the billboard. It flew up and about two feet from the top crashed—clear through the billboard. Dylan scrambled for the rope trailing after it.

"My god, what—oh right. You used to work out. You were training for a marathon or the Schwarzenegger-double contest or—" He caught her look.

"'Used to.' That was wrong, wasn't it. You still work out. Obviously." He looked up at the billboard. "Oh look! You smashed the baby's head in. Blessed art thou!"

"Oh shut up."

"Okay since I grabbed the rope, I think you should climb up it."

She looked at the rope. "You forgot to tie knots in it."

He looked at the rope. "I did at that."

She looked at the ground around the billboard, then back to her car.

"You know, I think I could probably just pull the car off the road, to here, and stand on the roof."

"Yeah?"

"Well, my 'Blessed be' would end up along the bottom of the billboard, but—"

"It would probably end up more legible. That's rather critical, isn't it?"

"It is, yes."

They headed back to the car.

"So, did you ever do your marathon?"

"I did," she sighed.

"And…"

"And," she said with mock brightness, "if I lived in Jamaica, I'd hold the national record!"

"Well, that's—ah. Not too many people in the tropics take up distance running, I take it. You still run? I mean besides to the corner and back. You did that quite well, I remember."

"No," she sighed, "I don't. Apart from the turning-into-cement thing, a few years ago, I realized that given my knees, I could either run for another five years or walk for another twenty. Didn't much relish using a walker when I hit fifty, so…"

They returned to her car, and she carefully drove it down the incline and over the field to the sign. So far so good. She jockeyed a bit to get it nice and close—and parallel to the sign. Then got out the passenger side after Dylan.

"Okay," she said, as she grabbed the can of spray paint and vaulted—okay, climbed—onto the bumper, then onto the hood, then onto the roof. "Wait. What do I do if a car comes and sees me?"

"Hit the deck!"

"But it's all sticky up here. Do you know how hard this stuff is to get off—oh yeah."

Dylan thought a moment. "I could go back up and pretend to be hitch-hiking. Then their attention will be on me. I'll be a decoy." He quacked.

"Shh!"

"What, you think the ducks are awake this time of night? We should be more concerned about wolves and bears. We'd probably make a nice, light snack."

"I'll need you to move the car," she said, having considered the logistics of their mission. "I can't reach the whole length of the billboard from here. So you can't be a decoy. Or a nice, light snack."

"Okay," he said cheerily. "Maybe another time."

"Okay." She began to spray. Dylan stood back and bit and looked on.

"Smaller letters, you're going to run out of room."

"But then they'll be too small to read. Look how big the other letters are."

"Right. Okay, narrower letters. Or start going up so you have room for a second line."

"I can't go up. I'm only 5'3.' Used to be 5'4,'" she added. "I hate this—"

"—growing old shit, I know. Here," Dylan vaulted onto the hood. And tripped. "Fuck."

"Here," he said after a moment, once he had crawled onto the hood. "I'm 5'10.' I know six inches isn't much—"

She snickered. "Actually, six inches—"

"Oh shut up."

He took the can from her and continued, reaching higher so they had room for a second row. She decided to jump off the car to take a look from a bit afar. So she—fell off the car. "Fuck."

She got up, took a few steps back, and took a look. "That's good, you're doing good," she said.

At about 'thy little ones,'she called out "'Car!'"

He stood still.

"What are you doing? Get down!"

"No, I'm blending in, pretending to be a tree."

"Trees don't grow out of car roofs. Rooves?"

"Well, if I jump off, the movement will catch their eyes."

"You think a frog is driving the car?"

By then, the car had reached their spot. It slowed down.

"Oh shit. It probably thinks we've had an accident. Hit a moose or something."

"And what, we've pulled over to the billboard to scrape it off the roof of the car?"

Sure enough, the driver pulled off onto the shoulder.

"You folks all right?" a man called out.

"Yes, thanks. We—" She couldn't think of anything. Neither could Dylan.

"Okay, then." He drove on.

"Think he believed me?" she asked.

"What, that we're all right?"

"It is rather unlikely, isn't it."

Dylan resumed their work. "Done!" he said after a few more minutes.

"Wait a minute," she said as she ran back up toward the highway, then back down to the sign.

"I think you need to do it again."

"What?"

"Just go back, each letter—it needs to be—thicker." She snickered again.

"Oh shut up." He shook the can and retraced the letters.

"Okay, done again," he said a minute later. "Good?"

Rev ran back up to the road. "Good!" she called out.

He went to jump off the car, thought the better of it, and climbed down the way he climbed up.

Rev climbed into the driver's seat through the passenger door, Dylan got in after her, and she started the motor. They managed to get back up the incline and onto the shoulder.

"I want to see it," he said. "But don't just reverse. Go up and around and back. We need the full effect."

She drove up the highway a bit, turned around in the emergency-only turn around, then drove back.

"Well," she said. "It's legible."

"It is that," he agreed lamely.

"You know," she said thoughtfully, "we may reach more people with this than I did in my whole teaching career."

"Nonsense. You didn't have a teaching *career*."

"Oh shut up."

JUST AS THEY WERE GETTING READY to leave the next morning, there was a knock at their motel room door.

"Check-out's not till eleven, right?" Dylan said.

"Yes and it should be illegal to require anything, of anybody, before noon," Rev said, as she went to the door, still coaxing her stiffened legs to—work.

A police officer was standing there.

"Good morning. Is this yours?" He held up their anchor and rope.

Rev opened her mouth, then closed it.

"Yes," Dylan stepped forward smoothly. "She had a little too much to drink last night," he nodded at Rev, "and wanted to stop the car from moving. So she threw the anchor overboard." He laughed.

The police officer did not. "And defaced a billboard in the process?"

"Well, her aim—actually," he turned to Rev, grinning, "yes, that's exactly what she did. She de-faced the billboard."

"I meant the graffiti."

"Graffiti?" Rev said, trying for innocently. And achieving only stupidly.

"I'm placing both of you under arrest for mischief and blasphemy."

"Blasphemy? How can it be blasphemy when it's true? I mean, it's not true, those who dasheth their babies' brains against the stone are *not* blessed, as far as I'm concerned. Actually, *no* one's blessed, because there's no such thing as *being* blessed, because there isn't a god to do the blessing—" Dylan shot her a look of—wonderment—"but I meant the 'Blessed is' line is from *The Bible*. So how can something from *The Bible* be blasphemous? And is blasphemy actually still a crime? What the hell is blasphemy?"

"Come with me, please." They picked up their already packed bags and followed him out to his vehicle.

"Wait a minute," she said. "Can we check out first?"

"You," he said to Dylan. "She waits here."

"Oh please. Like she's going to make a run for it."

"Oh shut up."

Dylan headed toward the office, but did an abrupt turn half way there.

"Why don't we just leave our stuff here," he said as he walked back toward Rev. Who had suddenly had the same thought. She handed him his bag. Then hers. As camouflage. "We might be all day, then get released on our own recognizance, then need a place to stay—right?" He looked to the officer.

"Suit yourself."

Dylan went back to their room, put their bags in, then locked the door. He and Rev got into the back seat of the police car.

"Don't you dare—" she said as she saw the grin starting.

"Can you turn on the siren?" Dylan asked, full-grin, as the officer started his car and pulled out of the motel parking lot.

HE DROVE FIVE MINUTES to what was apparently the police station. It doubled as the Legion hall. The floor was sticky, the tables were covered in cigarette burns, and the curtains were—despondent. The officer led them through to a small office. He went around a counter to a desk, then returned to said counter with a clipboard.

"Names?"

"Dylan O'Toole."

"Chris Reveille."

The officer wrote the information on the clean sheet of paper he had put on the clipboard.

"Address?"

Rev provided her address. Dylan remained wisely silent.

"Phone number?"

Rev pulled out her glow-in-the-dark cellphone with exaggerated pride, then realized her number wasn't on it. Or in it. And she certainly didn't know it by memory. She never called herself.

"223-6170," Dylan said. From memory. And thus with inordinate pride.

They continued to provide the information requested by the officer—dates of birth, driver's licenses, social insurance numbers. The fact that they were both single gave the officer cause to declare blasphemy again, but he did declined. Though apparently only with great effort.

He looked over the notes he'd made, probably checking for spelling errors, Rev thought, then asked them to wait in the bar.

They walked back into the empty room. "Is this the holding cell?" Dylan wandered over to the dart board.

"This is not good," she said.

"What, we'll get the charges dropped. You'll see. First offen—oh. This is not good."

"We should call a lawyer. Don't we get to call a lawyer?" she asked.

"Do you *have* a lawyer?"

"No. Do *you* have a lawyer?"

"No."

"Okay, we'll look in the yellow pages," she said. "There's gotta be a lawyer in this—county." Rev went to the doorway and called out toward the office. "Excuse me—do we need to call a lawyer? I mean, what's going to happen now—shouldn't we be able to call a lawyer?"

"Already done. Kosta's coming."

"Um—okay—thanks." She returned to the bar.

"Kosta's coming," she said to Dylan.

"Okay then. No need to worry," he said. Then after a moment—"And who's Kosta?"

While they waited, they played a game of darts—actually, Dylan tried to make a happy face on the dartboard with his darts, and Rev tried to send the dartboard through the wall and into the other room with hers. Dylan was alternately horrified and impressed when the glasses behind the bar shuddered.

"Okay game's over," he said, as one clattered to the floor. He went behind the bar to—"Oh for the love of god," he said, "it's plastic." He held up the glass.

A man about ten years younger than them came through the door just then.

"Hi," he said, extending his hand as he approached them. "I'm Kosta, your lawyer. If you like," he added. Dylan shook his proffered hand.

"Well, I'm not sure we have any choice. Are you any good?" Rev asked him.

"Well, I'm—Ms. Revei—Chris?"

She looked at him more closely. "I'm sorry, do I—"

"Dmitri. Dmitri Kosta. You were my teacher. Back in high school."

"Dmitri…Oh, Dim!" she smiled. Then look horrified. "You became a lawyer?"

"Yeah," he said, looking just a little miffed that she'd been so surprised. "When I regained control of my brain, I discovered I was actually rather intelligent. And I have you to thank."

"I helped you regain control of your brain?"

"No, age did that. I was pretty much a write-off from, well, all through puberty, actually." Dylan snickered. "But I've got you to thank for the law school thing."

"Cool," Dylan spoke up. "See? You *did* make a difference. Was he in your class when all that stuff about standing for the anthem happened? Taught him to think, you did!"

"Actually, no, I was in her grade ten class—when you—"

"Ah." Dylan said, grinning at Rev. Who was trying not to—

"Hey, if it weren't for that valuable lesson, I'd be paying so much child support I'd never've been able to *afford* law school."

"See?" Dylan turned to Rev. "You *did* make a difference."

"Oh shut up."

"Okay," Dim said as they arranged themselves around one of the small tables. "Want a drink?" He got up and went behind the bar. "On the house. Such as it is," he waved a plastic glass around the room.

"Actually, a Pepsi would be good," Rev said. "Thanks." Ever so politely and maturely.

"Can you make a Frosty Fuddbucker?" Dylan said.

"No, but come take a look and if they've got what you need, go for it."

Dylan walked behind the bar then and scanned the bottles. He took one off the shelf. "Tequila," he said to Rev, waving the bottle. She grinned then quickly wiped it off her face. Tried to put her responsible-teacher face on. Realized she didn't have one.

Dim popped open a beer for himself, took a Pepsi out of the fridge for Rev, and Dylan set about making a tumbler of Frosty Fuddbuckers. As he poured, he started humming 'I'm a Little Teapot' again. And doing the moves. A little Fuddbucker sloshed onto the floor. After the first one was successfully poured, he held up the tumbler and asked Rev, "Are you sure?"

"Yeah, one of us has to be—how long will we be here, do you think?"

"Oh I'm afraid the judge is out of town. Wife says he won't be back until tonight."

"Pour me a Fuddbucker," she called over to Dylan, giving it up.

"Okay," Dim said when the three of them had settled back at the little table. "Okay, the good news this is your first off— " he caught Dylan's look, saw Rev opening her mouth, and quickly held up his hand. "Don't tell me, I don't want to know," he put his fingers in his ears and started humming tunelessly. And loudly. Until he saw that Rev had closed her mouth.

"The good news is they have only dial-up. They didn't take your prints, did they."

"No," she said, thinking this through.

"No point. They can't search the database. At least not by the end of this century. Now I'm thinking if you offer to pay for a new billboard—you did it, right? I mean, it really sounds like something—no, wait, I don't want to know," he put his fingers in his ears and started humming again.

"If you offer to pay for a new billboard," he said after a moment, "Kurt will—"

"Kurt's the judge?"

"No, Kurt's the county prosecutor. He'll probably drop the mischief charge."

"And the blasphemy?"

"Yeah, about that..." Dim trailed off. "You picked the wrong county for that. Preston Manning's followers are still upset that he lost."

"They're still *alive*?" Dylan asked.

"*You're* still alive," Dim said.

"What's that supposed to mean?" Rev said.

"Well," Dim backpedalled quickly, "I just mean, you were my teacher. You know, when we grow up, we think all our teachers are long gone. Don't get me wrong, I didn't, I don't, it's not that I thought you were old. Actually, I thought you were hot. All of us did. No offense, man," he said to Dylan.

"None taken. I think she's hot too."

"Okay, so where were we?" Dim asked. Blushing.

"Blasphemy," Dylan said helpfully.

"Right. Jim's a bit—Jim's the arresting officer—he's a bit overzealous when it comes to this sort of thing. And Kurt was probably just bored. Thought this would provide a little amuse- But it won't," he said quickly, catching Rev's glare. "I won't let it, it's wrong, and I'll—"

"Stop," Dylan said, "have some of your beer." He handed Dim his bottle.

"I looked it up," Dim continued after he'd taken a swallow. "You were right. What you wrote on the billboard. I mean, not that I thought you might have gotten it wrong—" he took another slug of his beer.

"So even though blasphemy—well, technically, 'blasphemous libel'—even though blasphemy is still on the books—though it hasn't been used since 1935—and even though what you wrote *is* blasphemy—at least I think it is—there's actually not a definition in the Criminal Code—the fact that what you wrote is in *The Bible*, well, that—that—actually that confuses the hell out of things," Dim gave up. "Kurt's right."

"So are you still teaching?" he asked brightly.

"No. I write the questions that go on the LSAT," she said.

"Oh." He said nothing for a moment. And another moment.

"Any more of that Fuddbucker left?" He got up and headed to the bar.

Dylan burst out laughing.

"What if," Rev was thinking aloud as Dim poured himself a Fuddbucker, "what if you strike down the law of blasphemy once and for all here by arguing that it's internally inconsistent? As it is in this case. Sort of."

"Hey, we should call Clarence Darrow," Dylan suggested.

"He's dead," Dim said, coming back to their table.

"Of course he is," Dylan said glumly. "Doesn't mean we can't call him," he added.

"Okay..." Dim tried to go with Rev's line of thinking, "so if the intent of the blasphemy law is to protect religion, and yet its own words attack it...that makes *mens rea* contradict *actus rea*, which makes it..."

"But *mens rea* often contradicts *actus rea*," Rev said. "I can intend to save a drowning person and in the process drown him."

"So that means..."

"It means you have no argument. Yet."

"Right..." Dim said, drinking his Frosty Fuddbucker. Then trying again. "Subsection (3) adds a qualifier, it says 'No person shall be convicted of blasphemous libel for expressing in good faith and in decent language, or attempting to establish by argument used in good faith and conveyed in decent language, an opinion on a religious subject'—but that doesn't help us…" he trailed off. "I mean," he explained then, "you weren't really acting in good faith—"

"The hell I wasn't!"

"But you weren't attempting to establish anything by argument—and your language wasn't—well, most people would say it was inflammatory," Dim ducked.

"But I just quoted *The Bible*! It's *The Bible* that's inflammatory!!"

"Yeah, I get that—it's just—I don't see any way around it. What you *did* and what you *intended to do*—*both* attack religion. *Both* are blasphemous."

"But we just quoted *The Bible*," she said again. "That's typically not blasphemous."

"Not typically."

"Only because people pick and choose so judiciously," Dylan added his two cents. "So—wait—oh, oh—how about this: by finding us guilty, the judge will be saying *The Bible is* blasphemous."

"Yes!" Rev turned to Dylan. "Brilliant!!" She high-fived him. A moment later, Dim got it, and joined the high-fiving.

"Another round of Fuddbuckers," Dylan cried out and looked eagerly toward the bar. A moment later, he remembered there was no bartender. And a few moments after that, he was behind the bar again being a little teapot.

"So when did the judge's wife say he'd be home?" Rev asked.

"This evening some time," Dim looked at his watch. "Oh, it's—why don't we all go back to my place for some supper, then I'll call him, and we'll see where we are."

"Okay, thanks, that'd be nice," Rev said, Dylan nodding agreement. They headed out to the parking lot.

"We'll follow your car?" Rev suggested, looking at the nondescript brown car sitting next to hers.

"Sure. Though I'm actually two towns over—it's about half an hour—you know where Ardendale is?"

"No—"

"Well, just follow me. The turn-off's marked, then it's straight on for—just follow me."

ABOUT HALF AN HOUR LATER, after a quick detour back to the motel to pick up their bags and check out, Rev pulled in behind Dim's car. He led the way into his house, an old farmhouse, then into the large kitchen. He set his laptop bag onto a chair.

"Sue's probably out back," Dim said. "She's got horses." He went to the window and looked out the back at a barn and fenced in area. The gate was open. "Looks like she's out riding."

"Um," he turned back to Dylan and Rev, "have a seat, I'll see—" he opened the fridge, "um, we've got—" he started pulling out containers and setting them onto the table, "leftover lasagna, corn, green beans—you want them?" He clearly didn't. "Chicken salad," he continued, "rice something or other, mashed potatoes, gravy—if I heat it up," he said, opening that particular container—"otherwise it's—something else—" Dylan grinned at Rev. "And," he scanned the door of the fridge, "we've got pickles, and ketchup, what else?" He looked at the table, a smorgasboard of leftovers.

Rev got up. "Plates would be good—which cupboard?"

"Left," said Dim, as he went about opening all of the containers now sitting on the table.

"Fluids?" Dylan suggested, and started searching in the cupboards for glasses.

"Water from the tap's good," Dim said, "we've got a drilled well. Wine, if you like." He opened the fridge again. "No juice or anything," he said, looking, as he pulled out the bottle of wine. Then just as he was about to sit down—"Bread," he said, and moved a half-loaf from the counter to the table.

"There. Good?" he asked.

"Very good," Dylan said, as they all sat down then, and started passing various containers around.

WHEN THEY'D HAD THEIR FILL, Dim suggested that Dylan and Rev finish off the wine while he made the call to the judge.

"Porch or living room?" he asked, picking up the bottle of wine and gesturing to their glasses.

"Porch," Rev suggested.

Dim led the way to a comfortable screened-in porch out the back. "So," he said, refilling their glasses and setting the bottle on an end table, "make yourselves at home, and I'll make that call," Dim looked at his watch. "He should be home by now."

"Sounds good," they said as he left to go to his study.

"This is nice, eh?" Rev said as they looked out over fields ending in forest.

"It is. Maybe we could go for a walk before we head back—to—wherever it is we're going next."

"Or a ride. Ever ride a horse?" Rev asked.

"Of course I've ridden a horse," he said, grinning. "They're much easier to ride than cows," he added.

Rev considered that. "And chipmunks."

"Not that you'd want to ride a chipmunk."

"Of course not. Just saying."

He grinned at her, she grinned back, and they just sat for a while, basking in the fields.

"SO," DIM SAID, RETURNING TO THE PORCH.

"He was home?" Rev asked anxiously. "You told him how finding us guilty would be saying *The Bible* is blasphemous?"

"Yeah, he thought it was brilliant—"

"Great!"

"And he can't wait to pass that judgment."

"Gr—what?"

"He thinks that anyone who thinks there's a god, let alone that a supreme being wrote *The Bible*, or that *The Bible* is a good book, is 'a total idiot.' His words."

They were silent for a moment.

"Do you think it's better to be a total idiot or half an idiot?" Dylan wondered aloud.

"But we don't want to be found guilty," Rev was not distracted.

"Well, you *did* do—*if* you—" he quickly qualified, then just skipped over that part—"he said he'd suspend the sentence. He also offered to pitch in for half of the billboard, and dismiss the mischief charges, if you plead innocent to the blasphemy charge to so there can be a trial so he can find you guilty and make that statement."

"We *do* want to plead innocent to the blasphemy charge, don't we?" Dylan asked Rev. "I'm getting confused."

"Thing is," Dim continued, "he doesn't want the trial for another week or so. Gives him time to line up some media coverage."

"A week? We have to hang around here for a week?" Rev asked.

"But we'd get media coverage! That's good—isn't it?" Dylan said to Rev. "I'm getting more confused."

Dim looked back and forth between the two as they worked through the deal he'd presented.

"Yeah but—"

"We're almost at Algonquin Park, aren't we?" he looked at Dim.

"Half a day's drive."

"Okay, so," Dylan said to Rev, "we drive up to the park, spend a week there, as planned, then come back for the trial."

"I've got a tent and a couple sleeping bags you can use."

So at Dim's offer, heartily seconded by Sue, who had returned a little later, they stayed there for the night, heading out to Algonquin Park in the morning.

AFTER THE HORSE RIDE, Sue extended the invitation at breakfast and Rev insisted they accept.

"It'll be fun," Rev said, leading a reluctant Dylan out to the corral.

"Nothing before noon can be fun."

"Yeah, well, there's that." She too was suffering from the nine o-clock wake-up call.

Sue went on ahead into the barn and after a few minutes, led out two gorgeous red-brown horses.

"This is Jenkins," she introduced the horses to them, "and Pickle."

"Pickle?" Rev asked.

"What can I say," she shrugged. "Carrots hold no interest whatsoever for him."

"Should they?" Dylan asked Rev as Sue went back into the barn.

"Yeah! Horses love carrots. They're always nuzzling in your pockets to see if you have any carrots stashed in there. Once a horse started nibbling on my sweatshirt. It was orange."

"I thought it was rabbits that liked carrots," Dylan said. "Don't horses like apples? And sugar cubes."

She looked at him. "Actually, I think you're right. They nuzzle in your pockets for apples and sugar cubes. Okay then why did the horse nibble at my orange sweatshirt?"

"Good question."

Sue brought out a very, very big black horse. "And this is—"

"Darth Vader!"

"Snow White."

A silent moment. “That was going to be my second guess,” Dylan said.

“Wait a minute,” he said then, as he took in the three horses. And the three of them. “We’re each getting on a horse?”

“Well, that’s sort of required if you’re going to ride them.”

“Oh. I was expecting a—sort of a—you know—like at the circus. Someone holds onto the rope thing and the horse just walks around in a little circle. With someone sitting on it. You know—a horse ride.”

“Well,” Sue said, “we can do it that way. Or you can be adult about it.”

“Oh, well, when you put it that way. I’ll do the little circle thing.”

“I thought you said you’d ridden a horse before,” Rev said.

“Well I did. Sort of. Have *you* ever ridden a horse before?”

“Yes,” she replied without hesitation. “Sort of.”

“Okay,” Sue interjected, “I’m going to just pretend neither of you has ridden a horse before and you both would like to ride one now. So this is the saddle—”

“And this is the horse,” Dylan volunteered, pointing at Snow White.

“Right, but I’ll ride Snow White. You two will do better on Jenkins and Pickle.”

“Can I have Pickle?” Dylan asked Rev.

“And these are the stirrups,” Sue continued. “You get up by holding on here—” she demonstrated, “and here. Put your left foot in the stirrup, then heave your right leg over, and—” she heaved herself onto the horse. “Then put your right foot in the stirrup and take hold of the reins. Evenly. They’re your steering wheel. Okay,” she got back down, “who wants to go first?”

Rev stepped up to Jenkins. Sue stood nearby to hold the horse steady or to boost Rev, whichever was needed. It went well. Surprisingly well. Given.

“Okay, you’re next,” she said to Dylan.

Dylan approached Pickle. “Hi Pickle. Nice Pickle. Okay, that wasn’t exactly what I meant. Though,” he glanced under the horse, “I’m sure your pickle *is* nice.”

“You’re stalling,” Sue said.

“Yes I am,” Dylan said easily. He put his foot into the stirrup, decided it was best not to put it in so far, in case he fell off and his foot got stuck, pulled it back out a little, then reached up to grab on where Sue had indicated, and prepared to heave. Pickle snorted. Dylan quickly aborted his heave and stood back.

“He snorted at me. What does that mean?”

“I don’t know,” Sue said sweetly. “Maybe hurry up and get on already?”

“Okay, yes, hurry up and get on already.” He put his foot into the stirrup again, grabbed on, and heaved. When he opened his eyes, he found, much to his delight, that he was sitting on the horse. He was even facing the right way.

“Cool,” he said. “This is so cool,” he turned to look at Rev.

“Okay, stay there,” Sue said, more to Dylan and Rev than to the horses, who knew better, and quickly mounted Snow White.

“He’s moving!” Dylan cried out as Pickle took a few steps. “What do I do?”

“Nothing,” Sue quickly said. “Pickle knows what he’s doing.”

“Okay,” Dylan said uncertainly. “I don’t have to steer?”

“He’s not blind. I’ll take the lead, and Jenkins and Pickle will follow. If perchance they don’t, tug gently on the right rein to veer right, on the left to veer left.”

“Right to go right, left to go left. Got it.”

Sue gently dug her heels into Snow White and off they went. Jenkins followed Snow White, and Pickle followed Jenkins. They’d clearly done this before.

Sue led them out of the corral through the gate and into a field.

Dylan started relaxing into the ride. This *was* fun.

"You good?" Rev called back to Dylan half way across the field.

"Yee-haw!" Dylan shouted in response.

Sue came to a sudden and complete stop. Jenkins came to a sudden and complete stop. Pickle—had already come to a complete stop. Sue turned around to Dylan.

"What?" he said innocently.

"You're confusing the horse. 'Yee'—actually, 'gee'—means right and 'haw' means left."

"Really?"

"Really."

"But in the movies, everyone says 'Yee haw'—"

"Yeah, Hollywood always get things right."

"Point taken."

Sue turned again and continued leading the trio.

"Vroom vroom," Dylan was heard to say. Rev grinned.

The horses picked up speed as they made their way across the field, and Dylan realized Sue hadn't told them how to stop. He suspected it wasn't how you stopped on skis. At least he hoped it wasn't. Since his method involved falling down.

"Rock-a-bye baby," he began, "I'm riding through the—field—on a horse with no—a name," Dylan improvised then, "and the horse's name is Pickle. P-I-C-K-LE," he rushed the last two letters so it fit the B-I-N-G-O tune. "P-I-C-K-LE— "

"Desperado," Rev segued. Dylan grinned.

At the end of the field, they turned onto a trail through a forested area.

"There's probably a little creek up ahead where we'll stop to let the horses drink," Dylan said to himself. "Just like on the Ponderosa. There's always a little creek up ahead where they stop to let the horses drink. Because you *can* lead a horse to water."

Sure enough, there was a little creek up ahead where they stopped to let the horses drink. And sure enough Pickle didn't want a drink.

Dylan tugged down a little on the left rein. Then he tugged down a little on the right. Then he tugged down a little on both. He leaned forward on the horse. He stuck his left leg out and waved it around.

"What the hell are you doing," Rev finally said.

"I'm testing the theory."

"What theory?"

"That you can't make a horse drink."

"Trust me," Sue deadpanned. "When Pickle gets back to the barn, he's going to down a 40 ouncer."

Dylan burst out giggling. And Pickle started dancing.

"Woh, what's he doing?"

"I think he thought you were neighing at him just then."

"What? And what did he think I was saying? When I was neighing." Dylan giggled some more. Pickle danced some more. "You should be dancin,' yeah!" Dylan sang softly to himself. And Pickle.

"Don't—" Rev said. Too late.

Dylan threw his right arm into the air and let his left arm dangle, just like Travolta. Except Travolta wasn't holding on to a rein. That was connected to a horse. Pickle half leapt into the air, Dylan slid back, then lunged forward to grab on for dear life. "Stayin' alive," he squeaked. Pickle neighed. Then snorted.

When Sue turned around to see if everything was okay, Pickle acted like nothing had happened. As did Dylan.

So she guided Snow White back onto the trail, and Jenkins, and Pickle, followed. After a leisurely half hour, they were at the edge of the field again.

"Ready for the gallop home?" Sue didn't wait for an answer. Snow White took off across the field. Jenkins followed Snow White, with Rev yahooing—not yeehawing—and Pickle followed Jenkins. With

Dylan screaming Rock-a-bye.

Much to Dylan's relief, Sue guided Snow White through the gate and not over the fence. Jenkins followed. For a moment, it looked like Pickle might break precedent. He had astutely realized that now would be an exciting time to try the fence thing. It might have been Dylan's incipient hysteria that dissuaded him. Or Sue's glare. At the last minute—the very last minute—Pickle pulled up and sauntered through the gate, with a 'What?' look on his face.

"Wow, that was great!" Rev said, all fired up.

"Yeah," Dylan echoed weakly.

"Vroom, vroom," she said.

"Oh shut up," he said back.

Sue stood up in the saddle then and dismounted. She led Snow White into the barn, then returned to see that Rev and Dylan were still astride their horses. She waited, expectantly.

Rev stood up in the saddle and flexed her legs a few times. She looked down, way down at the ground.

Anticipating her problem, Dylan said conversationally to Sue, "Do you have a platform for disembarking?" He looked at Rev again. "Or maybe a haystack? Rev has a tendency to—"

"Oh shut up."

"Hey, I'm just saying—if you fall off you could get stepped on."

"Good point."

"By any number of legs," he continued, "each of which has a hoof on the end of it. And probably a horseshoe. Made of iron. Bearing god knows how many hundreds of pounds."

She sat thinking, then stood up experimentally. "Maybe I can just jump in the air and say 'giddy-up' at the same time. Jenkins will run out from under me."

"Might work. Wait. What does 'giddy-up' really mean?" Dylan asked Sue.

"Or," Sue suggested, "you can get off by the fence. Just step onto the rails. Can you handle that?"

"Oh shut up," Rev said. Under her breath.

She did manage to handle that. Dylan, on the other hand, overestimated the heave required to disembark and almost did a 180 off Pickle. Except for the foot in the stirrup. It didn't do the almost-180 with the rest of his body. Fortunately, Pickle turned his ass end toward Dylan at the last second, saving Dylan a badly twisted ankle.

"Thank you, kind sir," Dylan said to Pickle—well, to the horse's ass, actually, and bowed deeply. Pickle snickered.

Once the horses were safely back in the barn, and, more to the point, once Rev and Dylan were safely back on the ground, they readied themselves for their trip to Algonquin.

Dim had already left for the day, but had set the tent and sleeping bags he'd mentioned on the porch before his departure. They went inside to get their stuff, and loaded it all into the car.

Sue made sure they knew how to get back to the main highway. "About an hour north," she said, "you'll come to Bancroft. They have an outfitters store, or you can just get what you need at Zellers or Canadian Tire. Be a lot cheaper. There's a Foodland there too. Or you can get what you need in Whitney."

So they headed out. They made it back to the main highway, after just two wrong turns—which weren't really wrong turns, Dylan pointed out, so much as different, admittedly longer, ways of getting to where they were going.

ABOUT AN HOUR LATER, just as Sue had said, they came to Bancroft. The pulled into the mall, flanked at one end by the grocery store, and at the other by the Canadian Tire. On their way to the grocery store, they came across a bulk store.

"Oh, let's go in here. This'll be good." Rev walked down the first aisle, stopping to scoop up a bag of raisins. "And dried fruit," she said, looking ahead at the bins. "We need dried fruit."

"Right. So we don't get scurvy in five days."

"And peanuts. We should get some peanuts."

"Do you actually like peanuts?"

"No, I like cashews and pecans way better but they're more expensive."

"But surely you can afford the difference now. And if you can't, I can."

"You're right," she said after a moment. "Yes, I can afford it. Now. Why are habits so hard to break," she muttered.

"Because we're creatures of inertia," he said. "We follow the path of least resistance. Which is whatever rut we've made for ourselves."

"Okay, I'll get cashews *and* pecans!" she said. She marched away with enthusiasm. "And flour! Whole wheat, no—" she stopped in front of a bin, "*kamut* flour!" She looked defiantly at the bin. Having no idea what kamut flour was.

Dylan stared at her.

"I'm breaking my habits! Getting out of my rut! Normally I'd *never* take flour on a canoe trip—"

"And you're not taking it now." He took the scoop out of her hand. She managed to look crestfallen. "It'll get wet and sit there like a bag of—glue. And since I'm half paddling—"

"We could throw it overboard then."

"And probably kill half a dozen fish."

"You can't hit half a dozen fish with one bag of kamut."

"No, I was thinking they might eat it, you know, like they eat other junk we throw into the lake. And then—kamut!" He giggled.

"Okay. No kamut."

They continued up and down the aisles.

"Paprika!" Rev called out. "Let's get some paprika!"

"You are so lame at this. Paprika," he scoffed. Then he said, "Perspicuity." And giggled.

They continued to wander.

"Graham crackers!" Rev suggested. "Oh, oh, and animal crackers! Remember animal crackers?"

"I do! Pick out a lot of bears. And monkeys. The monkeys are good."

"But they all taste the same."

"I know, but the monkeys are still good."

"'Kaay..."

"And jelly beans," Dylan said after a few moments, and started looking for the jelly beans. "Can't go in the wilderness without jelly beans." He found them and scooped up a large bag.

"Anything else?"

"No, I think we're good," Rev said. "We've got raisins, dried fruit, cashews, pecans, animal crackers, and jelly beans. What more could we need?"

"NO WAY," REV SAID IN THE GROCERY STORE as Dylan put a can of spaghettios into their cart.

"You don't like spaghettios?"

"I've never actually had spaghettios. I object to the can. It's heavy. We have to carry this stuff. Or paddle it. And then we have to carry the damn can all the way back out."

"Yeah, but it'll double as a pot once we eat it." He paused, considering what he'd just said. "You know what I mean."

"Are we taking food that needs to be cooked?"

He looked into their cart. It was empty except for their nuts and raisins. And animal crackers and jelly beans. "We could."

"You're planning on building a fire?"

"You're not? How can you go backpacking and not have a

campfire?"

"I just—cooking food is more trouble than it's worth."

"Well we don't have to use it as a cooking fire. But we can't live on nuts and raisins for a week."

"Sure we can."

By this time, they were at the freezers aisle. The Sara Lee freezers aisle.

Dylan narrowed his eyes at Rev. "If you take a cherry cheesecake, I take the spaghettios. That has a box and a foil plate around it," he stared at the cheesecake she was staring at.

"Okay." She ran back, grabbed a can of spaghettios, tossed it into their cart, then took a cherry cheesecake from the freezer and set it lovingly beside the spaghettios.

They stared at their cart.

"Okay, anything else?" Dylan said.

"Coffee would be nice," Rev replied.

"You're planning on building a fire?"

"Oh shut up."

They got some coffee, and a few more things, then stopped at the bottled water.

"Hm," Rev said. "Last time I was in Algonquin, I just drank as I went, but—"

"That was long ago."

"Not that long—" she started to protest, "yeah, it was long ago."

He grabbed a six-pack.

"That won't last us a week. We need purification tablets."

"Well, we can boil the water. Seeing as we're planning to make coffee—"

"Right. So we need matches. Waterproof matches. And a pot."

"But—"

"Or a potholder for the can."

Dylan pulled out their old 'to do' list and started a new 'to get' list.

"Good idea."

AN HOUR LATER, THEY WERE putting their Canadian Tire and Zellers purchases into the car beside their bulk bin and grocery store purchases.

"Horshach!" Rev suddenly cried out.

"Where?"

"The oh-oh guy in *Welcome Back Kotter*! His name was Arnold Horshach!" She added then, "Do you know a Horshach?"

"No, do you?"

"No, but when I said 'Horshach' you said 'Where?' Not 'Who?'"

"What?" He looked at her in confusion. "When?"

AND A COUPLE HOURS AFTER THAT, they were pulling into one of the access points to Algonquin Park. One that had canoe rentals and a general store with over-priced freeze-dried packets of—

"Astronaut food!" Dylan cried out.

"What?"

"Let's get some." He chose a foil packet labeled 'Veggie Casserole,' then one labeled 'Grilled Cheese.' Rev reached out and grabbed one labeled 'Meat and Potatoes.'

"But you're vegetarian."

"I'm also curious. Perversely so."

"Right. Well in that case," he reached into a sale bin and grabbed another half dozen packets—unlabelled. "Could be fried ice cream in one of 'em," he said.

"Could be. Would we know?" she added.

"Do you still have your car cutlery?" He paused at the display of three-in-one jackknife-fork-spoon things.

"Yeah. Remind me to put it with our stuff though. It's currently in the glove compartment. Which we normally wouldn't put into our canoe."

"Not normally, no."

They went down to the waterfront next.

"Hi, we'd like to rent a canoe for the week," Dylan said to the young woman working the rentals.

"Okay. What did you have in mind?"

Dylan looked at Rev. Then back at the woman. "One that floats?"

"Okay. Good. We've got some that float," she deadpanned. Dylan broke into a grin. Then quickly sobered in case she was serious. About the some that didn't float.

She took them down to the canoes lined up near the shore. There were several kayaks there as well.

"Hey, how about a couple kayaks instead?" Rev suggested. "You know what they say about being anything but the lead in a dogsled team."

Dylan looked at her. "I know a great many things, but I don't believe I've ever heard what they say about not being the lead in a dogsled team."

"The view."

"Ah."

"Besides," she said, "you ever ride one of those bicycles-built-for-two?"

"Can't say that I have, no."

"Well, it's really—annoying. I'd rather walk."

"That wouldn't work too well here." He looked out at the water.

The woman waited patiently.

They walked over to the kayaks then.

"Can I have the red one?" Dylan said.

"OKAY, SO DO WE HAVE EVERYTHING?" Dylan said as they stood beside their now-loaded kayaks. "Tent, sleeping bags, food, water, our bags, paddles, life jackets."

"A map!" Rev said.

"Oh don't be silly. It's not like we can get lost."

Rev looked at him. "This is Algonquin Park. It's huge. There are no signs—thank god—and all the landmarks—look the same," she confessed. "Quite apart from the fact that I can get lost in an elevator."

"But you just follow the shore. And eventually—"

"Okay but what if we need to take the quickest route back. In case of emergency."

"Okay," he conceded. "We get a map, but we open it only in case of emergency."

So they went back up to the store and bought a map. Rev opened it immediately. And studied it as they made their way back to the water's edge.

"Is there a route we can take," she asked a young man who was squatting at one of the canoes, "that'll keep us on water for a week? I mean, with no portages?"

"We're old," Dylan explained.

"Sure," he said, standing up. Easily, Rev noticed. With a sigh. "You start there," he pointed to where their kayaks were waiting, "head off to your right, and just follow the lake around. Back to here. That should take you a day. Seeing as you're old," he grinned.

"But—"

"Then you do it again. Six more times."

"Funny guy," Dylan muttered as they got into their kayaks and pushed off. And headed off to the right.

THEY REACHED THE FAR END OF THE LAKE by early evening and decided that that was enough for the day. Rev nudged her kayak onto the sandy shore, stood up, and fell out.

Dylan burst out laughing.

“I’m sorry, that was—are you okay?”

Rev was swearing. “No I’m not okay, I’m fucking old!” She crawled onto the shore, turned herself around, and sat.

“Oh look, let’s watch the sun set before you set up the tent.”

Dylan noted the ‘you’ and grinned. Then sat beside her to watch the sun set.

ONCE IT WAS DARK, they decided to put up the tent. Dylan opened the bag and slid the contents onto the beach. Then stared at it.

“What the fuck is this?”

Rev looked at the various bits and pieces. “A cross between a bowflex and a geodesic dome?”

“What happened to aluminum poles and nylon rope? And grommets.”

She picked up a javelin piece, bent it experimentally, since it seemed to want to do that, and it shot out of her hands, spearing a nearby tree. Missing Dylan’s head. Barely.

“Oops.” She put down the other piece she’d picked up.

“What *are* grommets, by the way?” she asked.

“Grumbling hobbits,” he said, giggling. Then started to sort the pieces.

Rev saw the folded up piece of paper then and picked it up. “Instructions!”

“Good. We’re gonna need them.”

She scanned the piece of paper. “Okay, what kind of tent has a porch? And a closet?”

THEY GOT A VERY LATE START the second day, having slept till noon, having discovered it’s damn near impossible to put up a tent in the dark. Not to mention dangerous. They ate the cherry cheesecake for breakfast. Or lunch.

"This is just—perfect," Dylan said when they were out on the water.

"What's perfect?" Rev paddled up beside him.

"This," he said. He'd moved his seat into a reclined position, set his paddle across the kayak, and was just drifting. "Being here," he said, "the sun sparkling on the water, the trees, the quiet—is this what it's like at your cabin?"

"Often, yeah," she said, setting her seat back as well. "And it *is* perfect, isn't it."

So they drifted a while, the current and the wind taking them a little further along the lakeshore.

"I guess that's a portage spot," Rev said after another while, nodding at a spot up ahead. Two people carrying a canoe had come out of the forest. Dylan and Rev watched as they flipped the canoe onto the sand, then undid their backpacks and put them inside. In a moment, they pushed off and paddled away.

"Wanna try it?" Dylan asked. "See where it goes?"

Rev pulled the map out from her bag and opened it across her lap. "We could," she said. "It's only a quarter-inch."

"Surely we can carry these things a quarter-inch. We're not *that* old."

"It comes out to a little river, that has a bunch of criss-crosses on it, then it comes out to a lake. I wonder what the criss-crosses mean." She unfolded the entire map, looking for a key. Couldn't find one.

"Well, let's take a look," Dylan paddled ahead and pulled onto shore. Rev followed. Dylan got up and out of his kayak.

"Careful!" he called out to Rev, without turning.

"Oh shut up," she said, stretching one leg, then the other, then leaning forward to stretch her back. She put her hands on the cockpit rims, then pushed herself up and successfully out of the kayak.

The path into the forest looked well-worn. And level.

"Shall we?" Dylan asked.

"Sure, let's."

They unloaded, setting their stuff on the shore. Then stared at the empty kayaks.

"Okay, how do we carry these things?"

"Good question. I've only ever portaged with a canoe."

"Well maybe it's just the same. Same basic shape," he said. "Can't be any heavier."

"Okay," Rev grabbed the kayak near the front, and Dylan grabbed near the back.

"Okay, up—and over—"

"Ow," Dylan said. "My head's in the wrong place."

"How can—" she felt the kayak tilting down toward her. Severely.

"It's where the seat is. My head."

"Okay, let's put it down." They managed to flip it over and set it back onto the ground.

"Maybe it's easier when just one person does it." Dylan lifted the kayak over his head. The back end rested on the ground. He shuffled backwards, trying to find the point of equilibrium. The back end came up a bit, but he was clearly pulling it up with his arms. He shuffled back a bit more, and hit the seat.

"Your head's still in the wrong place," Rev said, observing closely.

He put the kayak down. They studied it.

"Maybe you don't carry it like a canoe. Maybe—" Dylan picked up the kayak's back end with his two hands.

"Yeah, this isn't bad. Pick up the other end." Rev did so. And faced Dylan.

"No way I'm walking backwards through the forest."

"Yeah, this can't be right. And if you turn around—"

"The pointy end'll get me in the ass. Plus, I can't dislocate my arms at will."

They studied the kayak again.

"This is ridiculous," she said. "Why can't we figure this out? We're not even stoned," she added.

"Maybe that's the problem." Dylan plopped himself onto the sand and started rummaging in his bag.

"Riiiight," Rev sat down beside him.

He rolled a joint, lit up, inhaled, and handed it to her.

"Maybe you don't portage with kayaks," Dylan suggested as he exhaled. "Maybe that's why all the canoes were there. Have you ever *seen* someone portage with a kayak?"

"No." She inhaled, held, then exhaled. "But you don't have to see in order to know. At least not if you're Kant. I wonder if he ever portaged with a kayak."

"Kant in a kayak," Dylan giggled.

*"Kan* in a kayak," Rev countered.

"Kant."

"Kan."

"Kant."

"Maybe we one-hand it—carry it like a shopping bag." Rev handed the joint to Dylan and got up to try it. She picked it up, but it dangled awkwardly against her knee. And she needed both hands if she held it higher, against her thigh. "This wouldn't work. I can only move sideways this way. And," she looked at the trail into the forest, "the trail goes forwards."

"So we need to find a sideways portage trail," he exhaled. "Does it say on your map which portages are sideways and which are forwards?"

Rev put the kayak down, got the map out, sat back down beside Dylan, reached over to take one last toke, then studied it. The map, not the joint.

"Well," she said after a while, "it doesn't say, but some look like sideways portages. 'Course, if I turn the map sideways," she said as she did just that, "the ones that were sideways turn into forwards. And the ones that were forwards turn into sideways. Woh." She turned the map unsideways, then sideways again, then unsideways, then—

"What if," Dylan got up after he extinguished the joint in the sand, then buried the very little bit that remained, "what if I grab it here as close as possible to the back, and you grab it as close as possible to the front, like a double-personned shopping bag?"

"No," Rev got up, "wouldn't a double-personned shopping bag be a shopping bag big enough for two people to get in?"

"Well we probably could both fit into the kayak."

"Yeah." She stared at the kayak, clearly having forgotten why she had gotten up. "What did you want me to do?" she asked after a while.

"Wait a minute, I'm trying to remember." Dylan stood there holding the back end of the kayak in his one hand. "Oh yeah, pick up the other end of the kayak."

"Oh. Right." Rev grabbed onto the cockpit rim at the front with her left hand and picked it up.

"No, turn around. So you're facing forwards. Or at least so you're facing the same direction I'm facing."

"Well it's not the same thing, you know," Rev said as she switched hands and turned around. "One's an absolute, the other's relative. *Big* difference."

"What are you talking about? They're *both* relative. *Everything's* relative because we don't have a place to stand from which to move the Earth."

"And even then—can you back up a bit? Distribute the weight

better?"

"The seat's in the way. There's no place to grip—oh wait a minute—there's a hole behind the seat—"

"There's a hole in my kayak?"

"No, it's more a space than a hole—though—" he peered into it. "I wonder if it's a wormhole."

"Put your hand in it and see."

He did so.

"Is your hand still here?"

"Yes! And so am I!"

"Good. I like it that you're still here."

"Me too."

"Okay, let's—" they took a few steps forward.

"Well, this would work," Rev said.

"Awkward as hell, but yeah, it would work."

They put the kayak back down.

"So we leave all our stuff here, take the one kayak," Rev struggled to work through the process, "then come back, get our stuff, then—" she lost it.

"Then come back and get the other kayak. It's just a quarter inch long, you said, right?"

"No! Look at it! It's gotta be at least eight feet long!"

"Not the kayak, the portage."

"Oh. Right. The portage is only a quarter-inch."

So they picked up the kayak again. Rev took a step forward with her right foot, as Dylan took a larger step forward with his left, and the kayak bumped uncomfortably against both of them. Dylan took another step, before Rev had taken another step—

"We have to step together," Dylan said.

"You think?"

"Ready? Right, left, right, left—"

"Good thing we've got just a right and a left," Rev said cheerily.

"Good thing."

Just as they made it the twenty feet up the beach to the trail's entrance, they heard someone call out, "Coming through!" They stopped then and stared in amazement as two young things came out of the forest, each carrying a kayak slung over one shoulder.

"Hey, how's it going?" the first one waved to them with the paddle in his free hand.

Dylan nodded. "Good," he managed to say. They continued to stare as he lifted the kayak off his shoulder with the hand that had been holding it there, and set it gently onto the sand. The woman behind him did the same thing.

They stared at Rev and Dylan then, still standing there holding the one kayak between them, down around their legs. They quickly set it onto the sand. Pretending they hadn't been so stupid. Didn't manage to pull it off. At all.

"Your first kayak portage?" the woman said, taking her backpack off and setting it into her kayak.

They nodded, mutely.

"Well, have a good one!" the man called out, and then they were gone.

So Rev enthusiastically picked up her kayak and slung it over her shoulder. The back end swung around and hit Dylan in the chest.

"Oof!" he said, stumbling back.

"Oops, sorry," she said, turning to him. The front end swung and banged into a tree.

"Oops." She used her free hand to steady the kayak, but that had the effect of unsteadying her, and she—fell over.

"Shit! Fuck!"

Dylan watched, barely managing not to laugh, as she picked herself up out of the kayak.

"You know," Dylan said, "we could just go around the lake six times."

"Or we could just camp here. For six days."

They considered both options for a while.

"I'm hungry," Dylan finally said.

"Yeah."

So they sat down on the sand, pulled out the bag of animal crackers, and ate them. Especially the monkeys.

THE NEXT MORNING, LOOSELY SPEAKING, they managed to make the portage.

"This is nice," Rev said, looking at the little river before them. "Which way, do you think?" She looked to the right and to the left. Not much could be seen in either direction.

"Well, this way," Dylan pointed to their right, "looks easier. That way looks like it's going against the current."

"Yeah."

So they set off on the river to the right.

"This is *really* nice," Rev said, as she drifted along. "We don't even have to paddle!"

Dylan drifted along beside her. "Well, except to keep straight," he said, dipping his paddle in from time to time.

After a minute or two, he said, "Are we picking up speed?"

"I think so. Must be the wind. Can you hear it?"

"Yeah...but I don't see it." He looked at the trees lining the river on either side. "Are you sure that's the wind we hear?"

"What—oh shit." They'd come around a curve—to the rapids.

"Now what?" Dylan called out, already some distance away from Rev. "How do I—"

"Aim for the clear and calm spots!" Rev shouted. "Stay away from the rocks!!"

"Right—"

The rapids pulled them along quickly as they tried to navigate safe passage. Within seconds, they'd both pretty much lost control of their kayaks and resorted to navigating upright passage. They bumped and scraped and zigzagged and—

"Yee haw!" Dylan shouted.

Perspicuity, Rev thought.

"Yee—" Dylan disappeared. How could he disappear? Oh. Rev hoped it was a short waterfalls. She lay her paddle across the cockpit and held on tightly to the kayak underneath. Then she hoped she didn't land on Dylan.

She went over just in time to see Dylan's kayak do a nose-dive into the water. She leaned back, trying for a belly flop instead. Well, a back flop.

Whoosh slam. That's what she got instead. A whoosh slam.

"Are you okay?" She paddled up to Dylan, whose kayak was tilting to one side, water rushing in.

"I think so," he was leaning over the other side, trying to counterbalance. She reached out and tried to help him untilt. They managed to get the lip clear of the water, but he was sitting dangerously low. The current was still pulling them along, but not quite as quickly.

"Can you get to the shore before you go completely under?"

He paddled gingerly.

"Give me your pack. And the tent."

"I'm afraid if I move around too much, it'll go under again. And if it sinks completely—"

"Right. Okay," she looked ahead, "you're almost there."

He paddled a bit more, and got carried a bit more, but managed to make an oblique path more toward the shore then away from it. Rev tried to stay close enough to grab on, in case, but not so close she bumped him over. Eventually, he was close enough to reach out to grab a branch hanging over the water. The bank was steep though, with no place to pull onto shore.

Rev grabbed onto a branch a bit further up. "It looks like there's a bit of a sandy section a bit further on," she called out. She pulled herself back along the branch until she was right beside him, then reached in and tried to tug—they managed to get the tent and his pack out of his kayak and into her lap. Her kayak sank considerably. But it was still higher than his.

"Okay?"

"Yeah."

"Really?"

"Yeah," he looked at her. "In fact, let's do that again," he grinned.

"Right. Okay. Yeah. But let's empty the kayaks first." She let go of the branch and steered her kayak toward the sandy section. Dylan followed. Once there, they pulled their heavy kayaks onto shore and got out, sitting heavily on the sand beside them.

"So I guess that's what the criss-crosses mean," Rev said.

"You think?"

Once they'd recovered, they unloaded their kayaks, then turned each one over. Water poured out. Most of it. Dylan lifted the front end of his kayak, but the water in the front end just ran down to the back end. So he lifted the back end. The water ran down to the front end.

"How—?"

"We need to bail. And we don't have a pail." She giggled.

"But we've got a can!" Dylan rummaged in his waterlogged bag for his can of spaghettios.

He pulled it out triumphantly. "Aha!"

It took a moment. "We don't have a can opener, do we," he said.

"We have a plastic knife," Rev said. "Wait a minute," she said then.

"How are we going to boil water to drink?"

"Well, I don't know about you, but I think I swallowed enough water to last me a couple days. That was fun, eh?"

"In a scared-shitless-kind-of-way, yeah," she replied. "Oh, oh!"

"Horschach?" Dylan looked around him.

"No, the cheesecake plate! We can bail, and heat water, in the foil pie plate thing the cheesecake was in. Good thing we ate it already, eh?"

"Well, if 'we' hadn't, I'm sure that wouldn't be much of a problem at this point."

"Well, let's—" she got up and surveyed their stuff. "Geez, did *everything* get wet?"

"It'll dry out. By the time we—we're staying here, right? We're setting up our tent and—"

"Oh yeah. We're staying here. We'll put an SOS in the sand and they can come fly us out."

Dylan considered that. "That'd be cool. Do you think they'd let us sit in the kayaks when they stork-lift them out?"

SO THEY HUNG CLOTHING ON TREE BRANCHES, unpacked other bits and pieces to dry on a nearby rock—and set up the tent.

"At least we don't have the door on the sand this time," Dylan commented when they were done.

"No. Still, it'd be better if it weren't on the top."

"Yeah. Well."

"I'll bail," Rev offered. "Do you want to do the fire thing?"

"Sure." Dylan set about finding small rocks to make a pit in the sand, then headed into the bush for sticks and, hopefully, a few larger chunks to burn.

After an hour or so, they were quite comfortable, sitting in dry clothes by their little fire. A pie plate of water was steaming, and

Dylan was reading the instructions on the astronaut meat and potatoes pouch, while munching on jelly beans. Rev was munching on nuts and raisins.

"Okay, so apparently when I pull the ripcord on this thing, it heats itself, and then it's edible."

"Well, let 'er rip!"

He did so. A puff of steam rose out of the pouch.

"It smells—actually, it smells like meat and potatoes," Dylan said. He held the pouch toward Rev for a sniff.

"It does." She pulled a spoon out of her bag and handed it to him. "Here."

He scooped out a spoonful of—brown paste. "You first," he held it toward Rev.

"Why me first?"

"Because you're the one with aspirations to become the Ship's Philosopher. On the Enterprise. You'll need to eat astronaut food," he spelled it out.

"Oh right. Okay." She took the spoon from his hand and tried it. "It's disgusting!" she grimaced. "Possibly the most disgusting thing I've ever tasted! Give me some of your jelly beans," she said, and quickly tossed back a handful.

Dylan then tried a spoonful of the 'meat and potatoes.'

"Well?" she said, chewing vigorously.

"Not great. But not disgusting." He considered further. "But not great. But I'm hungry," he said. "You want any more?"

"No, knock yourself out," she said.

"You know," she said a bit later, staring into the fire, "if I hadn't've still been a little stoned, it might've occurred to me."

"What?"

"That the easy way, the current, was *because* there were rapids up ahead."

"Yeah, well. The sound should've been a clue too. We both missed that."

"We're never going to make it back up, you know."

"We might not have to. We'll see where this river leads—being ever vigilant for increasing currents and rushing noises in the distance—"

"Or we could just look at the map." Rev had pulled the map out again. "Oh."

"What?"

"That's what the thick black line must mean."

"There was a thick black line on the map? To mark the waterfalls? And you didn't notice that? Was there a skull-and-bones too?"

"Hey, you said it was fun."

"Well," he grinned, "it was."

"Okay, so, if that's the rapids," Rev traced her finger along the river, "and that's the waterfalls, we're here—which means, yeah, it opens out onto a lake."

"Well that makes sense. Rivers do that, don't they. They flow into lakes. Any more criss-crosses or thick black lines on the way?"

"Nope. No skull-and-bones either."

"Okay, so tomorrow, or the next day, we head to the lake."

A LITTLE LATER, AS IT WAS NEARING DUSK, Rev got up and went into the forest to scrounge for another armful of firewood. Dylan poured a cooled pie plate of boiled water into one of their empty water bottles, scooped up another plateful from the river, and set it over the fire.

When she returned, he rolled and lit a joint.

"This is nice," she said, starting out at the water.

"It is. Very nice."

A few minutes later, there was a rustle at the far end of the stretch of sand. Dylan turned, then cried out happily, "Bob!"

“That’s not Bob, silly. It’s a bear.”

When her words reached her brain, a few seconds later, she scrambled to her feet. “It’s a bear!”

“Well it’s not going to—” the bear started walking toward them. “We just need to—” Dylan casually pulled a twig from the kindling pile, reached for one of their many bungee cords, put it across the fork of the stick, loaded a jelly bean—and fired.

The bear kept coming.

He loaded another jelly bean and fired.

“What the hell are you doing?” Rev cried.

“Trying to dissuade it. They’re not really dangerous.”

“The hell they’re not! It’s probably hungry and—it’s *not* dissuaded.” She picked up the can of spaghettios and whipped it at the bear.

It let out a high-pitched wail and put its paws to his nose. Then it stared at them in—disbelief—and ran off crying.

“My god! I think you broke its nose!”

“I know, I—”

“I supposed you used to play baseball as well?”

“No, if I did, my aim would’ve been better,” she moaned.

“I’d say your aim was pretty spot-on.”

She looked at him, horrified. “I didn’t *mean* to hit it in the nose! I meant to hit it in the shoulder or something. It was coming straight for you, and it looked like the jelly bean slingshot wasn’t going to do it. Who taught you that brilliant trick, by the way?”

“A bunch of drunken Indians.”

She snorted. “Figures.”

“Well I don’t think it’s coming back. Poor thing,” Dylan said. “It’s probably crying all the way to mom.”

“Quit it,” she said. Grinning. Sort of.

THEY STAYED THERE THE NEXT DAY as well, but the day after that, they decided to pack up and venture down the river. All their stuff had finally dried, except for their shoes.

Dylan insisted on hugging the shore, propelling himself hand over hand by grabbing at tree branches. Rev drifted freely in the middle and was soon much further ahead.

"Scream if you hear rapids," Dylan shouted to her. "Scream louder if you hear waterfalls."

After a short while, Rev shouted back to him, "The lake! We're at the lake!"

He paddled up beside her and took in the breath-taking view. "We are indeed," he said, awe-struck. The lake glittered. Absolutely glittered.

"Let's go that way," she said, nodding to her right. A small island was in the distance, across the sun-sparkled water.

"Okay."

"You're paddling too fast," Dylan cried out a little while later. "Slow down! Listen to the flowers, smell the birds!"

She grinned. And when she looked back, she saw that Dylan wasn't paddling at all. He'd adjusted his seat and was leaning back, his feet up on the front, paddle resting across his thighs. She followed suit.

"Look!" Rev whispered loudly a little while later, nodding toward shore. A deer had entered the water and started swimming.

"Cool," Dylan said softly They watched until it was about a third of the way across to the island.

"Wait a minute—isn't that—there's a little one with her," Rev cried. "And it's in trouble! Oh god—" she started powering toward the deer. Dylan followed. The baby deer went under. It bobbed back up. Rev paddled faster. It went under again. Mama tried to nudge it up, and it managed to struggle to the surface, but then it floundered again, bleating in distress. Mama circled, helplessly. Rev stood up and shot out of her kayak. Well, it was more of a topple, since the kayak slid out from under her as she pushed off, but as soon as she hit the water she started swimming. Hard. By the time the baby went under for the third time, she was there. She saw it, limp and lazily sinking, a couple feet below the surface. She managed to scoop it up and get its head out of the water. Dylan was there already right beside her, so she treaded water as best she could as she handed it up to him.

He gently took the baby, then screamed, "Look out!" as he saw Mama heading straight for her. Rev went under.

"Rev!!" Dylan screamed even as he held the baby deer up by its hind legs, water streaming out its nose.

"I'm here, I'm okay," she gasped as she came up on the other side of his kayak and held on.

Relief flashed across his face for just a moment before he went into rescue mode again, laying the baby across his backpack. It wasn't moving. He puffed into its muzzle, then laid his hand on its chest and started gently pressing. One, two, three...

"I think—" he blew into its muzzle again and resumed his gentle pressing. "Come on," he said encouragingly. He blew once more into its muzzle and it let out a wailing "Baanh." Dylan relaxed with joy—just as Mama hit the kayak.

"Shit! Now what?" He steadied the little fawn and grabbed the sides of the kayak.

"I don't know! If you put it back, it'll just—it's too little—"

Mama was in great distress, as she circled the kayak and rammed it again.

"What if we lay Baby across Mama's shoulders?"

"Well, we can try." As Mama approached the kayak again, Dylan lifted Baby out. He set it across the deer's powerful neck and shoulders as it swam alongside. But as soon as he let go, Baby slid off into the water. Rev grabbed it again, as it kicked weakly, and lifted it back up to Dylan.

"Baanh!"

Rev glanced then at Mama, heading her way, and dove under the kayak again to come up on the other side. Dylan set Baby on his backpack again.

"Start paddling!"

"Get in!"

"I can't. It'll take too long. I'm okay."

"All right—no wait—where should I go?" He looked to the shore they'd left. It was closest, so he started in that direction. Mama barreled toward him ready to ram.

"Okay not that way!" Rev called out.

"Got that." Dylan turned his kayak away from the shore.

Rev looked around as she treaded water. "The island—it's the closest shore—"

"Okay. Good." He started paddling. "No, wait. Are you sure you can swim that?"

"Yes! Go!" Dylan rummaged in his kayak and threw her his lifejacket. Then he started paddling for the island as quickly as he could.

Mama let out a scream.

"Dylan wait!" Rev called out, as she wrestled to put the lifejacket on. "Lay Baby across the back so Mama can see it."

"Good idea." He stopped paddling and carefully laid the baby deer across the back of the kayak. Mama swam close and saw that Baby was there. She let out, or breathed in, a big huff.

"Is it still okay?" Rev had swum up beside them.

"Breathing. Beating. I think so." He started paddling again.

"Careful," Rev said. "And slow. Let Mama keep up. She's tiring too."

So Dylan paddled carefully, slowly, toward the island. Mama kept pace behind, eyes on Baby. And Rev swam behind Mama.

After a while, seeing Mama get slower and slower, Rev called out, "She's really tired, Dylan. But I don't know what I can do. Think I can put my lifejacket on her?"

"Don't even try," Dylan yelled back. "You'll get a hoof in the head. It's several hundred pounds, Rev. It wouldn't make a difference anyway."

Rev swam closer to Mama then, trying to encourage it.

"If Baby cried once in a while—might give her the strength to keep going."

Dylan reached around and poked Baby.

"Dy-lan!!"

"Baanh."

Mama surged onward. But then quickly faded again. Its once powerful kicks were soon barely moving the water. Rev kept trying to encourage it, but about fifty feet from shore, she was near tears as Mama's shoulders and neck were now submerged. Its head was barely above water as it struggled to keep going, to not drown.

"Poke it again!" she yelled at Dylan. "Make the baby cry!" Then a moment later, "I can't believe I said that!"

Dylan reached behind and gave it a good poke.

"Baaaaanh."

He saw then how badly off Mama was and raced to the shore. Mama found one last ounce of adrenalin and pushed on after him.

Dylan's kayak touched ground. He quickly got out, lifted Baby off the kayak, and set it on land in clear view of Mama. It stood on unsteady legs. Mama floundered, but in a few moments got the sandy shore under her feet. Her knees buckled then and she collapsed in the shallow water. But her head was out of the water. Dylan helped Baby take the few steps across the sand to get to her. "Baanh." Mama groaned.

Rev waded onto shore, Dylan rushing to her side.

"You're okay?"

"Yes. No. Please don't die," she whispered, looking helplessly at Mama. They stood there, arms around each other.

After a few very long moments, Mama pushed to her knees then and started licking Baby. Baby toppled. Dylan approached and gently moved it so it was lying securely on land. Mama heaved herself a little closer to it, also getting securely on land. She let out a huge sigh. And closed her eyes.

"Please don't—" Rev repeated.

"She won't—look." Dylan pointed to her heaving chest. She was breathing. In and out. In and out.

"Baanh," Baby cried out after a few minutes. Mama opened its eyes and snorted weakly. After another minute, Rev and Dylan watched in amazement as Mama heaved herself to her feet. She nudged Baby, who also stood. The two of them swayed slightly, then stumbled off into the bush.

"Ah. Well. All's well that—" Dylan sat down heavily on the sand. Rev took off her lifejacket and sank onto the sand beside him.

"We did it!" she said. "*They* did it!"

"It still had its spots," Dylan said. "It was so tiny!"

"It was. She must've given birth just a few days ago. What the hell was she thinking, making that swim?" Rev's relief and joy flashed into anger.

"Maybe she didn't have a choice," Dylan said. "Wolves? Unlikely in the afternoon," he looked out at the still sunny day, "but—"

"Then where the hell was Dad!!" Rev shouted at Dylan.

"I don't know!" he shouted back. "Maybe he gave himself to the wolves so—"

"You're right," she said, deflating. "You're absolutely right."

They sat there for a while then, leaning on each other.

"We're staying here, right?" Dylan asked. "I mean it's only

afternoon, but—this is a nice place, right?"

"It is. Oh," she said then. "The tent's in my kayak." She looked out at the water and saw her kayak sitting serenely a couple hundred yards out.

"But I've got the sleeping bags. We don't need the tent."

"Yeah, but—it's calm now. And it's right there. Who knows where it'll be later—or in the morning."

"Good point."

"Besides, we don't want to wake up tomorrow morning to find the coast guard dredging the lake for my body."

"Another good point. Okay, I'm convinced. Go get it. I'm tired," he explained. "I've had an exciting day."

Rev burst out laughing. "*You're* tired? *I'm* the one who swam the whole way."

"Yeah, with a life jacket."

"But you just paddled. And not very fast," I might add.

"But I had extra weight. Must've been a whole twenty pounds," he laughed. "Okay, ten. At least."

He groaned as he got up. "God I hate this growing old shit," he said and headed for his kayak. Rev watched, happily, as he pushed off. She waited a minute then called out.

"You should take the life jacket."

"I'm not going to—"

"Just in case. You might hit some rapids. Or a waterfall." She grinned.

"Right." He kept paddling.

"You might fall overboard when you try to tie the kayaks together."

"Oh." He stopped. "I thought I'd just sort of nudge it to shore." He looked out at the floating kayak as if he might really do it that way, then sighed as he paddled back in to get the life jacket.

"I'll have camp set up by the time you're back," she called out.

"No you won't. Since I've got the sleeping bags and the tent is out there."

"Oh, right. Okay then I'll just—wait—here."

THE SUN WAS JUST ABOUT TO set when Dylan got back. They decided not to bother with the tent. Or a fire. They had a bit to eat and drink, then just lay in their sleeping bags on the sand and watched the sun set.

IN THE MORNING, STILL ASLEEP, Dylan felt a nudge.

"Go away it's too early," he mumbled. He was nudged again. He opened his eyes to see Mama standing over them. "Uh-oh." He nudged Rev.

"Go away it's too early," she mumbled. He nudged her again. She opened her eyes. My what big hooves you have.

"Either Baby didn't make it and Mama's here for revenge—"

"Baanh." They turned to see Baby standing unsteadily in the bushes.

"Or Baby *did* make it and Mama's here—for a ride?" he said incredulously.

Mama took a step backwards then and sat down.

"Okay…," Rev said. "I didn't know deer could sit like that. We're still stoned, aren't we?"

"No we were too tired to get stoned last night, remember? What with being old and all."

"Oh yeah."

"Well, let's get up. Slowly. Maybe she's just investigating, and they'll dart off as soon as we move. As deer do." They got up. Slowly. Which wasn't a problem for Rev.

They didn't dart off. As deer do. In fact, Mama pointedly looked in the direction of their kayaks.

"No," Dylan said in disbelief.

"Unbelievable."

"Well, maybe not," he changed his mind. "If Pipsqueak's not strong enough—" I named him Pipsqueak, he explained. "Just now. If Pipsqueak's not strong enough to make it here, he's not strong enough to make it back. Or anywhere else. And I guess there's not enough food here for them to stay until he's old enough to make it. What do deer eat, anyway?" he asked.

"Probably not jelly beans."

"Probably not."

"Okay, so how are we going to do this?" Rev asked.

"Can't we have a cup of coffee first? A swim?"

Mama snorted.

So they loaded their kayaks, which didn't take too long, seeing as they hadn't really unloaded them, and waded with them into the water.

"Okay, so maybe we should do it exactly like yesterday. So she knows, understands, doesn't get too stressed out."

"That's good. Okay, come here, Pipsqueak," Dylan said, squatting down and opening his arms.

"Baanh." Pipsqueak stayed put. Mama nudged it.

"I don't believe this," Rev whispered.

Pipsqueak leaned into Mama. It wasn't getting into Santa Claus' lap. No way. Uh-uh. Strange man.

"This isn't going to work," Dylan said, standing up.

"So, what, we start paddling, they start swimming, and we wait until Pip starts drowning again for him to understand that he's in trouble and should accept our help?"

Dylan shrugged. "What else can we do?"

"Hm," Rev said, considering. "Okay this time I'll start in the water. I'll swim along with them and, say, twenty feet out, let's just try to lift him into your kayak. As soon as he starts getting tired, but before he starts drowning."

"Okay. That might work," he said, pushing off. "No wait," he stopped. "Let's think this through a bit."

"Quickly, Mama's getting antsy."

"Well, where are we going? I mean once we get Pip in the kayak, where should I go?"

"I don't know. I kind of thought Mama would lead the way and you'd just follow her."

"Hm. Could do. Okay, so you're going to lift Pip up to me and I'm going to put him across the back—"

"Better across the front so Mama can see him when she turns around to check?"

"Okay...but he's not half unconscious today—I'm not at all sure that'll work. You'd better be ready for another rescue."

"Good point. Okay. She waded out into the water again."

"No wait. Can't you take your kayak with you this time? Tie it to your wrist or something this time so it doesn't drift away?"

"But then I won't be able to dive into the water. If I have to. To get Pip."

"Right. Okay what if you used a very long rope."

"Do we have a very long rope?"

They start rummaging in their kayaks. Mama pawed the ground impatiently.

"Here. Dylan held up a rope about fifteen feet long. It'll have to do."

Rev started tying it around her waist.

"And put your life jacket on."

"But then I won't—"

"Okay, tie it to the rope so you can reel it in or something."

"Yeah. That's good." She untied the rope, strung the lifejacket on it, then tied it around her waist again.

"Okay. All set."

"All set?" Dylan asked Mama. She snorted.

"I don't believe this," Rev said again.

Dylan got into his kayak and paddled out a bit. Mama entered the water and started swimming, with Pipsqueak right by her side. Rev got in behind them. They weren't doing too badly, but it was clear Pip wouldn't be able to make it too far. He had already fallen behind.

"Ready?" Rev said softly to Dylan.

"Ready," he rested his paddle across the kayak. Rev swam up to Pip, put her hands under him, and lifted him up to Dylan.

"Baanh."

Mama turned and started swimming toward Dylan's kayak as it drifted away while he tried to lay Pip across the front. Pip didn't want to lay down.

"Shh, it's okay," he tried to soothe Pip, but still couldn't get his legs to fold under him.

"Mama's concerned," Rev said, as she circled Dylan's kayak.

"I've got him sitting between my legs," Dylan said softly to Rev. "Where's Mama?" He turned to see Mama heading toward him. She pulled up alongside the kayak, managed to somehow reach over and nuzzle Pip, then, apparently satisfied, veered away.

"All right, where to?" Dylan said to her. But Mama kept circling.

"Mama isn't taking the lead," Dylan said.

"Maybe she wants to nudge you in the right direction."

"Well," Dylan looked around, "we don't have much choice. Either they go back to where they were yesterday," he nodded to that shore, "or they go across to the other side."

"Well they must've left that side for a reason. I'd say across to the other side?"

"But that's at least twice as far."

"Well, let's find out if that's where she wants to go."

Dylan started paddling to the far shore. Mama snorted and came barreling toward him.

"Okay, wrong way." He turned and started paddling toward the shore they'd left the night before. Mama eased off and followed.

After just a minute, Dylan called out softly to Rev, "Pip's getting distressed."

She could hear him bleating. "Stroke him between the eyes. Like Sue did with Pickle, remember?"

"Can't. I left my third arm at home. Dad said it would make me stand out," he added.

A second later, Rev saw him stop paddling. Pip's bleating calmed a bit.

"Did you stroke him?"

"I gave him a jelly bean. He seemed to like it."

Dylan started singing 'Rock-a-bye Baby.' Pip seemed to calm even more.

"Okay, now Mama's getting distressed," Rev called out. "I think she needs to hear Baby. Pip. Or see him. Can you paddle backwards? So she can see him?"

Dylan turned the kayak around and paddled backwards.

"Okay, you need to steer me," he said, zigzagging wildly until he got the hang of paddling backwards.

"No, Mama's steering you, remember?"

"Oh yeah." He looked at Mama, swimming behind him—or in front of him—a little to the right. He veered so she was directly behind him. Or in front of him.

"She looks like she's doing good," Dylan said.

"Yeah."

"So's Pip."

"Good."

"And you—why don't you put on the life jacket? I don't think Pip's going to need a rescue, and you're towing your kayak for pete's sake."

"Yeah. Remind me never to do this again." She reeled in the life jacket and put it on, the kayak jerking about as she did so.

They were about two-thirds of the way to the shore, and Mama had made only minor corrections in their path.

"Maybe that's where home is," Rev suggested, "and whatever made them leave—the danger has passed?"

"Maybe. She's still doing good, looks like, yeah?"

"Yeah. I'm glad we're almost there, but I don't think she's in danger of not making it."

"And how are you doing?"

"Fine. Lifejacket was a good idea. How's Pip doing?"

"Really good—actually I think he's about to curl up and take a nap." The kayak rocked back and forth a bit as Pip apparently did just that.

Mama suddenly snorted.

"She can't see him anymore," Rev said from the water.

Dylan poked him.

"Baanh."

"Good. Okay. Do that every now and then. And maybe go faster."

So Dylan paddled a bit faster, zigzagging a bit more, and kept singing 'Rock-a-bye-Baby,' stopping every now and then to give Pipsqueak a poke. Mama followed, or led, more or less okay with things. And Rev swam along in the rear, towing her kayak.

"You could probably just get in your kayak," Dylan suggested.

"No," Rev said, having clearly already considered the idea, "I don't think I could."

"Oh. Right. Okay."

Another ten minutes, and they were there. Dylan nudged his kayak gently onto the shore, then waited a minute for both Rev and Mama.

Rev held his kayak steady as he got out, carefully, then Mama supervised as he gently lifted Pipsqueak onto the beach. She nuzzled him. He bleated and wagged his tail—Dylan and Rev looked at each other in amazement—and then they took off into the bush.

"Did you see—"

"It actually wagged its tail?"

"Well, it was happy," Dylan said.

"Well. So am I."

"Are you going to wag your tail?"

"I can't even wag my arms." She took off the life jacket. Had some difficulty doing so, what with having turned to cement.

Dylan tried to help, but really just made it worse. "Sorry, my backwards muscles as well as my forward muscles are toast."

"Toast. Do we have any toast? I'm really hungry."

"Here." He pulled the bag of jellybeans out of his pocket. "Pip ate all the red ones though."

"So now what?" Rev said after a bit. She and Dylan were lying on the sand exactly where they had sat down.

"I'm inclined to stay right here," Dylan said. "For the rest of the week."

"Okay," Rev agreed.

"You know we might have just saved Pip for a death much worse than drowning," Dylan said after a long silence.

"You think they took to the water to get away from wolves?"

"What else?"

"Why can't we all just get along," she muttered.

"Because Daddy Wolf had three kids to support," Dylan suggested.

"Well he should've thought about what exactly he'd have to do to feed them before—" she broke off with a chuckle.

EXHAUSTED, THEY SPENT THE REST OF THE DAY in a leisurely fashion.

Mostly getting stoned.

"We don't have any Doritos, do we," Rev said.

"We might," Dylan exhaled. "We still have a few packets of mystery astronaut food. One of them could be Doritos."

"Well let's find out." She took the proffered joint, inhaled, gave it back, then crawled into the tent. After a while—quite a while—she came out with a couple packets.

"You got lost in there, didn't you."

"Oh shut up."

She pulled the ripcord on one of the packets, and dipped her spoon into it.

"Well?"

"Not Doritos."

He took the other packet and ripped it open.

"Well?"

"Hm." He licked the spoon thoughtfully. "This is—spinach, mustard, and—shortbread cookies. Is that—possible?"

"Let me see." She dipped her spoon into his packet and gave it a try.

"Wow. You're right about the spinach and mustard. But I'd say," she took another spoonful, "arrowroot cookies."

"Hm. But not Doritos."

"No, alas, not Doritos. "

NEAR DUSK, THEY HEARD BEAVERS slapping their tails and loons calling.

"And you hear this every night? At your cabin on a lake in the forest?"

"Yeah. Well, no, not anymore. The weekenders and summer people consider it party time, remember? Or a never-ending home improvement project. So between the lawn mowers, and the whipper snippers, and the nail guns, and the chain saws, and the motor boats, and the kids screaming—did I have a point?"

"You always have a point. You're a very pointy person."

"And you're a very—jello person."

He giggled. "Lime jello?"

"Lime jello."

"But sometimes red jello?"

"Sometimes red jello."

"Okay," he leaned back happily.

"SO WE SHOULD PROBABLY FIGURE OUT how we're going to get back," Rev said a little later.

"Yeah. Good thing we got the map, eh?" He grinned.

"Good thing," she grinned back and crawled into the tent to get the map. After a long while, she came back out.

"You got lost in there again, didn't you."

"Shut up."

"Okay," she studied the map for a very long time. Then turned it the other way around.

Dylan burst out giggling.

"Okay," she studied the map for another very long time. "I think we're here."

"I *know* we're here." He giggled.

"Which means we either go back the way we came—"

"Or we go another way."

"Right. Good." She nodded at him, impressed. Then she studied the map again. "One other way, which is not the way we came, is we take the portage at the other end of the lake, which looks like it leads to the lake we started from—which *is* the way we came." She looked at Dylan with great confusion. "How can that be?"

"Maybe when you smashed the dilithium thing, you warped space just a little bit."

"Or maybe your Dad's trying to get you home."

"You think?" he said eagerly.

"No."

"You're cruel. Pointy and cruel." He sulked for a minute.

"Maybe it's a miracle," he giggled.

She snorted.

"Okay," he said a while later," so how long is this portage? At the other end of the lake?"

"Three inches."

"Right."

"Oh, oh!"

"Where?" Dylan looked—up.

"Or we take the trail!" Rev said excitedly. "On the other side of the island which leads to a parking lot."

"There's a trail from the island to a parking lot? How can *that* be?"

"It's not on the other side of the island, it's on the not island part that's on the other side of the island."

"Perspicuity," Dylan said. And giggled.

"And how long is this trail?" he asked. "The one that's on the not island part on the other side of the island."

"Half an inch."

"Hm. Any criss-crosses on it?"

"Well there wouldn't be—let me check. No."

"Any thick black lines?"

She looked at the map again. "No."

"And any skull-and-bones?"

"No."

"And once we get to the parking lot?" Dylan said. "What do we do then?"

"Hm. Good point. It's hard to paddle a kayak in a parking lot."

"You've tried?"

"Well, no but—you want to try?"

"Well, no but—"

"We could hitch-hike back to where we left the car, drive back to the parking lot, load the kayaks onto the car, drive back to—" she was losing it, "and return them."

"Does your car have a roof rack on it?" he asked.

"No. I was thinking they might just—stick there."

"Hm. Actually, they might do."

"Or," she had a brilliant idea, "we could call the outfitters place and ask them to come get their kayaks in their kayak-carrying pick-up truck! We could tell them we're old—"

"And ask them to come get us as well!"

"That would work."

"Do you know their number?" Dylan asked.

"No. Do you?"

"No. We didn't put it on our little ID things."

"Do you still have your ID thing?" Rev asked.

"No."

"So it's a good thing we didn't put their number on it. 'Cuz then we wouldn't have their number."

"But we don't have their number now."

"Right. How did that work?"

AS THE GUYS UNLOADED THEIR KAYAKS, Dylan and Rev put their stuff back into their car, then headed to the outfitter's office to do the paperwork.

"Hey look," Dylan stopped in front of the bulletin board at the door. A sheet of paper was tacked onto the bulletin board. It had a photograph of a bear with his nose all bandaged up.

"Billy the Bear broke his nose," he grinned at Rev.

"Yeah," one of the guys said, coming in behind them, "Billy came out of the forest one afternoon, crying and holding his nose."

"Billy?" Rev said.

"Yeah, Billy's a bit of a mascot. We've known him since he was just a baby. His dad took off," Rev slouched with guilty remorse, "then his mom got killed," she winced, "and all the other bears made fun of him because he was such a little runt—"

"Oh please," she said then.

The guy looked at her. Intently.

"He's just a bear," she said by way of explanation.

"Bears have feelings too," the guy said. "Anyway, people started feeding him, and—generally we discourage that, but he was so cute, and we really didn't think he'd become a danger—I mean he was almost—he'd never learned how to survive in the wild, so there was no reason to think he'd ever—anyway so he showed up one day, I don't know, four or five days ago?" he called out to the other guy.

"Yeah, sounds about right."

"Poor Billy was wailing away as he came up to the shop, he knows Greg and me, and it turns out the poor little tyke's got a broken nose."

"The poor little tyke's got a broken nose," Dylan said to Rev.

"Bit of a puzzle really. Can't really imagine him running full tilt into a tree or anything—"

"But he's okay?" Rev managed to say.

"Oh sure. We took him to a vet and got him all bandaged up. But the little guy looked so cute, we had to take a picture of him."

"The little guy looked so cute," Dylan said to Rev. "Poor little Billy the Bear—"

"Oh shut up."

WHEN THEY GOT BACK TO DIM'S PLACE, they discovered that their trial wasn't going to take place in the little town of their transgression or even in the city closest to that little town, but in Ottawa.

"Ottawa?" Rev said as they gathered around the kitchen table.

"Yeah. Hey do you guys want a Pepsi or something?" Dim stood in front of his open fridge. "Are you hungry? I can make a couple sandwiches."

"Actually, a Pepsi and a sandwich would be good," Dylan said.

"So good," Rev said.

Dim looked at them. "You guys've been living off nuts and seeds for the past week, haven't you. Okay, so," he put a huge bottle of Pepsi on the table, and a couple glasses, then set about making sandwiches and coffee. "Okay, so the judge got a change of venue."

"But—Ottawa?"

"Well, it's a big thing, striking down the blasphemy law once and for all. And he wants it to be noticed."

"But he can't actually strike down the law, can he?" Dylan asked. "I mean, he doesn't have that power, does he?"

"No, but if he makes it look as ridiculous as he hopes to, that might be only one step away. Someone somewhere will file the—or propose the—I don't actually know what the process is exactly—"

"You don't know how laws get changed?"

"No."

"But you're a lawyer."

"Right. Lawyers can't do anything to get laws changed, so—"

"But you are. I mean, isn't that why you took on this case?"

"Well, no, not really," he said casually, but then when he turned from the counter, he saw Rev's face. "Yes! That *is* why I took this case!"

"You know," Dylan said, "we never actually talked about your fee."

"Yeah—um—well I usually charge around $300 an hour."

"Right. And how many hours have you spent so far on the case?"

"Well, none really."

Dylan and Rev turned to stare at him.

"Sliced ham okay? You want ketchup?" Dim asked.

"You haven't spent any time on the case so far?"

"Well," he began to see the problem, "there were those phone calls to the judge. Ten minutes, maybe." He just didn't see the solution. "I don't have to prepare a defence, remember?" He finished lamely. Which was about the way he began. "The judge tried to get the venue changed to Washington, but—"

"Washington's in the States," Dylan said.

"Yeah. He found that out."

Dylan and Rev stared at him.

"Just kidding," he sort of choked on his laugh.

"About the judge not knowing Washington was in the States or about the judge seeking a Washington venue."

"The first. He *did* seek a Washington venue, but just to make a point and to get the media's interest from the get go. He called the *Post*—"

"Which is in Toronto—"

"Yeah," they were all sitting at the table now, munching on their sandwiches and a big bag of potato chips Dim had set out. "But it's the paper everyone reads. So that's where we want coverage. So the Judge called the *Post* and told them about the case and said he was going to seek a venue in Washington because they were bigger idiots than us when it came to religious beliefs—"

"And billboards advertising same—"

"Especially in connection to abortion—"

"And the *Post* guy laughed his head off, but of course wrote up a little piece and now everyone knows about the trial."

"Cool," Dylan said, smiling at Rev. "So how long will we have to stay in Ottawa?"

"Oh, probably just a day'll do it. You plead guilty, the judge finds you guilty, end of story."

"I thought we were pleading innocent."

Dim paused as he refreshed their glasses. "Oh yeah."

"Don't you think," Rev said, "that as our lawyer you should be clear about our plea?"

"Well, yeah," he had the good grace to be a bit embarrassed, "it's just that it wouldn't really make a difference what you plea. Either way the judge's going to find you guilty and—he just wants a plea of innocence to draw the trial out and make his judgment more—noteworthy."

"Right. We're being theatre," Dylan said. He turned to Rev, "We should get costumes!"

"So, what," Rev ignored him, "a couple days?"

"Well," Dim thought, "actually, now that I think about it, since you *are* pleading innocent, we'll have to hear the case in full—better count on a week."

"A week?" Rev said. "We can't afford a hotel in Ottawa for a week. *And* your three hundred."

"Oh, the judge is paying for your room."

"Isn't that sort of a conflict of interest?"

Dim snorted. "It's Ottawa."

Rev stared at him blankly.

"Who's going to notice?" he said by way of explanation.

"Good point," Dylan said.

"Okay, so," Rev was processing it all, "this finding us guilty—you said the judge was going to suspend the sentence, right?"

"Right. At the critical moment, I pop up and ask that the sentence be suspended and the judgment be stricken from the record."

"So we won't even have a criminal record," Dylan smiled at Rev.

"Can he do that? Just strike it from the record?"

"I guess."

"On what grounds?"

"On the grounds that he's the judge?" Dim suggested.

"No, I mean on what grounds are you going to ask that the sentence be suspended and the judgment stricken from the record?"

"Oh. 'Extenuating circumstances.'" He apparently relished the phrase.

"What extenuating circumstances, exactly?"

"What do you mean?"

"What circumstances do you consider to be extenuating?"

"Oh I don't know. It just sounds good. 'Extenuating circumstances.' Everybody accepts extenuating circumstances as—an excuse."

"Right."

"What I don't get," Dylan spoke up, "is how he's going to find us guilty."

"Well, if blasphemy is defined as anything that challenges religious beliefs, and *The Bible* itself does so—'Blessed are those who dasheth their babies' brains against the stone' sort of challenges the notion of God as all-good and all-loving—then *The Bible* itself challenges religious beliefs, so you've got religion challenging itself, so the blasphemy law becomes internally inconsistent."

"Yeah, I get all that—and it's good to see you do too—" Rev grinned to herself as Dylan continued, "but what I meant was how will he find *us* guilty of blasphemy? They haven't got any proof that *we* put the quote on the billboard. Do they?"

"Hm. That'd be Kurt's responsibility. He's the prosecuting attorney."

"But shouldn't you know what his case is so you can present a defence?"

"No," Dim said. "I'm not defending you, remember?"

"But you're our lawyer—"

"But if I defend you, I might succeed—" Rev stifled a snort, "and the whole point is that you're found guilty. So if I make a case that you're innocent—"

"Got it," Dylan said.

"Which is why I haven't spent any time on the case," he finished somewhat sulkily.

So THE NEXT DAY, they made the drive to Ottawa. Sue decided she'd come along for a bit of a holiday, seeing as that's what Dim was apparently planning, so they took both cars.

"The Ritz?" Rev said as they pulled into the parking lot of the hotel Dim had given them directions to. "Is this the message we want to send?"

"What, atheists have to be poor?"

"Well, no, but—I don't know. If we want to change people's minds—people don't like rich people."

As soon as their car had come to a stop, an armada of uniformed hotel employees descended upon it.

"You know, by the time we tip everyone we're expected to tip, it'll probably cost us more than if we stayed at a motel on our own dime," Dylan commented. They didn't open their car doors just yet.

"Not a problem," Rev said. "I don't tip."

"You don't tip? But—"

"It just encourages—it justifies the employer not paying a decent wage. And it makes trained seals out of the customer service people," she opened her window. "Aarf! Aarf!" she said to the bellboy. "And how demeaning is that?"

"What, barking at the bellboys?"

"No, calling them bellboys."

"But—"

"They're men, for god's sake. Adults. And *bell*boys. Like they're supposed to hop to it when they hear a bell?"

"Maybe that's why they're also called bell*hops*," Dylan grinned.

They continued to sit in their car trying to decide what to do as the service people milled about making gestures. After a while, rude gestures.

"That one's certainly not getting a tip," Rev said.

"When you don't give a tip," Dylan tried again, "they assume it's because you think they don't deserve one. Or you're walking away without paying for what you got. So of course they're going to—do shit like that," he nodded to the most enthusiastic bellboy.

"If you're not going to tip," Dylan continued, "you should at least give them a little card or something, explaining that you're boycotting tipping so they'll get paid enough not to need to kiss your ass."

"That one's not kissing my ass."

"No," Dylan looked out the window, and winced, "I don't suppose he is. *And* you should send a letter to their boss also explaining. Otherwise—"

"Otherwise I'm tilting at windmills."

"Well, I wouldn't call it tilting. Ramming is more like—what you've been doing—your whole life—sort of—" he cringed, anticipating the jab. That he got.

"Okay," Rev said, "so we either go somewhere else or we stay here, don't tip, get up to our room, then make up a bunch of cards to pass out."

"We could even call room service for the supplies we'll need," Dylan grinned.

"Could you pass me the Red Violet?" Dylan asked, as they were spread out on the bed with a bunch of little cards and a box of Crayola crayons. The big 64-er box.

Rev took another toke and passed him the Red Violet. She was working with the Blue Green.

"Are we going to write the letter to the CEO in crayon too?" Rev asked. "Might stand a better chance of him being able to understand it," she added.

"Hm..." Dylan was concentrating.

"Okay, so do we have a message that fits yet?" Rev tossed her Blue Green attempt into the pile of once-blank business cards filled with incomplete sentences.

"How's this?" Dylan held up the card he'd just finished, 'Boycott Tipping—Increase Wages' printed on it in Red Violet.

"But doesn't that sound like we're asking *them* to boycott tipping?"

"Right. Okay, hand me the Periwinkle."

"You think Periwinkle will do it? When Red Violet didn't?"

"Well I'll change the words too."

"Oh. Okay. That might work." She handed him the Periwinkle. And then the joint. He'd need both, she was sure.

An inordinately long time later, Dylan held up his Periwinkled card, exhaling at the same time. "'Boycott Tipping to Increase Wages' Whaddya think?"

"You just added a word. One word."

"But the word I added was 'to.' 'To' is a very important word. It's way different from 'from.' For instance."

Rev looked at him suspiciously. She wasn't buying it.

"It's got homonyms," he boasted. "'Two' and 'too.' Which means it's got *two* homonyms. 'To' has two homonyms," he added, just in case she wasn't getting it. She wasn't.

"Yeah but does it have any cinnamons?"

Dylan had no answer to that question.

"Try the Cerise," Rev suggested.

Dylan took the Cerise crayon out of the box. He started humming 'I'm a Little Teapot.' Rev smiled. At the 64 colors in the Crayola box.

When he got to the end of the song, for the third time, he held up his Cerised card: 'TIPPING BOYCOTT to increase wages.'

"Ooh, nice use of capital letters."

"Yes, and note that it's on a line all by itself—like a title. Then the rest is on a separate line. Like an explanation."

"You've really thought this through."

"Don't have two degrees for nothing, do I."

"Well, yes, you do. But—"

There was a knock on their door.

"That'll be our pizza," Rev said, as she got up. Then she turned back to Dylan. "What if he hits me? When I don't tip him?"

"Here," he said, shoving their pile of discards at her, "give him all the discards. The dis-cards," he giggled. " They're the cards we dissed. Diss-cards. Miss-demeanor. Perspicuity," he said then and giggled again. "And close the door real fast," he remembered what was going on.

"The door *is* closed." She was suddenly puzzled. Well, not suddenly. But puzzled nevertheless.

There was another knock on the door.

"Oh yeah." She too remembered then what was going on. "Why don't you do it?" she suggested.

"It's your idea."

"Is not."

"Is so."

"Is not."

When she finally opened the door, the bellboy was gone and their pizza was sitting elegantly on a little serving table.

"THIS IS REALLY PATHETIC PIZZA," Rev said as she picked up her fourth slice.

"It's designer pizza. Probably cost $50."

"Really?" Then she added, "I hope the judge is paying our *whole* bill."

"We could order out."

"Do we know how to do that?"

"We did it in Montreal all the time," Dylan said.

"Oh yeah. But the phone there didn't need a nine."

"We could use our cell phones."

"Would we get service in here?" Rev asked.

"We just did."

"Not room service, silly, cellphone service."

"You want to call a bellboy to make a phone call for you?"

"No. He'll hit me for sure. Let's go out. There's gotta be a pizza place near here."

"Okay. We can get Doritos and cinnamon buns too."

So they put on their jackets and made sure they had their hotel room key. Rev put her hand on the door knob.

"Wait!" Dylan said. "We don't know where we live!"

"Good one! Okay, write down the room number."

Dylan got a piece of paper and a pen. "Okay, what is our room number?" Rev read it off the key she put back in her pocket.

"Okay, ready," he said, putting the piece of paper in his pocket. Rev opened the door.

"Woh," she said, when she saw the hallway full of doors. "We're never getting out of here." When she turned to Dylan, she saw that the hallway in the other direction was also full of doors. "My god!" she jumped back.

"We could leave a trail of jelly beans."

"I thought we finished the jelly beans."

"We did. Maybe there's something in the room. Don't they leave mints?"

They went back into the room and found two mints on the little table.

"We can't really make a good trail with two."

"Two might be enough for to, but not for from."

"Isn't it the same?"

"How can it be? To and from are completely opposite."

"And yet—they *are* the same. Isn't that interesting." She sat down to figure it out. Dylan joined her.

After a while he said, "What if we crumble them up and sprinkle mint dust to mark our way?"

"We might end up in Kansas."

"That would be bad?"

"Well, given the extenuating circumstances."

"Oh yeah. Good thing the judge didn't get the venue changed to Kansas."

SO THE NEXT DAY, Dim met Rev and Dylan at the courthouse. Sue was off shopping. For horse things.

"Bet you they don't have dartboards in their holding cells here in Ottawa," Rev said, taking in the grandeur of the courthouse.

"Probably that's a good thing. This is Ottawa."

"Right."

They walked through the halls looking for their courtroom. They should have just followed the crowd. People were streaming past all the rooms in the main corridor, turning right at the end, walking right past Rooms 110, 111, and 112—well, not quite past 112, since 113 was already full to the max and the overflow packed the hall in both directions. Dim, Rev, and Dylan eased their way past a great number of reporters and camera people, past an even greater number of sign-carrying people, and past a few homeless people sensing an uninterrupted six hours of sleep in the back of the room.

"'Keep Christ in Christmas'?" Dylan read aloud. "Must've brought the wrong sign."

"'The multitude shall stone they that blasphemeth, Leviticus 24:16,'" Rev read another sign. "Not that guy."

"Wow." Dylan turned to Dim. "Are we going to need security to get out of here alive?"

"Oh, they're not serious," Dim laughed.

Dylan looked at him. "You were jacking off during grade ten History too, weren't you."

"Yeah," Dim laughed. Then stopped short. "We'll grab one of the uniforms when we leave."

"Hey, look," Rev pointed to a cluster of sign-carrying people off to one side.

"'God is no respecter of persons, Acts 10:34.'"

"'The congregation shall stone him who gathers sticks on Sunday, Numbers 15.'"

"'Thou shalt eat the fruit of thine own body, Deut. 28:53.'"

"Ah. Those must be the ones who've actually read *The Bible*."

Once they reached the front of the room, they took a seat at the defence table. Which was a bit ironic.

A few moments later, Kurt, the prosecuting attorney, walked in. Not one, not two, but three assistants trailed behind. The first one was wrestling with a huge pile of files and books. The second was wrestling with an even huger piles of files and books. The third was efficiently pulling a cart neatly piled with even more files and books. He was clearly the gifted one. The four of them crowded their table.

After a few minutes, the clerk announced, "All rise" and the judge walked in.

Rev and Dylan looked at each other in disbelief. The judge was Johnny Fever. From *W.K.R.P.* They both started grinning, but then Rev had a thought. About Magnum P.I. singing showtunes.

She turned to Dim. "You're sure the judge is on our side? He does intend to strike down the blasphemy law."

"Well, that's what he told me."

"And you just believed him?"

"Well, he's a judge—he wouldn't—"

"I'm calling Alan Shore," Rev pulled out her glow-in-the-dark cellphone. Which was, appropriately enough, glowing.

"But he's just a character."

Rev nodded to the rest of the court.

"Point taken. But he's just a make-believe lawyer."

"Well a make-believe lawyer will do a better job at this point than—"

"BUT WE DON'T WANT A BETTER JOB. We want to be found guilty, remember?"

"Oh yeah." She put her phone back in her pocket.

"Will the defendants please stand?" the clerk said.

Dylan and Rev stood.

"Please state your names for the record."

"Dylan O'Toole."

"Chris Reveille."

"You are hereby charged with one count of blasphemous libel, Section 296 Subsection 1 of the Canadian Criminal Code. How do you plead?"

"Innocent."

"You may be seated."

They sat back down.

"Shouldn't you have stood with us?" Rev whispered to Dim.

"What? Oh. No, I'm not the one who—yeah, I guess so. But if you get two years, I'm not going to jail with you," he grinned.

"Two years?" It was louder than a whisper.

"Well, that's the maximum—"

"TWO YEARS??" Considerably louder than a whisper. "But I thought—"

"Well, yeah. Just saying."

"Now the interesting thing," the judge was speaking, "is that although blasphemous libel is still a crime in Canada, there is no definition of blasphemy in the Criminal Code. However, there is no shortage of definitions in other countries, and I found a good one in The General Laws of Massachusetts."

"Did he say Massa*chu*setts?" Rev whispered to Dylan? "That's it. I'm definitely calling Alan Shore." She pulled out her cellphone again.

"Note, however," the judge looked out at the many reporters, "that Massachusetts is not a country. It's a state. In the United States of America. That's a country. And it's not our country."

"You don't know his number," Dylan whispered to Rev.

"No, I don't." She put her cellphone back in her pocket.

"'Whoever wilfully blasphemes the holy name of God by denying, cursing or contumeliously reproaching God, his creation, government or final judging of the world, or by cursing or contumeliously reproaching Jesus Christ or the Holy Ghost, or by cursing or contumeliously reproaching or exposing to contempt and ridicule, the holy word of God contained in the holy scriptures—' Did you get that?" The judge grinned devilishly at the media.

"Contumeliously," Dylan said. And giggled.

"Here's another one. It's much shorter. But it doesn't use the word contumeliously," he grinned at Dylan. Who grinned back. "'If it excites contempt or hatred against God, Jesus Christ, *The Bible*, *The Book of Common Prayer*, or the Church, it's blasphemy.' That's from Byrne.

"And here's an even better one. From Bouvier. It'll serve us excellently. Blasphemy 'attributes to God that which is contrary to His nature and does not belong to Him and denies what does.'

"Now is there anyone in the court—and I include everyone—" he looked at the combustible half of the sign-carrying audience—"who does not accept that definition? We're all good with that?"

There was some sporadic nodding. And praising the Lord.

"Okay, I just want to be sure. All right Kurt, you're up. What have you got? On what grounds should I find Ms. Reveille and Mr. O'Toole guilty?" The judge sat back, prepared to listen to the prosecuting attorney's sure-to-be-lengthy address.

The prosecuting attorney stood up, straightened his tie, cleared his throat, then said, "Because no one else did it."

"That's your case?" Rev turned to him and said in disbelief. "They did it—because no one else did?"

"How do you know no one else did it?" the judge asked.

"Well, sir, we have twenty witnesses—" he turned to face the crammed courtroom—"to attest to the fact that this is what the billboard looked like at 7:00 p.m. Tuesday, August 2." He keyed his laptop and a picture appeared on the screen at the side of the court. It was a picture of the billboard—before.

"Ooh," the court said.

"And we have twenty witnesses—" he turned to face the courtroom again—the same twenty people, it seemed—"to attest to the fact that this is what the billboard looked like at 7:00 a.m. Wednesday, August 3." He keyed his laptop again.

"Aah," the court said.

The Judge smiled. At Rev and Dylan. "That just proves that *someone* did it," he said.

"Yes, sir, but that's prerequisite. If I may continue—"

"Please do."

Was that sarcasm?

"The local police happened to be doing radar surveillance of that stretch of highway that night. Only two vehicles appeared."

"Wait a minute," the judge interrupted. "The police were monitoring a stretch of highway all night long that had only two cars on it? All night long?"

"Yes sir. The first car has license plates matching those of the defendants."

"But that just makes a 50-50 chance we did it," Rev couldn't help saying.

"And the other car is licensed to a Reverend Daniel Ellis."

"Of course," Rev couldn't help saying.

"Now Reverend Daniel Ellis is responsible for putting up the billboard in the first place."

"Of course," Dylan helped her out.

"And we have twenty people who can attest to that. They had a prayer meeting at the site when the board went up. The Reverend himself put the finishing touches on it. So it is unlikely that he himself would deface it."

"Counsel?" the judge looked at Dim. "Your turn."

"Oh, um," Dim got to his feet, "okay, um, so—oh! oh! If they were praying, they probably had their eyes closed! So they wouldn't've actually *seen* this Ellis guy put the billboard up."

"And the radar evidence?" the judge asked.

"Oh. Right." Dim sat back down.

"Plus," Kurt spoke up, "there's the other matter."

"The other matter?" the judge asked.

"An almost-empty can of spray paint containing paint matching the defacement of the billboard was found in the car of Ms. Reville and Mr. O'Toole."

Rev and Dylan looked at each other. Oops.

"We know the paint matches because we had the lab test it." He sounded smug.

"And fingerprints?"

"We assume the fingerprints on the can are those of Ms. Reveille or Mr. O'Toole."

"Ah. You assume. Well then."

Okay, that was definitely sarcasm.

The judge looked pointedly at Dim and waited.

"Oh! Oh!" Dim finally jumped to his feet. "Then you don't know, do you? And you don't know because you didn't take their fingerprints at the time of the arrest!" he said triumphantly.

"No, but we can take them now, can't we?" Kurt asked the judge.

"Well, we could, but really, that would simply prove mischief. You agreed to have that charge dropped. Remember?"

"Oh yeah," Kurt said.

"Oh yeah," the judge echoed. "I think it's time for recess. *A* recess, I mean." He stood up.

"All rise," the clerk's voice boomed with authority. All rose and the judge left.

AS SOON AS REV AND DYLAN STOOD UP, they were mobbed by the media.

"Is it fair to say you don't believe in God?"

"Don't you believe in freedom of religion? Freedom of speech?"

"Are you in favour of dashing babies' brains out against the stone?"

They decided to sit back down.

"ALL RIGHT, DIM," THE JUDGE SAID, "it's your turn. What's your defence?"

"Nothing, Your Honour," he called out. Cheerfully.

"All right then," the judge said, smiling. Just a little. "Seeing as Kurt and his assistants didn't do their job..."—each had the good sense to wither, except for the third one, who remained perky and inordinately pleased with himself—okay, so maybe he wasn't gifted—"What Mr. O'Toole and Ms. Reveille wrote on the billboard was most certainly blasphemy. It *does* excite contempt or hatred against God, Jesus Christ, and *The Bible*. And if it doesn't, why the hell not? People who bash babies' brains out are *blessed*?

"I like to wander among those who attend my court," he continued. "Mr. Denner, would you please step forward? You can begin our parade of sinners."

A man walked to the front of the court, carrying a sign that said 'The Lord told Nebuchadnezzar that he'd conquer Tyre. He didn't. Alexander the Great did.'

"And Ms. Ranier."

A woman walked to the front of the court. Her sign said 'It is impossible for God to lie. Hebrews 6:18.'

"Mr. Mason."

'Behold, here is my daughter a maiden ... do with them what seemeth good unto you. Judges 19:24-5.'

"Ms. Peabody, if you will."

'God is all-forgiving. And apparently sending us straight to Hell.'

"And Mr. Morrow."

'And David said unto all the congregation of Israel, if it seem good to you and that it be of the Lord our God, let us send abroad unto our brethren everywhere, that are left in all the land of Israel, and with them also to the priests and Levites which are in their cities and suburbs, that they may gather themselves unto us. I Chronicles 13.'

"All of this is blasphemy. They all 'attribute to God that which is contrary to His nature or deny what is His nature.' The first one calls into question his omniscience, the next one, his omnipotence, the next, his morality, and the next, his logic." The judge paused a moment as he looked again at the last one. "I don't know what the hell that last one is saying." Mr. Morrow shrugged. Cheerfully. "And they're all from *The Bible*." Several people in the court were busy flipping through their bibles.

"So you see? *The Bible* is *full* of blasphemy. Soundbite!" Several reporters stood straighter—some woke up—and got their pens ready. "*The Bible is full of blasphemy.*" The judge waited a moment. "Which is a good reason—a really, really good reason—to reject *The Bible*, as a book of—" he waved vaguely, "anything worthwhile. Or a good reason to reject once and for all the blasphemy law. Or both.

"To the matter at hand," he resumed after a moment, "there can be no doubt that Ms. Reveille and Mr. O'Toole are guilty of blasphemy." He looked pointedly at Dim. Who wasn't paying attention.

Rev jabbed him so hard he almost fell off his chair.

"Oh! Oh!" Dim popped up. "Your Honour, I ask that the sentence be suspended and the judgment stricken from the record."

"On what grounds?"

"On the grounds of extenuating circumstances," he said proudly.

"All right," the judge said agreeably and pounded his gavel.

"All rise," the clerk said.

THE ROOM ERUPTED. As the judge tried to make his way to Dylan and Rev—he was going to ask if they wanted to join him for a beer—he was swarmed by media.

"Do you believe in God?"

"I believe people who ask stupid questions won't go heaven when they die."

"Do you think the Supreme Court was listening?"

"Well, if not, I've made arrangements to send them the transcript."

Rev and Dylan were being swarmed as well.

"Good for you," one man reached out just to shake their hands.

"'Bout time!" another person congratulated them.

"My prayers are with you both—God forgives all sinners!" A church lady with scarlet lipstick reached out a gentle hand.

"You will rot in hell BITCH!!" A man practically spit on them.

"Him too?" Rev asked the church lady.

"Well—" she looked doubtful for just a moment, then glazed over in a beatific smile. "God forgives all sinners!"

"Hello, my name is Phil Brightson," a man pushed his way toward them, "and I'm a member of an atheist alliance group. Would you be interested in a speaking tour? We book at all the Bible colleges."

"The Bible colleges book you?" Dylan was understandably surprised.

"Well," he tried to lead them away from the fray, "we call the series 'Bible Enlightenment.' They don't get past the title."

"Ah."

"I don't know," Rev said, "I'm not much into preparing lectures anymore."

"Oh don't be silly," the man replied. "They usually start throwing things at us after the first two sentences. So that's all you'd have to prepare."

"Excuse me," a woman pushed out of the madness to approach them. "I've just gotten approval from my acquisitions editor," she was putting her cellphone away, "would the pair of you be interested in writing a book about this whole experience?"

"A book?" Rev said. Dully. "You're offering to publish a book if I write it?"

"Well, makes more sense that way. I mean, it'd be stupid to offer to publish a book if you didn't write it," she grinned.

"Do you think you can get us a movie deal too?" Dylan was joking.

"Excellent idea!" The woman pulled out her cellphone again and started dialing enthusiastically.

"Call me tomorrow," Phil gave them his business card, before he got jostled away. The woman on the phone also reached over with a business card, and nodded at them to indicate they should call her as well.

Rev was stunned. "You think these are legit?" she asked Dylan, holding up the two cards.

"Won't know until we call tomorrow," he replied.

"Hm."

Several reporters had finally made their way to them, microphones outstretched, camera people in tow.

"Excuse me, Ms. Reveille, Mr. O'Toole, a few questions please—"

EVENTUALLY, WHEN ALL OF THE REPORTERS seemed to have gotten what they wanted, and Dim had said his goodbyes, and they decided that the born-again snipers had gone somewhere to pray, Rev and Dylan made their way outside. They sat on the courthouse steps and looked out at the summer day.

"Well," Rev said after a while.

"Yeah," Dylan agreed.

"This turned out better than I'd thought." She grinned at him.

"It did, didn't it." Dylan grinned right back.

www.ingramcontent.com/pod-product-compliance
Lightning Source LLC
Chambersburg PA
CBHW051255210726
48287CB00002B/505